the TRUTH of DIFFERENT SKIES

By Kate Ling:

the TRUTH of DIFFERENT SKIES

KATE LING

LITTLE, BROWN BOOKS FOR YOUNG READERS

LITTLE, BROWN BOOKS FOR YOUNG READERS

First published in Great Britain in 2018 by Hodder and Stoughton

1 3 5 7 9 10 8 6 4 2

Text copyright © Kate Ling, 2018

The moral right of the author has been asserted.

*All characters and events in this publication, other than those
clearly in the public domain, are fictitious and any resemblance
to real persons, living or dead, is purely coincidental.*

A CIP catalogue record for this book
is available from the British Library.

ISBN 978-1-51020-020-3

Typeset in Minion by M Rules
Printed and bound in Great Britain by
Clays Ltd, St Ives plc

The paper and board used in this book are
made from wood from responsible sources.

Little, Brown Books for Young Readers
An imprint of
Hachette Children's Group
Part of Hodder and Stoughton
Carmelite House
50 Victoria Embankment
London EC4Y 0DZ

An Hachette UK Company
www.hachette.co.uk

www.hachettechildrens.co.uk

For C, my sky

Absolute Zero

'The fact is, there's no way to be sure that all humans experience time in the same way. Five minutes for me could seem like five days to you, so maybe you really do feel like you've been in this classroom for millennia.' I shrug. 'It's a matter of perception.'

Around the edge of our back-to-back terminal screens, I watch Micah's beautiful mouth as he does this slow half-smile and says, 'You know, Karlo, for a nerd, you're pretty hot.'

And I say, 'Hilarious, Bexley,' when what I'm really thinking is: *Stop it. Please. You're killing me.*

'All you need is some glasses and you'd have that whole sexy librarian thing going on,' is what he says next, still leaning to the side and tipping back a little in his chair the way he does, every movement full of lazy grace. I go back to staring at my screen, even though I don't have a chance of actually concentrating, not with him looking at me like this, talking like this. Under the table he gently kicks my foot.

'Stop ignoring me,' he says. God. If only he knew. I couldn't ignore him if my life depended on it. I'm aware of his every move to a distance of a thousand kilometres. Probably more.

'Mr Bexley ...' Dr Griffiths frowns over at him from his desk. 'Are you using your access time on the science database wisely to research the quantum properties of light, or merely frittering it away on studying the more mysterious properties of Miss Karlo, who you could observe in her natural habitat at some other point?'

Micah doesn't answer, just raises a hand in apology, before rolling his eyes and smiling as he turns back to his screen.

Science Research is the only lesson we've had together this year, which is annoying because it's my favourite, which means that I've spent all year in this constant battle with myself about whether to concentrate or to allow myself to be completely distracted by the proximity to Micah Bexley.

When the beeps finally go, I'm expecting the whole place to basically explode with joy that school is over for the summer, but actually there's something flat in it, almost as if now we're at the finish line all anyone wants to do is get out of here. There's the sound of every single one of Gower Gate Academy's three thousand students pushing stuff into our bags against which Micah says, 'You don't have to go to work today, do you?' But just as

2

I'm about to answer, Dr Griffiths says, 'Miss Karlo, can I have a word before you go?'

'Catch you outside,' Micah says, almost killing me with a half-wink before he leaves, me watching him all the way.

Dr Griffiths leans back in his chair, hands clasped over his stomach, the room emptying around us. 'Remember me mentioning the 2050 project?'

I shrug, even though I do.

'At Abertawe University. They want to –' he waves his hands around like he's looking for the right words – 'encourage more applications, particularly for the sciences. They asked me to nominate my most promising student, for a summer workshop that could lead to a place at university. So I nominated you.'

I'm shaking my head. 'Dr Griffiths, I . . .'

'If you're worried about finance, don't be. The workshop only carries a nominal fee. And scholarships are possible for university places.'

Yeah, they're possible. But they still only pay some of your fees, and there's no way I could afford the rest. University is for the rich; not for people like me.

'You have so much potential, Beacon – you do know that, don't you?' He takes his glasses off and chews on the arm of them, frowning a little while he watches my face for clues.

'Thanks,' I say, 'but I have to get to work now.' And I walk out, feeling Dr Griffiths' disappointed eyes follow me.

By the time I get outside, the rain is coming down so hard that everyone is sheltering around the edges of the building, waiting for it to slow. Jam is waiting for me. Although Jam is technically my stepbrother, I never call him that, or think of him that way. I guess I don't really think of him at all; he's just always been there, or that's how it seems, even though actually my mum only married his dad a little over five years ago.

He stands there all moody, with his hood up, gazing out at the low brown clouds that press in over the basketball court like a lid.

'Where were you?' he says, looking at me as I approach. 'We missed our transport.'

'I'm sorry. Griffiths was off on one.'

I try not to look for Micah, but I see him anyway, standing under the hoop at the far end with his arm around Mali's shoulders. While I'm watching, she does this little dance that bumps against his side and he kisses her head. It still sinks through me like a stone to see them together, even after three years of them being madly in love.

Even though she's my best friend.

If I could cut away the dark-hearted part of me that wants him, if I could carve that pain right out of me, I would. I would give anything not to feel the way I do, not to want him so much it hurts, when I know that it can never be. She looks round then and catches my eye, smiles and runs over through the rain.

4

'You're sick,' she says, and for a second I'm terrified she saw it right there on my face before I could hide it. 'You've just come down with something really gross,' she adds, and then she's grinning, and I see where she's coming from. 'There's a party in Bradoc and neither you nor Jam are missing it, so I'm calling in sick for you.'

Even though she's my best friend, Mali is another person who holds certain misconceptions, like thinking Jam and I are the kind of people who can call in sick to the job that is the only reason we get to eat. Like it's even an option. I watch her big eyes batting for a few seconds.

'We finish at midnight,' I say, stepping closer to tidy her rain-smudged eyeliner with my thumbs. 'How about we catch up with you then?'

'Bea, come on!' She takes hold of my shoulders. '*Please*, I need you there.'

Micah arrives behind her, but I don't dare look at him.

'We'll come as soon as we're finished, won't we, Jam?' I look over my shoulder at him, but his face is mostly covered by his hood and I can only see his mouth, grumpy and downturned as he says, 'Mm-hmm,' pretty unconvincingly.

When I look back at Mali, she couldn't seem more disappointed with me.

To distract her I say, 'How's mine?' closing my eyes so she can check my eyeliner too.

5

'Perfect cat flicks,' she says, grudgingly. 'As always.'

'I had a good teacher,' I say, threading her arm under mine and trapping it there so that she's close.

'I know you did,' she says, putting up her little pink umbrella over both of us. 'You learned from the best.'

We're all waiting on the same transport platform, heading to AcePrice, where Jam and I work, which is also the only place you go if you're underage and want to buy a shedload of alcohol. When I worked in Payment, this used to make life really difficult, as kids I knew would come to my station, knowing that I would punch in the code to authorise the purchase, risking getting sacked every time while they anxiously gripped the necks of their bottles of schnapps or vodka. It's not such an issue since I got moved into Electronics. Now the worst part of it is that they see me in my ugly red AcePrice uniform and probably never shake the image again. Bea Karlo: AcePrice girl. Bea Karlo: the girl who has to work full-time while still at school and take home out-of-date bread just to keep from dropping off the map completely.

Even though we are deep underground, rainwater runs down the wall on the far side of the transport tracks, on its way down to the water table to get pumped away so that we can only have it back at a premium. I tend to try not to think about that too much, or about Centralisation or the Information Collapse or any of the million other ways in which our world has been mismanaged into a mess by those who are meant to be in charge, because it doesn't do an awful lot for my mood.

The transport hums in, high-pitched. It's already busy but we cram on, losing each other and falling apart in the damp press of coats. This is how come I end up looking over a stranger's shoulder at Micah, raindrop-dotted sunglasses pushed up into his hair, eyelashes dark, the golden tone of his olive, Mediterranean skin only slightly drained by the fluorescent lighting. In an ugly place like this I always think he looks superimposed from somewhere better, like a tropical island. His eyes shift from me to Jam behind me.

'What shall we get you? To drink later, I mean, at the party. The usual?'

I feel Jam shrug; feel him go to his pocket for money. Micah shakes his head. 'Sort it later, man.'

We jolt round the hard left that brings us out of the tunnel and into the light for a few seconds. We are skirting the perimeter of Gower Gate, looking out across the vast, square fields and the ocean of sheep that is the reason this town was built. It's nearly twenty-five years now since they cleared the local villages and farms and rural cottages and relocated everyone here to make way for the Agri-Tract – a new area dedicated to industrial sheep farming. 'Centralisation' is what

7

they called it. More land for sheep, the efficiency of shared services, economies of scale. Families who had worked and lived on this land for generations were torn up by the roots and transplanted into brand-new tower blocks, employed by massive multinational conglomerates to go back and work on supersized versions of the farms they once knew. Sometimes I think it's a blessing that those of us that were born here never knew any different.

Rain sweeps across the land in grey curtains, filing in from the sea. And this is at the end of July.

We dive back into the bowels of the transport tunnel, and stop in Evans Block. A few people shove to get out around us and it makes enough space for Mali to slide in next to me.

'I'm debating coming to get you when your shift finishes. I need to celebrate with you today, Bea. I don't care if you are falling over from exhaustion – you are coming to this party.'

'Aw, so sweet.' Micah tilts his head. 'That's real friendship for you.'

'Shut up,' she says, but you can hear the smile in her voice.

At the AcePrice terminus, the whole train empties and we kind of lose track of each other on the way up the stairs. I hear Mali calling me at one point, but I kind of not-quite-on-purpose ignore her. School and

AcePrice have become like two worlds to me, two separate worlds, and only Jam, who knows me better than anyone, is allowed to follow me from one into the other.

Event Horizon

I've just managed to shove my stuff in the locker in the break room when I realise Taylor is standing behind me. 'Miss Karlo –' he shakes his head – 'you should have been on the floor three minutes ago.'

'Sorry Taylor, it's only that—'

'If you're to have any future here at AcePrice, you're going to have to respect our rules.'

He's in my space now, breaking into a smile. And I think, not for the first time, about how I could tell him something that would wipe the smile clean off his face. But I don't.

'You know I'm just messing with you,' he says, sitting back on a box, watching me. 'What held you up anyway? Boyfriend?'

'I don't have one.' *Urgh, why did I say that? To him of all people.*

'Wow.' He shakes his head. 'You know, I just find that so hard to believe. Girl like you – clever, pretty ...'

I look away; pull the ties at the side of my tabard tighter. 'I should go. Martin's alone in Electronics.'

'Run along then,' he says, and I feel the weight of his gaze watching me like prey as I leave.

'Would you take a look at this crap?' says Martin as I arrive next to him amid the sea of televisions that make up the walls around us.

On the screens, some band are jumping around on a beach, the lead guitarist on his knees in the sand, mid solo.

'I remember these guys when they were cool,' says Martin, even though he's barely five years older than me.

I fish the universal remote control out of my tabard pocket and flip channels.

'Ah man, Bea, not the news, please,' he whines. 'You know how agitated you get. You'll be ranting about development gaps and the environment and water export all night.'

I shoot him a look. 'You're a father now, Martin – you should know what's going on in the world.'

'Why?' He laughs. 'It's not like it's ever anything good.'

I get to Global News Network and am just clicking through the menu to get the subtitles on when I freeze, breath stolen by the image on-screen – a vast, partly skeletal structure, in orbit, with a slowly tracking Earth as backdrop.

'That's . . . ' I hear myself say, and then I'm blipping up the volume.

'Not another stupid cargo hauler,' says Martin, but I'm shushing him, stepping closer to the bank of screens as the sound fades in.

' . . . *announce the technical completion of its eponymous space traveller. The Ventura has been under construction in Earth orbit since the mysterious radio signal, thought to originate from star system Epsilon Eridani, was discovered seventeen years ago at the La Verdad space research facility in southern Spain. This clearly deliberate and manufactured attempt at contact, although remaining enigmatic to this day in its content and meaning, was our first irrefutable proof that we are not alone in the universe, and is often cited as the most significant scientific discovery in human history and the key to unlocking our future as a space-faring civilisation. This afternoon, officials at the facility announced that, though the core crew of the traveller will be recruited from within existing employees of Ventura Com and sister haulage company Concordia Industries, up to three hundred suitable volunteers will be sought from the general public over the coming weeks. These pioneering individuals will make up the first generation of a space mission slated to last over seven hundred years, one that many around the world are calling the most scientifically significant project humanity has ever undertaken. The cynics amongst us have noted with interest the convenient timing of the announcement, coinciding as it does with the launch of Ventura Com's much anticipated new personal device for the Post-Information era – the Pod, which comes on to the market worldwide this week.'*

Martin laughs and kills the volume.

'Hey, I was watching that!'

'Don't you get it –' he shakes his head – 'it's just a publicity stunt,' he says, indicating the huge liquid-crystal display advert for the Pod behind me – all dancing colours, ridiculous smiling people and the swirl and star of the Ventura Com logo. 'It's genius, actually. I bet that signal isn't even real. These people would do anything to shift product, you know that.'

'No, you're wrong.' Words start tumbling out too fast. 'You don't understand – it's not like that. Ventura Com is a corporate sponsor, but it was La Verdad Space Research Facility that discovered the Epsilon Eridani signal in the first place, that have spent all these years analysing it. They used to be run by the European Space Agency and the Spanish government. They only sought sponsorship because they lost their funding when their economy went to hell.'

Martin blinks, open mouthed, like a particularly dumb and hairy fish. 'How the hell do you know all that?'

'Library database. School science database. Journals. The news. I've been following this story my whole life. It happened the year I was born, so it's always felt . . . I mean, there is *life*, other beings – out there – trying to reach us. Aren't you even a little bit curious about that?'

'Wow, you're really into it. You should volunteer, Bea,' he says, gazing back up at the screens, where suited Ventura Com execs, military white-coated scientists and astronauts in ESA jumpsuits are sat behind a long table giving a press conference, strobed by camera flashes. 'To be fair, it would be completely hilarious to see you in a spacesuit.'

I roll my eyes at him as I walk away, but as soon as I lose myself among the screens, I have to lean against a shelf and I'm frowning at the floor, breathing through it, trying to get my heart to stop pounding against my ribs.

Later I'm out in Dispatch looking for Jam, when I see the delivery truck come in driven by Dylan Jones, who, at thirty-eight, still hasn't given up getting stupid asymmetrical haircuts, so that he looks more like a vain big brother to Taylor, rather than his father.

His father, who also happens to be my father.

As soon as his first foot hits the tarmac I tell him, 'You have to tell Taylor; you have to.'

He looks around to make sure no one is watching us, then back at me. 'You know I can't.'

'He needs to know. He keeps ... it seems like he ... '

Luckily, he gets it without me saying any more. 'Oh God, I'm sorry,' he says, looking at his feet. 'Just make it clear to him you're not interested and that's the end of it. There's really no point in stirring all this up.'

'No point for you and your happy family you mean,' I say bitterly.

'No point for any of us, Beacon.'

'Don't call me that,' I almost snarl, and I can see the half-second of shock in the brown-green eyes, the same as mine, which are the only thing he ever gave me, before he blinks it away.

'It's your name,' he says, but quiet now. 'And I like it. It's … meaningful.'

'Not to you, it's not.'

'You're wrong.'

'Am I?'

He sighs, shifts from foot to foot while we both avoid eye contact. I've nearly given up waiting for him to speak again and am about to walk away when he says, 'I know I have no right to ask you for anything, but I know you'll do what's right. Do you need money?' he reaches into his back pocket, spooling some coins out into his dirty palm.

'Don't do that,' I say, throwing him a look of disgust as I walk away.

Stellar Evolution

Even though he's not even a little bit up for it, I drag Jam along on the transport to Bradoc Block at midnight and up to fifteenth to where the party is. As if he's making a point, he yawns all the way there – those big, shaky, eye-watering yawns – and he won't take his hood down, even though it isn't raining.

'Don't you think it's amazing though?' I ask, because I've spent the whole way here telling him about the Ventura. 'Don't you remember watching all those TV shows about the signal when we were kids? And suddenly it's ... happening. They're really going.'

'Yeah, it's pretty cool,' he says, between yawns, but I can tell it's only for my benefit.

At number 15-501 there are people spilling out of the door on to the walkway, standing around or leaning on the railings where the service pipes and rubbish chutes drop away deep into the innards of Gower Gate.

People from school greet us like we just got back from

the war. They're all like, 'Jam! Bea! You made it!' even though they never normally speak to us. It's only right now that I'm remembering I don't like parties at all, because they're mostly full of people you don't really know or like.

'You're here!' It's Mali, shrieking from the kitchen door as she weaves through the crowd to get to us, like someone swimming upstream. She shoves a cup of something that smells like coconut in my hand and one into Jam's before reaching up to push his hood off his head and yell, 'Dance with me, Eeyore!' Jam rolls his eyes, shakes his head and pulls his hood up again, but not without a flicker of a smile.

Mali was the first person to point out to me how rarely Jam smiles, and she came up with the ridiculous pet name for him that she's teased him with ever since. Ironically, it does seem to raise a smile from him, but then Mali can make anyone smile.

'Leave the poor man alone,' says Micah, just appearing through the crowd. 'He's exhausted.'

'YOU dance with me then,' she whines at him.

'There's barely enough space to stand upright, or hadn't you noticed?' He laughs, resting his chin on her head in such a way that means our eyes meet. I look away.

As soon as I can, I slip away, looking for a TV and finding one in the quiet back bedroom, turning it on in the dark, sitting on the carpet and leaning my head back against the coat-covered bed behind me. I see Jam walk past the door but then stop, come back, lowering himself down next to me. The light from the TV plays across his face and his cup is clasped loosely between his raised knees. I turn back to the TV and watch the subtitles scroll:

'Volunteers should be between sixteen and twenty years of age, and speak fluent English or Spanish. They will need to travel to the La Verdad space research facility in Spain within the next ten days, where they will undergo stringent testing.'

'We should do it,' I say to Jam.

He turns his head a little. 'What did you just say?'

'Well, I'm going to.' I laugh.

'You're joking.'

'No, I'm serious, Jam – why not? All we've ever wanted to do was get away from Gower Gate. And we're never going to do that. I mean, seriously – how are we ever going to do that?'

He doesn't answer at first, just stares at me, but in the end he says, 'Nothing's keeping us here.'

'Jam, everything's keeping us here. We don't have any money. We never have any money. You know I'll never be able to afford university. And I can't spend my life working at AcePrice. I just can't. It'll kill me, I swear. And what's the alternative? Shearing? The abattoir?'

Jam takes a slug on his drink, swallows slowly, before

he says, 'We could save enough to get to one of the cities. Get a better job.'

'And then what?' I shake my head. 'People like us can't afford to live in any of the cities. Rents are three times what we could ever earn, even if we could get a job.'

'So you're going to outer space?'

'Don't you think it would be amazing? To be a part of answering the call of whoever or whatever it is that messaged us? To know you're heading out on the first mission to actually make contact with extra-terrestrial beings? It's . . . ' I run out of words, or maybe I have too many to get out.

Jam sits up, watching me from under his hood, his eyes wide in the dark; it's the first time I've felt like he was really listening to anything in a long time.

I lean into him, take hold of his sleeve as I say, 'I mean, you've been saying for the last year that we should try out for the space hauler training programs. What's the difference?'

The look on his face changes, his mouth falling open in surprise. 'Haulers come back every few years, Bea. If you go off on this thing, you'll be gone for ever. You may as well be dead.'

I don't know what to say to that, but before I get a chance to form a response Mali bursts into the room. She drops drunkenly to her knees on the carpet in front of us. 'I have amazing news. You are about to love me so much.'

'I already do, Mals.' I grin and she kisses me so hard on the lips I accidentally bite my tongue.

'You are going to love me even more then. I just managed to con my sister's boyfriend out of four rec passes for the Peninsula for tomorrow! He says the weather's going to be crap – as if that matters!' She waves the little transparent sheets in front of our faces. 'Don't tell me you're working. I mean, I know you will be working, you always are, but you can't be working for the whole day.'

We share a look. 'We're on lates,' I tell her. 'Four until midnight again.'

She shrieks. 'Perfect! So we get up super early and we go.'

'We haven't got a car.'

'We do! We have Micah's dad's. He's . . . away right now. So, pack your bikinis!'

'Don't you mean our coats?' smirks Jam.

Mali pulls his hood up right over his face. 'Come on, Eeyore – you are going to damn well have fun – even if I have to make you!'

Micah steps into the doorway, leaning against one side, glancing at the TV, then at Mali and Jam, then at me, before sitting on the bed behind me. I feel the leg of his jeans, warmed by body heat, against the skin of my shoulder, and reflexively twitch away.

'That's that space place you always talk about, right?'

he says, and when I turn my head he is squinting at the TV, at the aerial images of the space research facility on the screen, shifting his eyes to me for a microsecond and then back before he says, 'Your space nerd alter-ego taking over from your party-girl tonight, Karlo?'

I hit his leg and steal his drink, while trying not to notice how good he looks when he laughs as I push myself up and out of the room.

In the kitchen I bump into Jac Ashley, who I know from when I used to be in the running team. I'm not sure how we end up kissing but at some point we do, and I've basically got to that point of being drunk where I can't quite focus, and he smells so good I put my hand inside the back of his shirt, pull him closer. Then someone kicks my leg and says my name and when I turn it's Jam, leaning against the counter next to me.

'We're going home now, Bea – come on.'

And Jac Ashley says to him, 'Man, you're killing me here.'

And Jam doesn't say anything, just stares at him from under his hood.

Jac leans in and kisses my neck in a way that makes me not want to go, but Jam kicks my leg again. 'Bea, I'm going.'

'I can bring her home later,' says Jac, into the skin on my throat.

'That isn't happening,' says Jam. 'Bea, let's go. We have to be up in two hours.'

I groan then and set about the long process of unwrapping myself from Jac's octopus-like grip, during which time I realise he has one of those horrible thin moustaches like the ghost of a moustache yet to come, and suddenly I can't actually believe I was kissing him.

Outside it's cold and the clouds are tinted orange on the underside. Once we get away from the party, the world is empty and suddenly spinning, the only sounds coming from the rubbish compressors down in the sublevels as they grind and creak and feed the furnaces that heat Gower Gate. I link my arm through Jam's and he slows his pace to match mine.

'I wish you wouldn't do that,' he says.

And even though I know, I say, 'Do what?'

'Hook up with whoever. You should hear what people say about you.'

I sigh. 'I've told you, I don't care what they say about me.'

'But I do.'

'Aw, Jam, that's sweet.'

He stops. 'No, it's not! I'm the one who has to hear it. If you ever want someone to treat you right, you're going to have to stop giving it all away, Bea.'

'Giving it all away?' I say, and I can't help laughing. 'This isn't a Brontë novel. This is Gower Gate.'

He shakes his head and walks off without me, then slows until he sees I'm following him, but keeps a gap, just out of reach.

When we get back to our flat in Hydref Block, Joella's asleep at least, and there's no sign of her idiot boyfriend, but I know better than to hope that she's rid of him for good.

Once I've brushed my teeth, I lie on my bed and roll into a ball before I hear Jam's voice from beyond the thin plasterboard partition wall that makes this tiny room into two minuscule bedrooms, with half a window each.

'Jac Ashley's an idiot.'

'I get it, Jam, but I honestly don't feel like I'm giving something away. If anything, I feel like I'm taking something.'

'Taking what?'

I think about it. 'A piece of their souls maybe. You should try it some time.'

'Taking souls?'

'You've got zero game, Jam – you don't even try.'

'We weren't talking about me.' I hear his bed shift as he rolls on to his side.

I stare up at the polystyrene planets and wire orbits of the model solar system I made for the science fair five years ago and have kept screwed to my ceiling ever since.

Jupiter drifts, brownish in the dim light. 'Maybe I do it just because I can,' I say eventually. 'It's the only kind of power I have.'

'Power?' I can hear the face he's making. 'That's all kinds of wrong.'

'OK, maybe that's not it. It's more like ... getting someone to show you who they are when they stop pretending. When they're being real. Seeing the side of them nobody else gets to see.'

There's a silence while he thinks about that, then: 'OK I get that, but surely that would be better if it was someone you actually liked?'

'Of course it would,' I say, immediately thinking about Micah. 'But you can't sit around waiting for life to happen to you.'

'You always say that,' says Jam, sounding mostly asleep.

'Do I?' I frown.

But he doesn't answer. I swallow the dryness in my throat and reach to lift the corner of my blind so I can see the grey of growing light in the sky. Strange to think that the stars are always there, even when you can't see them.

Luminosity

We meet in the sub-garage at Caradoc Block, where Micah's dad keeps his car. It's this ugly green Tesla, and here in the mostly darkness of the sub it looks like there's basically no way it will start.

'How long is it since he used it?' I ask him, pulling cobwebs off the door that are so thick they're like movie props, while Micah goes around to the back and unhooks it from the charge.

'I don't think he's paid for the charge for a while, so it's just a matter of whether it stored.'

Jam groans. 'Please tell me there's somewhere to get food on the Peninsula. I'm going to die.'

'It's all in the mind, Rees. Man up,' laughs Micah, but he is for sure several shades paler than he normally is this morning. 'Where the hell is Mali?' he says, just as the sub door beeps open and emits her, arms full of sandwiches and drinks.

'Everybody relax,' she sings into the echoes. 'I'm here!'

Jam and I have just got into the back seat when Micah takes a deep breath and says, 'Here goes,' as he turns the key. At first there is only this series of clicks, this long drawn-out beep, then nothing. I guess I didn't realise how much I actually wanted to go to the beach until that moment. We all look at each other and Micah even says, 'I'm sorry, I should have realised it wouldn't be charged,' before suddenly it beeps again and all the lights on the dash flicker on, windscreen wipers swishing, indicators flashing, so that we are all laughing, all smiling, Micah grinning and slapping at the wheel.

And Mali says, 'Let's hit the beach, kids!'

Micah isn't that great a driver (as well as being hungover and everything) so he almost crashes into a pillar before we even get to the exit gate, where he pulls up too far from the keypad and has to get all the way out to punch in the code scrawled on the back of his hand in biro. Then suddenly, like that bit in *The Wizard of Oz*, the sub-garage door cracks open, rises bit by bit, nearly blinding us, and we are out.

We drive out through the Agri-Tract, all along the one straight road that replaced all the trunk roads when they centralised everyone from this once-rural area into the urbanisation. The muck-streaked, soaking wet shepherds waiting for pick-ups and drop-offs from Fleece and the Abattoir watch us pass. Rain teems in glum curtains across the sheep-studded fields. Sometimes we pass old places that used to be people's houses, crumbling into the dirt.

Our passes take us to Rec Unit 4, and we beep in to the nearly empty car park. I find myself looking back across the Agri-Tract at Gower Gate in the distance. From here it's a wall, a vast grey wall, right the way up from Caradoc block at the northern tip to Celyn Block at the southern end, twenty-two blocks long, twenty-seven levels high, nine hundred housing units in each, plus commercial and services on the ground floor, basement and subs; top floors and external flats are where you get to live if you're in Research or Management, lower levels and internals for those of us less fortunate. Basically all I've ever known of the world if you don't count a couple of holidays in England and some school trips to the North.

We edge along the path that winds down the side of the bay, wind and rain battering against us. Down on the hard-packed cement sand we lay out our towels and sit on them. Mali shucks off her coat and even pulls her hoody off, lies back in her bikini top, ravaged by goosebumps, sliding on her sunglasses while we all laugh, even Jam. For a moment she's like a movie star from the old days.

'This is perfect!' she says.

Micah closes her coat in his fist, leaning in to kiss her. 'Crazy girl,' he says against her lips.

'Aw man,' says Jam from somewhere inside his hood. 'Can we go home yet?'

'Eeyore,' yells Mals, 'my gorgeous little raincloud – get those jeans rolled up and come paddling with me.' She's up and pulling on his hand.

'Where even *is* the sea?' he says.

'Trust me, it's out there,' she says, dragging him up and off, even though there is no actual evidence of it, beyond the mist that's just rolled in. I notice there's another few people on the beach then, the only other people as crazy, or as desperate to get out, as us – an old couple in plastic jackets and trousers striding past us. They raise a hand each.

Mali and Jam disappear into the mist and Micah opens a bottle of Coke with a hiss.

'So where's your dad?' I ask, uncomfortable in the thick silence between us. 'Is he . . . '

'Yeah, they put him in the Psych unit again, over in Abertawe,' he says.

'I'm sorry, I did wonder,' I admit.

'Aren't you going to ask what he did this time?'

'Only if you want to tell me.'

He hands me the Coke. 'I suppose it doesn't really matter in the end, does it?'

I hold his eye contact; shake my head. 'This place does it to all of us in one way or another,' I say, swallowing a mouthful, the sugar and fizz making my ears ring. 'It just … gets you down. I mean – of course it does.' I hold my hands up and look around at the mist. 'Did you hear what they're saying now? Apparently the sun is never going to shine here again. We missed the boat on climate change by, like, minutes, and now it's non-reversible. So Wales will most likely be stuck in a permanent mid-autumn from now on, and whatever else comes along with that.'

He shifts his eyes to the side. 'Whatever else like what?'

I shrug. 'Oh you know, the usual … failed harvests, food shortages, loss of many species of wildlife causing a breakdown of what remains of the ecosystem. Basically some form of apocalyptic, slow-burn Armageddon, that kind of thing.'

He laughs. 'So no big deal, then.'

'I just like to bring you the good news, Bexley.'

I watch him slow-smile, his rain-cooled skin so lovely I can hardly bear it.

'I'm starving,' I say, to break the tension.

He reaches behind him for the brown paper bags of sandwiches Mali brought, pulling a triangular half out and handing it to me. 'Looks like cheese.'

I take the sandwich and study it for a few seconds before I say, 'So anyway, I've been thinking about volunteering for that Ventura thing.'

'What?' He's just taken a bite from his half and he

coughs and almost chokes before he can swallow it. 'For real?'

'Yep,' I sigh. 'I'm planning to take Jam with me, of course – he wouldn't last five minutes without me looking out for him.'

'Man,' he says, shaking his head. 'I mean, I'm pretty desperate to get out sometimes, but that's extreme. You wouldn't . . . you wouldn't ever come back. Like, ever.'

'I know.'

I feel him studying the side of my face.

'It would be like you . . . died or something.'

I take a bite out of the sandwich and the mayonnaise in it squeezes out, landing on my chest. I scoop it off with my thumbnail and wonder whether sucking it off is too gross. Luckily Micah looks away, towards the sea.

'I know science is your thing, and whatever,' he muses at the mist. 'Space and all that. But you're clever. You can get to university, I know you can. Get a job at a research facility or . . . ' He trails off as he watches me shake my head. 'Why not?'

'I'm never going to university, Bexley. I'm so far away from being able to afford it, I'm not even in the same time zone.'

'But all those hours at AcePrice . . . '

I'm still shaking my head. 'Nowhere close. And then I saw this on the TV yesterday and I knew. I mean, in a way, I've always known. This is just what I have to do. This is my way out of here. This is my chance to do something that matters. It's amazing when you think about it. I mean . . . space. *Living* in space. Your whole life dedicated to a mission, to reach out into the universe, to be a part of making contact for the first time.'

He studies each of my eyes, then laughs.

'What?'

'I've never seen you look like that.'

'Like what?'

'Like you really want something.'

But I know that isn't true, even if he doesn't.

'Wait –' he frowns at the sand – 'so how do you . . . don't volunteers have to go down there? To Spain?'

I nod.

'Well, if you're serious about this, maybe we should all go?' he says, and he grins, raising his eyebrows. 'Road trip?'

I get up, leaving the rest of my sandwich on my towel. 'Let's go check out the dunes.'

He follows me, saying, 'Don't change the subject. We could get the ferry and then drive through Spain in my dad's car . . . camp out.'

'Bexley, why would you . . . I mean, can you even afford to do that?'

'Probably not, but we could work it out somehow. How cool would it be to take a trip somewhere?'

'Yeah, Barry Island maybe. Not Spain.'

31

He touches my arm, making me turn to him. 'How are you planning to get down there? Don't you want us to go with you?'

We're just at the edge of the dunes. I crouch to look closely at a pretty blue-leafed plant that hunkers against the ground.

'*Eryngium maritimum*,' I murmur. 'Sea holly.' I smile up at Micah. 'Look how pretty the blooms are. It's like a blue from a dream.'

'Think how many plants we could see if we hit the road. Just imagine ...' He smiles at me, and he is heartbreakingly beautiful just then, a flush along his jaw from the wind, sheened in droplets of mist. So much so that I have to look away, back down at the blue holly leaf, which I pinch between my thumb and forefinger.

Suddenly Mali dances out of the mist like some kind of sea spirit. 'What is this crazy talk? Eeyore says you want to go into space! We won't let you do it. We'll never let you go.'

'It's OK, Mals, it's not going to happen.' Micah catches my eye and does this half wink, destroying me. 'We're going to go to Spain with her and have such an amazing time on the way that she'll change her mind about going.'

'Now *that* sounds like a plan!' squeals Mali, taking hold of my arms and dancing me in a circle.

*

Micah and Jam are down at the shoreline looking for sand crabs, and we are sunbathing in our coats when Mali turns her face my way on the beach towel and says, 'You and Jac Ashley?' raising her eyebrows.

'Urgh.' I make a face. 'Don't remind me.'

'You can't be single for ever, Bea.'

'I just … I just haven't met anyone I like that much. That's all it is.'

She studies me for a few seconds of silence. 'You like someone. I can see it in your eyes. You like someone!'

'No,' I say, but I flush. 'Really, I don't.'

She sits up and points in my face. 'Oh my GOD – you DO! You like someone and you're not telling me! Spill, instantly!'

'No, Mals, really, it's nobody,' I say, and I turn my face away from her, just as she hauls on my arm to make me turn back.

'OK, so it's a secret love? Now, let me see, who can it be? AcePrice? School? But who?'

She is staring at my face so hard that I swear I am shrivelling up in the heat from her eyes. They're like lasers. This is it. She is going to see it. We know each other too well for her not to be able to read it on my face. It's amazing she hasn't called me out on it before. Oh God. What am I going to say?

She sits back, realisation dawning. I can't even breathe. All I can do is tell her I didn't mean for it to happen. All

I can say is that she and I are made of the same stuff, we always have been, so it was inevitable that we would love the same boy. I open my mouth to speak, and then she says, 'It's Taylor, isn't it? That guy at work?'

It takes a moment for my mouth to form words. 'What?'

'I've been thinking about it for a while actually. Wondering about it. I mean, he's definitely semi-hot. He's on the hot spectrum,' she laughs. 'Hey wait, you're not – is it, like, already a thing?'

I guess I'm just sitting there open-mouthed all the time she is talking, but I only realise when I close my mouth and it is so dry my tongue sticks to the roof of it like Velcro.

'N-n-n-no,' I manage in the end. 'No. Really. No. Taylor is . . . God, no.'

'Well, OK, if it's not Taylor then who is it? And why won't you tell me?' She leans forward with her hand on my leg, pressing there, eyes so wide and blue. 'When did we start having secrets from each other, Bea?'

'It's not . . . ' I choke and cough and have to start again. 'There's no secret. This is all in your head. Seriously. You don't have to feel sorry for me because I'm single. I'm OK with it. I'm young! We don't all get to find the love of our life when we're fourteen.'

She smiles, drawing circles in the sand between us with her finger. 'You think Micah's the love of my life?' She sits up straighter. 'Oh my God, am I going to go through my whole life only having had sex with one person?' She makes a face. 'Wow, that kind of seems like ... doesn't that seem like a bit of a waste?'

And I'm wondering how being with Micah could ever, in any universe, be considered a waste, but instead I say, 'Yeah, there should be a global day of mourning for all the people who are never going to get to sleep with you,' just before she flicks sand at me and I flick some back and we end up chasing each other into the dunes.

Blue Shift

We get home from work that night and the front door is open. Down here on five you get a lot of fumes and you also get noise from the commercial floors, so you don't tend to keep your door open. Especially after midnight and everything, with the sketchy people that wander around these levels late at night. So this is how we know that Joella is pulling some version of her usual crap.

As it turns out, she's just wasted and is passed out on the sofa with Ianto, her loser boyfriend.

'Hey babes,' says my mother, waking up and shifting. 'You're home.'

'Looks that way,' I say, going into the kitchen.

'Hey, kids,' says Ianto, stretching, his voice sleep rough.

One of the kitchen light bulbs is blinking and there are empty paper bags and wrappers all over the surfaces. Ianto always makes Joella order takeaway from downstairs when he comes over (that she pays for). Then he eats everything in the fridge too. Then he drinks everything. Then he goes for her purse. I study the one dried-up lemon in the crisper before pushing the fridge door closed.

Jam is sitting in the armchair while Ianto tries and fails to shake his hand three times. It's always a mystery to me how he manages to get himself into such a state. I lean against the doorframe and watch it all play out.

'You're OK, man,' says Ianto, pointing at Jam. 'You're OK.'

I roll my eyes. 'What are you doing here, Ianto?'

'Bea!' says Joella. 'He's my friend!'

'Is that what we're calling it?'

'Things have turned around for him, Bea. I told you that the other day. They've taken him on down at Fleece with me, in Shearing. Part-time.'

'Part-time meaning when he feels like it? When he's not too wasted on TCA?'

Ianto holds his head in his hands and rolls back on the sofa, dirty trainers scrabbling for purchase. 'Ah, why is she so shrill? Make her go away.'

I laugh. 'Don't worry, I'm going.'

I stand in the shower, ranting to myself, slamming my hands on the tiles until, less than two minutes in, the stream clicks off because clearly nobody's put any credit on the water meter. Then another light bulb starts to strobe and I have to get out in the flashing dark, scramble for my towel, stagger out across the hall and into my bedroom.

'Put the world to rights in there?' Jam says through the partition.

'Water ran out. And another bulb's gone.'

There's a knock on the door.

'Bea –' Joella opens the door without even waiting – 'don't be cross.'

'I'm not cross. I'm just naked and trying to go to bed.'

'Babes,' she says, as she taps the doorframe with her nail. 'He's trying. He's turning it around.'

'I don't care, to be honest,' I tell her. 'If Ryan finds out about him, he'll be dead soon anyway.'

She sighs, tucks the long side of her asymmetrical blonde hair behind her ear. 'And how would Ryan find out about him?' she says, shifting her eyes to the partition wall. 'Joram would never tell his father something that would upset him for no good reason at all, would he?'

'Leave me out of this,' says Jam from behind the wall.

Once she's gone I switch off the light. Polystyrene Saturn drifts wide on an undetectable air current.

'And you wonder why I want to be a few million light years away from here?' I sigh. 'How can someone be so selfish and so helpless all at the same time? It's a miracle she even made it to thirty-seven.'

Jam sighs. 'Ultimately Joella does what Joella does. Don't let it get to you.'

I punch at my pillow. 'That's easy for you to say,' I tell him. 'She's not your mother.'

Deep into the night I wake up with it knotting my stomach. I know this feeling; it's always the same – a clenching that gets tighter and tighter and there is only one way it is going to release. I haven't had the feeling in a while, but I knew it would be back, it always is. I get to the bathroom just in time for it to ping inside me like a snapping rubber band, for the vomit to paint the toilet bowl in every shade of red. I cough up the last of it, pant, slide on to the floor where I can let the shivering subside and the sweat turn cold against the tiles.

'Babes?' Joella's nails against the door. 'Babes, you OK?'

I realise now that she's still awake; she often is, all night, like some kind of creature of darkness.

'I'm fine,' I say, wiping off my mouth and staring at the dark streak of blood on the back of my hand. 'Go to bed.'

'Do you need anything?'

'Go to bed, Joella.' I roll my eyes so that you can hear it in my voice, and I listen to her walk away. I try to flush the toilet but it just grinds emptily. No water.

It's OK, I tell myself. According to the Many Worlds

Interpretation, there are millions of other versions of this universe where none of this is happening. In some of them Joella is a better person. In some of them Ryan never went to jail. In some of them we have money. In some of them my body isn't destroying itself from the inside out.

Antimatter

Sunday night's always dead at AcePrice. I watch the latest report from La Verdad three times. People are already gathering at the gates, even though the deadline for volunteers is eight days away. There are endless interviews with the tanned, sweaty, windswept teenagers who are just pitching a tent on the sand outside the facility gates close to a huge brushed steel version of the star and swirl Ventura logo.

'I want to make the future,' says one girl, in broken English. 'I want to live with the stars. I want to die with them.'

Later, I'm wiping dust off the big screens when Taylor appears behind one. He makes me jump so hard that it's like a cartoon and he laughs.

'Miss Karlo.' He chews noisily on his gum. He's had his head freshly shaved on one side, left it long and hanging on the other. He must spend so much time thinking about this stuff; it's ridiculous.

'Nice haircut,' I tell him, sarcastic.

'Why thank you,' he says, missing it. He rests his hand

on the top of the TV next to me and leans in, surrounding me with the overly sweet mint of his breath and his nose-burning aftershave. 'What are you doing later?'

'Sleeping.'

'Before that?'

I just look at him.

'Let me take you to the Star and Whistle,' he says. 'Just for one. I want to talk to you about something.'

I shake my head. 'No thanks, Taylor.'

He raises one eyebrow, won't let me break eye contact. 'Night Supervisor job is coming up in Electronics. It's significantly more money, you know, for doing basically the same thing.'

'Doesn't that seem like the kind of thing we could talk about in your office?'

He laughs, just one loud sound. 'You'd think that,' he says. 'But I have my own way of doing things. It's got me this far.' He taps at his badge, flicks the corner of it, where it says FLOOR MANAGER.

I go back to wiping the TV, but end up thinking about that one dried-up lemon in the fridge, the grind of the empty toilet flush. 'One drink,' I say.

'Good girl,' he says as he leaves.

The Star and Whistle is only three doors away, but on the way there we still manage to run into Dylan as he comes round the corner, just getting off shift.

'Where you going?' he says, frowning as we pass him in the wrong direction.

'Star and Whistle,' says Taylor.

Dylan struggles to arrange his face as he looks from my face to Taylor's and back again. 'Good idea,' he says eventually, forcing a smile. 'I'll come with you.'

'No, Dad. Mum's waiting for you,' Taylor says, ushering me to the door. 'We're only going for one, I'll see you at home soon.'

I glance back at Dylan as he watches us walk away.

When Taylor gets to the table with two pints of beer, I find myself grabbing mine and slurping at it hard. He watches me, a smile growing.

'Thirsty, Miss Karlo?'

'You can call me Bea, you know. "Miss Karlo" makes me feel like I'm at school.'

'Well, I don't want to make you feel like that.' He watches me over the rim of his glass while he drinks, his green-brown eyes so similar to mine. I'm amazed he's not worked out the truth.

Being near the external transport trunk line, the Star and Whistle at this time of night is all about the dirty, worn-out workers who don't want to go home. I don't come here a lot but when I do it's always after my shift, gone midnight, and they'll be sitting around, often still in their muck-smeared overalls, smelling like sheep dip, or worse if they're from the Abattoir. There's a row of televisions bolted up behind the bar and almost everyone else in here is watching one of them. Mostly they show football matches and some endless bicycle race somewhere on the continent, but tonight one of them shows aerial shots of the spaceport at La Verdad, where a scheduled supplies shuttle is about to launch, thrusters blasting plumes of flame. When I turn back to Taylor, I find him staring at me, half-smiling. He leans forward over his knees, into my space. 'Look, Bea, I should probably admit that I didn't really bring you here to talk about the supervisor job.'

'You didn't?'

He shakes his head. 'You can have that, you know you can, if you want it. Martin's not going to love it, but whatever. I'll tell him it's because you've had less sick days.'

'I've had no sick days.'

'Exactly. Right. No sick days.'

'Am I even allowed sick days on my contract?'

He laughs. 'Probably not.'

'Am I allowed sick days now I'm a supervisor?'

He laughs again. 'You know, this is what I like about you, Bea. You're funny.'

'You want to make me supervisor because I'm funny?'

'No, I don't mean . . . God, you're not making this easy.'

My scalp creeps under my hair. 'Making what easy?'

He puts his pint down and scratches his forehead. I

notice that he accidentally catches his eyebrow stud as he does it. Then his hand is on my leg.

'I know I'm not your usual type or whatever, Bea.'

I shake my head, remove his hand from my leg, my skin crawling. 'Taylor, I . . .'

'Please let me finish. I've seen all your –' he makes air quotes – '"alternative friends" and stuff. And Rees already told me I have no chance.'

I'm shaking my head harder. 'Taylor, seriously, we don't need to have this conversation. It'll just embarrass us both.'

'Wow . . .' He loosens his AcePrice tie. 'Won't you even just let me say my piece? I just said I'd give you a promotion – more money – and you won't even let me speak?'

I lean back in my chair, catch the eye of a woman at the next table as she peers over her shoulder at me.

'One date is all I'm asking.'

'No, Taylor.' I'm burning with the horror of it now, shrugging on my coat.

'Where are you going?'

'Home.'

He laughs. 'Why are you being so weird about this? Man, sit down.'

'Goodbye, Taylor.'

But he follows me, a fact I don't even realise until I'm along the walkway, heading down the low tunnel that leads down to the transport line and he catches up to me, takes hold of my shoulders, pushes me against the wall, holds on to the front of my coat in his fists.

'Don't be like this,' he says, his breath on my face. 'You told me, you already told me there isn't anyone else.'

'Taylor, get off me, please.'

'I know you like me, Bea. I've seen you watching me. You don't need to be shy about it.'

'Get off me, you freak – this is not how this works.'

'I'll tell you how it works.'

Which is when he takes my face in his hand and kisses me hard on the mouth and I enter this, like, second or two of shock in which I am so angry at my body for betraying me the way it does by just shutting down and doing nothing. And then suddenly I get it to do what I need and I knee him in the groin, as hard as I can, but it doesn't quite work because we have too much clothing between us, so I do it again and obviously get a better shot in because he crumples away from me, bends at the waist, coughing, and I run.

He calls after me, but I'm running for the transport line because up ahead there are voices and I don't even care who it is, I just need someone else, anyone, to be there before he catches up to me. I don't even realise how hard I'm running until I get round the corner and crash hard into two guys coming the other way and it's only when I do and one of them starts holding on to me that I freak out, start yelling, battering him off me until I properly hear his voice and I look up. And it's Micah.

'Karlo ...' He looks worried, pained, melting into a small smile. 'What is it? What happened?'

I can't even speak. I take a step back and look from him to the other guy he's standing with, his younger brother Seth, then back up the tunnel behind me, where shadows move in the sodium light. My mouth is moving but nothing's coming out. He goes to take my shoulders, but I don't let him.

'Easy,' he says then, hands up, like someone approaching a wild animal. 'Just talk to me, tell me what happened. Come on, where are you going? Where's Rees? Didn't he wait for you?'

'It's OK,' I hear myself say, but my voice is so small. 'I'm just ... I'm going home. I'm OK,' and I set off down the yellow-lit tunnel. He takes my arm.

'You know this is the external transport line, right? This isn't the way back to Hydref Block. You know that, right?'

His brother looks awkwardly at his feet, but Micah is looking at me, and smiling, and something about his smile breaks me and suddenly breathing is hard and my eyes are burning, and he is shushing me, pulling me in between the sides of his coat where he is warm beneath his shirt, wrapping his arms around my head so that it is dark and quiet and safer than anything ever was.

'Come back with me,' he says close to my ear. 'It's on the way. Come back to mine and we'll sit for a bit and then I'll take you home. How about that?'

And even though I don't answer, we are walking then, and the only reason I am walking at all is because he is holding all of my weight with his arm around my ribs. We have to walk back past it then, back past the entrance to the tunnel where Taylor was the last time I saw him, and I hear my breathing speed up again but he's not there; he's gone.

Micah lives in Caradoc where AcePrice is, but on twenty-one, and on an outer wall, so it's quiet when we get out of the lift, cool, a wind slicing along at us as we head down one of the side passages to where his front door is. He stays holding on to me, just as tight, for the whole time that he is going through his pockets for his fob key. He even says, 'You OK?' again, watching me nod just before he holds the fob up to the pad, and then we're inside, in the dark, the only light coming from the extractor hood over the kitchen hob.

'You want a drink or anything?' he says, as his brother heads for a door and closes it behind him, and I am shaking my head. He leans against the counter for a minute and watches me, then says, 'Oh, hey, there was this song I really wanted to play you anyway. Come on.'

And even though I pretty much know he's making it up just to distract me, I go with it and follow him to his room.

These outer units are bigger so he has his own normal-sized room. It even has a window. An external window. I've always been amazed by this, ever since the first time I came here. This is how come I end up the same way I always do, kneeling on his bed, looking out at the long line of lights that mark the road and transport line to Abertawe Bridge in the distance, the sea of darkness beyond.

I hear him pressing buttons on the laptop behind me and a song starts. I've heard it somewhere else recently, but can't place it at first. Micah has the most amazing collection of old music because his dad, despite only being a teenager at the time, was sensible enough to download and store as much as he could before the Information Collapse. There are all these old-looking hard-drives stored along the shelves in his living room and apparently they're eighty per cent music. He always jokes that this is one of the benefits of his dad being a paranoid manic-depressive, and we always laugh, even though it's not funny.

'Roxy Music, "More Than This,"' he says, even though I didn't ask.

'You put this on Jam's data key, didn't you?' I watch my breath steam the window. 'He's been playing it.'

'I could put some music on yours again some time, you know,' he says, a smile audible in his voice. 'Then you wouldn't have to listen to it though the wall.'

I almost smile at the thought of that, despite everything. He did it once before, about a year ago, and it felt like being inside his head, or having him inside mine. I listened to it so much that in the end Jam confiscated my data key.

For some reason this is what finally makes me lose the tension that's been the only thing holding me upright and I turn, fold, until I am sitting on his bed with my back to the window.

'It was my fault,' I say, shaking my head at my knees.

'What was?' He sits on the edge of his desk, shrugs off his coat.

I mess with the end of my sleeve. 'Taylor Jones. I've known for a while ... or thought anyway ... that he liked me. But tonight, when he asked me to go for a drink with him, I said yes and he thought ... And anyway he –' I feel myself make a face – 'like, grabbed me and kissed me.' I swallow.

'Grabbed you and kissed you?' he says, his voice loud. 'Are you serious?'

I carry on messing with my coat sleeves. 'Yeah, it's fine –' I shake my head – 'I got him off me. I kicked him in the balls pretty hard. I just ... I'm mad at myself, really.'

'What? Why are you acting like this is your fault, Karlo? That guy is clearly a total scumbag.'

'I know that.'

'Nobody has the right to do that.'

'I know. I know that. I should have just told him the truth, though.'

'The truth about what?'

And I don't know why I do what I do next. I have no idea, except that there is something about Micah Bexley, and the way he tilts his head when he looks at me, that breaks me open.

'Taylor's my brother.'

He frowns. 'He ... who ... what?'

'We have the same dad. It's a secret because he had an affair with my mum, which ended as soon as she got pregnant with me. He didn't want to hurt his wife and kids, so ... ' When I finally look up at Micah, he is watching me with his mouth partly open and his forehead creased and perfectly still, like a statue of himself, so much so that I laugh.

'God, I don't have any idea why I just told you that. I'm so sorry. Mali doesn't even know. You know how hard she finds it to keep secrets, so I never ... I just got used to the fact that I was never going to tell anyone that. Ever.'

Micah runs his hand up his face and into his hair, pushing it back, before he looks at me and shakes his head.

'God, Karlo, that is –' he holds his face in his hands for another few seconds – 'that is so messed up.'

'I know.'

He looks at me; shakes his head again. 'And nobody

knows this? I mean – *what*? You just carry this crap around all by yourself?'

'Well, my mum knows of course, and Dylan, my ... my father. And Jam. Jam knows. Jam knows everything.'

'And how long have you known for?'

I look up at the ceiling. 'I don't remember a time I didn't know, I guess.'

He's still watching me with his mouth open as he nods. For some reason now we both laugh, just a little.

'Man, Karlo, you're hardcore. I am constantly amazed by you, do you know that?'

'I don't feel hardcore,' I say, feeling a rash of goosebumps course over me.

'Oh, but you are.' He holds eye contact with me so long I stop breathing, and only just manage to start again by the time he laughs and says, 'No wonder you want to go to outer space. When are we leaving on our road trip, by the way?'

I sigh, pull my coat back around me. 'I want to. I want to so badly but ... ' I shake my head.

'But what?'

'Jam and I jacking in our jobs, spending the only money we have, which is basically nothing anyway, when maybe we won't even get picked and then we'll be ... ' I hear myself laugh. 'If we didn't get picked, we wouldn't even be able to afford to get back. It's just a dream really – pretending there's a way to escape this place.'

Micah shrugs. 'I'm a fan of dreams,' he says. 'I'm also a fan of crossing bridges when you get to them.'

I make the mistake of looking at him then, of falling down the rabbit hole. It's like there are these pathways in my brain that only he can activate. As a scientist, the whole thing defeats me. I always wonder how long you need to be in love with someone before it becomes a part of who you are. If you fall in love with them aged fourteen and live with it every day for almost three years, those three important years, are you a different person from who you would have been otherwise? Is it woven into the fabric of you by then? Have you spent so long leaning into their light that you'll stay bent that way for ever?

The song ends and we sit a moment in silence, before he says, 'I'm going to make hot chocolate.'

'I should go,' I say.

'Please don't,' he says. 'I make great hot chocolate. It's the one thing I can do in the kitchen.'

'I should just go get the transport. I'm so ...' A yawn steals away the rest of my sentence into random sounds. It's only after it's passed all the way through me in a series of shudders that I manage to say: ' ... tired.' I get to my feet, even though it's so hard, I nearly don't make it.

He smiles, a big one that fades slowly, but then all the way into a sad frown. Having come in from the cold to the heat, he's a little flushed across his cheekbones and having one of his particularly beautiful moments right then. I'm so absorbed watching his face that I guess I'm smiling dumbly, because he mirrors it back at me and says, 'What are you looking at me like that for?'

And so I shake it off as quick as I can, which isn't quick enough. 'No, it's ... nothing. I'm going.'

His hand on my arm. 'Stay for some hot chocolate, then I'll take you home.'

In the end I'm so flustered I just nod.

'I won't be long,' he says, and shuts the bedroom door. His bedroom door. So now I'm alone in Micah's bedroom.

I get up off the chair and walk around for a minute, breathing deep, taking in the smell of him like medicine. His clothes are piled in a heap over the back of his desk chair, which is kind of slobby, but all I can do is focus hard on resisting the temptation to bury my face in them. He doesn't smell like other guys my age – feet and sweat and cheap body spray. He smells sweet and warm and clean, like laundry fresh out of a dryer. Or maybe that's just the way he smells to me; maybe to other people he does smell like socks. Humans are programmed that way, calibrated to each other in certain pairings. Even when it's impossible.

His laptop sits on his desk, one window open on the English summer project we have to write about *Wuthering Heights*. On the wall is a pin board full of pictures of Mals, of him and Mals. One is so old that he looks almost exactly the way he did the moment I first saw him. He was the new kid, thirteen years old, just transferred from Abertawe Bridge Academy, his hair too long after summer, staring at my apple so hard that in the end I gave it to him, then watched him eat it out of the corner of my eye, juice dropping on to his shirt, before both of us got thrown out of the library because we were laughing too hard. Funny that my first instinct was to take him straight to Mali, introduce him to her like I was showing her the treasure I just found. Or, as it turned out, putting it right into her hands. I have always wondered if he was almost mine. In any number of other universes maybe that day went differently.

The most recent photo is one of them here, right here, lying on his bed. There's something different about both of their faces in it – something smudged and swollen – something entirely private. I swallow the tightness in my throat and turn to look at the bed behind me.

Suddenly I'm exhausted, so tired that I find myself unable to resist lying down, turning on my side so that my face is against his pillow. Right where he lies each night. I breathe in and close my eyes.

Dark Matter

I wake up warm, sighing into it, smiling before I open my eyes. It's only when I do that I realise.

I'm still at Micah's.

It's the morning and I'm still at Micah's.

I sit up, fear shooting up my spine. He's lying on the carpet down next to the bed. I peer over the edge at him for a minute – lying on his back with his face turned to the side, away from me, a blanket pulled diagonally across his stomach, his chest and shoulders bare, golden and flawless, so beautiful it derails me completely. He has this dip in his chest where his bottom ribs come together that I don't think I'll ever be able to stop thinking about. All this is why when he opens his eyes and catches me watching him, it takes me a few seconds of stuttering before I manage to get to the real issue.

'I'm-I'm-I'm still here. What time is it?'

He shunts his elbows behind him and levers himself up, his hair all standing up like a fan even after he pushes a hand through it. He presses the space bar on his laptop and squints at the screen.

'Ten to eight,' he says, his voice rough so that he clears his throat.

'Oh my God.' I lie back on his bed.

'Yeah,' he says, sitting up with his back against the edge of the bed. 'Don't worry, I called your place to say you were here. You were so deep asleep – I couldn't bear to wake you.' He looks at me over his shoulder.

'Thanks,' I say, though it barely makes it out of my throat.

I stand and go to the bathroom, smearing toothpaste on to my teeth with my finger, glancing at myself in the mirror twice before I spit, then leaning forward across the sink to study the smeared panda mess around my eyes, the shining flop of hair across my face that has escaped my ponytail. I take the band out and rake my fingers through it, pulling the mess of it back while I take long, deep breaths that shudder in, then shudder out.

I creep back past the open kitchen door and luckily Seth and their mum are too busy arguing in Spanish and burning toast to notice me darting past the doorway and then momentarily slowing my steps to listen. I always forget that his mum's from Spain; I forget that family life happens in a whole other language for Micah, one that I've never even heard him speak. I'm all the way in his room and leaning on the back of the door when I realise he's in the middle of getting dressed, just finishing pulling his jeans up.

He looks up at me, then turns to reach for the shirt that's hanging on the back of his desk chair, so that I watch the secret bones and muscles that slide beneath the skin of his back, the way his trousers slip low on his hips down to where his skin gets paler.

I need to get out of here. Now.

'I'm going to get going,' I say, speaking too fast.

'I'll walk down there with you.'

'So are you going to tell Mals, or shall I?'

'Tell her what?' he says. 'Bea, maybe you don't know this about her, but she gets really jealous.' He pushes a hand through his hair, slides his sunglasses on, walks over to me and places his hands on my upper arms so that I glance up at him. 'We know it's all cool, so let's just not mention it, huh?' he says, leaning in so close I can hear him breathing.

Down at the transport tunnel, I find I am acting like a criminal, walking along ahead of him and checking over my shoulder. He even laughs at me and I know why. I feel so guilty, but at the same time the intense charge of last night is running along under the surface of my skin. I spent the night in his bed. I smell of him. I'm dizzy with it. God, this is awful.

I go to duck down the tunnel without saying goodbye, but he gently takes my arm.

'I've come up with a plan,' he says. 'And I think I might actually be a genius.'

'Not that you're blowing your own trumpet or anything.'

He smiles. 'Go to work tonight and tell Taylor that you won't report him as long as he gives you and Jam two weeks' holiday. That way you can go to Spain but keep your job in case you don't get selected. What do you think?'

'I . . .' I laugh, head spinning. 'I can't do that.'

'Why not?' He frowns, steps into my space. 'I really think we should do this. None of us have ever been anywhere really, seen anything. My family are from Spain, and I've never even been there. The only thing I know about the world is that it's messed up and there has to be more to it than that.' I watch the expressions that fleet across his face, watch his throat move as he swallows, his grip tightening a little on my arm. 'I've got money from when my grandparents died, Mals can get some, and you two must have something to show for all those hours. And if this whole thing with Ventura is something you feel like you have to do, then it's worth it. It's worth whatever it costs.'

I raise my hand to my forehead, press it there. 'You really think I can do that? With Taylor?'

'Of course,' he says, like it's the easiest thing in the world. 'Want me to come with you?'

That makes me smile, but I shake my head.

'Pack your stuff and let's just go,' he says, grinning. 'As soon as possible. You tell Jam and I'll tell Mals. Whatever happens, this trip is going to be amazing.'

The flat seems empty, thank God, except for Ianto's mess and stench, and the way it looks like it's been searched. I hear Jam shift in bed before he calls through the wall.

'Jesus, I was about to go out looking for you when Micah called. What happened with Taylor?'

I don't answer; I just flop face first on to my bed, because Jam is highly likely to lose it if I tell him about it. I hear him get up and open his door, come around to mine and stand there in the doorway.

'How did you end up at Bexley's?' Neptune orbits past, almost hitting him on the head, set in motion by the pressure shift.

'I just ran into him.'

'And you stayed there? All night?'

I smile secretly into my sheets, but then swallow it.

'Was that a good idea?'

I roll over and stare at the ceiling. 'God, it's not like anything happened.'

'OK, but I know how you feel about him.'

'It's just a fact of life, Jam. One I've learned to live with.'

'That's not true. It's making you ill, Bea. You realise that, right? You don't eat enough. Or sleep enough. Swallowing something like this for as long as you've swallowed it. It's aggravating your condition, and in the end it'll get too much. Sometimes I get scared it'll kill you.'

I laugh like that would never happen, when what I'm really wondering is if it might.

'Just one of the reasons why I'm better off leaving and never coming back,' I find myself saying.

He sits on my bed, sighs, pushes his hair behind his ears. Jam has the most beautiful hair – shiny and dark and heavy. When it isn't hidden under his hood, it's hard to resist touching it.

'Are you really serious about this?' he says.

'I need to get out of here,' I tell him.

'I know.' He makes this noise that is almost a laugh. 'But a one-way trip to outer space seems a bit extreme.'

'Extreme, yes.' I watch polystyrene Mercury, arcing out on a sudden eddy, trailing a cobweb, before meeting his eye. 'I can't explain why, Jam, but it just ... feels right.'

He blinks a few times before he leans forward over his legs and stares at the carpet.

I kneel up on the bed next to him, my hand on his shoulder. 'Micah wants us all to go. To drive down to Spain. Camping, sun, beaches ... If we do everything cheaply, I think we can just about afford it. I just want to go there, to La Verdad, to see it, and let's face it, this is the only chance I'm ever going to get.'

He frowns. 'Not necessarily, Bea.'

'It is,' I say, sitting back on my heels and sighing. 'When will an opportunity like this happen again? Someone offering to drive us, the possibility of getting time off work. And we have a little money saved for the journey. There's probably no chance of us actually getting picked, but isn't it worth a try?'

He looks at me. 'Us?'

'Look, I'm going, and I want you to come with me.'

He sighs. 'To Spain or to space?'

I grin. 'Both, you idiot. Or would you rather I left you here to scrape Joella and Ianto off the floor every day and night?'

He looks from me down to his hands, clasped between his knees.

'Look, the fact is, I can't think of anything about our life here that I particularly care about leaving behind,' I say. 'Can you?'

He breathes out through his nose, one long breath, and shakes his head.

Right Ascension

I stand across from Taylor where he sits at his desk.

'What?' he laughs. 'You're on zero hour contracts. You don't get holidays.'

'We're not asking to be paid,' I tell the wall behind his head. 'We just need the time.'

'And who's supposed to cover for you both?'

'School just finished,' I say. 'There are loads of people on the temp lists.'

Taylor nearly chokes. 'Yeah, who need training.'

'You don't need much training to do our jobs,' I say.

He laughs again. 'Damn straight you don't.'

I glance through the internal window at Jam, who's waiting outside, and something about just looking at him gives me strength again.

'I tell you what, Taylor, how about you let us go and I won't go to HR and tell them about how you've been sexually harassing me.'

His face falls for a moment and he swallows, looks

away into the corner of the room; then he forces a smile that doesn't spread to his eyes. 'Whatever, babes,' he says, shunting his chair closer to his desk and tapping on his keyboard. 'Take your two weeks and get out of here.'

We get about twenty metres away from Taylor's office before we turn to each other and I'm jumping up and down on the balls of my feet as Jam grabs my hands.

'Oh my God, how did you do that?' he says.

'You don't want to know. What matters is, we've done it – we're getting out of here.'

'OK, so what are we looking for?' I study Jam in the weird light of the lift as we sink through the innards of Hydref Block to the basement, but his hood's up and his head's bent over, as usual, so I can hardly see his face. I can only see his mouth and it's motionless, until he says, 'Joella said there was a tent down here, which is the main thing. But the volunteer requirements list said we need to bring eight to ten printed photographs of ourselves in Earth locations.'

I make a face. 'It did? What's that about?'

'Apparently it's to promote a sense of connection and belonging in the future crew.'

I stare at the doors of the lift while I'm turning it over in my mind. 'I don't think there'd be any down there,' I say eventually. 'We've never had many reasons to take photos.

There's a couple of us as kids on the fridge I think, and some of me and Mals that she printed for me, but apart from that ...'

'So much for a sense of connection and belonging,' says Jam.

'Yeah,' I laugh, even though it's not funny.

The lift doors slide open and we are in Sub-2, otherwise known as Personal Storage. Every unit in Gower Gate has its own storage locker down here, but mostly it seems like a place people put things they don't use, don't need or want to forget. I wonder how much of the stuff down here belongs to the dead. It's a maze. It's basically the Minotaur's labyrinth with low ceilings and strip lights.

Jam looks up at the little plastic sign on the wall that tells us which way the numbers run. 'Come on,' he says.

There's the sound of someone rolling up a shutter somewhere out of sight. We walk for a while before we pass a locker that's open. There's a tall, bald guy inside staring at a piece of paper in his hand, while all around him the walls are lined with boxes of chocolate bars. A black market trader, clearly, who only shoots us the briefest of looks before he hauls his shutter down to hide our view.

When we get to our locker, we scan the fob and there is a beep and the flash of a small green light. Jam reaches down and hauls the shutter up and it emits the cold, stale air of a tomb, just before the light inside flicks partly on, gets stuck in a half-lit stutter and stays like that. Boxes crowd us out, not even leaving standing room for one.

'Wow,' I find myself saying. 'I'm guessing Ianto never got his hands on this fob then.'

'Either that or everything here is crap.' Jam pulls a box down from the top, struggles and almost drops it before putting it down on his feet and prying open the flaps. 'Man, that's heavy,' he says, and then with a laugh through his nose, 'Well, I wasn't expecting that.'

Because it's books. He picks one out and looks it at, fans its pages in his face like he's smelling it. 'Have you ever seen Joella read a book?'

I shake my head, pick one out for myself. '*Wuthering Heights*,' I read off the cover. 'I need this for English.'

Then I notice, round the back of the box where Jam can't see, that this box is marked *Shayma Rees*. Jam's mother. He follows my gaze. I watch his face for clues, and don't find any. All he does is grunt, slide the box to the side with his foot before pulling down another.

I squat next to the first box and trail my fingers across the spines of the books inside, slide another one out: *Tender is the Night*.

'Did you know these were here, Jam?'

Still nothing. I look behind me and notice that at least three more of the boxes are marked with Shayma's name. As we shift them down and open them, we find that they're all books.

'Your mum read a lot?' I try then, sitting back on my heels.

'Looks like it,' he says, deadpan.

'Did you know this stuff was down here?'

He shrugs, and carries on rummaging.

I watch him until he looks back.

'What?' he says, his face strained. 'Can we just look for the tent, OK? This place gives me the creeps.'

I give up and stand, which is when I spot something all the way on the back wall, crushed in.

'Oh my God – look!' I lean right over towards it and grab it by the neck, but gently, like it's an animal, manoeuvring it out until it's in my arms. A guitar. 'Whose was this?' I breathe.

'My dad's,' he says, but without even looking.

'Ryan's?' I can't keep the surprise out of my voice. 'You remember him playing it?' I cradle it like a baby. 'Because I don't.'

He doesn't speak, not really, just grunts, the way Jam does. I sit cross-legged on the floor and gaze at it in my lap.

'I'm keeping it,' I tell him. 'How could it just be left down here? That's so wrong.'

'Do what you want,' he sighs, stepping in towards the back of the unit.

I run my fingers along the strings, hoping and at the same time not daring to believe that they will make a sound. But they do. And it makes me smile.

'Would you believe it?' says Jam, and I watch him reach in over a box at the back, flexing, straining until he pulls something out that is bulky, bagged in blue cloth, clunking as he lowers it to the ground. He unties the strings at the top and peers in, like it's a Christmas stocking. 'It's a tent,' he says.

'Cool,' I say, laying my hand on the warm wood of the guitar. 'Then there's only one thing left to do before we can go.'

'Why would you need your full medical records?' says the doctor who just took over from my old one a few months ago, having moved here from Caerdydd. She is sitting there with smudged eye make-up that makes it look like she's been crying. It's not like it's surprising; I'd be crying too if I'd had to move here from the city.

'We're being assessed for eligibility to a space program,' I tell her.

'Haulage?'

'Not exactly.'

'Let me guess –' she sits back in her chair – 'that First Contact mission.'

'Ventura,' I confirm.

'You have to go down to Spain to enrol, I understand? What if you have a flare-up? You could be far away from medical attention.'

'I won't have a flare-up.'

68

I turn to Jam and see it on his face. 'Don't look at me like that,' I tell him. 'It's my body. I get to decide about my body.'

The doctor sighs.

'I have warned you before that you need to avoid stress,' she says. I think about how easy that must be to say when you don't have my life. Basically what she's saying is: don't have your life, don't be you.

'I'm afraid I am going to have to note on your record that you're travelling against my advice,' the doctor says, all doleful eyes.

'That's fine.' I fold my arms across my chest, breezy, like it's no big deal.

'Bea . . . ' Jam says, and I turn to meet his look, hold it just long enough so that he knows I want him to let it go. Then I turn back to the doctor and say, 'Please just give us the records.'

'You realise this means you won't be able to take out any insurance, and you would only be entitled to the minimum of treatment over there if you needed it?'

'That's fine,' I say, and I swallow it, swallow everything, just like I always do.

Joella gets home about seven and stands in our doorway, watching us pack for a while before she says, 'What – wait – why aren't you at work?'

'We got two weeks off to go to Spain.'

'How can you just go on holiday?' Her pale pink frosted lips look metallic as they start to turn down at one edge.

Neither of us has mentioned Ventura to her because I know she'd only try to stop us.

'We just decided we needed to get away for a while,' Jam says. 'See some of the world.'

'I took you to Macclesfield last Christmas, you ungrateful little ...' she trails off before starting up again. 'You need a holiday? *You* do?' She shakes her head. 'Who's going? Just the two of you?'

I clear my throat. 'And Mali and Micah.'

'You're supposed to be saving your money for the future, Bea,' she says, her tone suddenly soft, coming close to stand behind me, gathering my hair into her hands and moving it to behind my shoulders. I can smell the stale sheep-dip smell from working at Fleece that she never manages to shake. 'You've got chances, opportunities that other people don't have. What about that science workshop?'

I frown. 'How do you even know about that?'

She flaps her hands. 'Doctor whatever-his-name-is called me. You know I'd give you the money if I had it, but you obviously have some money saved if you can go away. So why don't you use it for that instead?'

She sits down on my bed and I resist the urge to tell her that there is zero point paying for the workshop when there's no way I'll ever be able to afford university. I also don't tell her that if she wasn't always 'borrowing' money off us and then giving it to Ianto there might actually be some food in the fridge sometimes.

'And you, Joram,' she says, looking at him as he leans in the doorway, and I notice he's nearly as tall as it – he's outgrowing this flat as much as I am. 'You told me you were saving to get yourself a housing permit.'

There's a lot of things he could say right now, and I watch them move across his face like clouds before he settles on: 'We've still got another year of school, Joella.'

She stands and shakes her head at the floor, her long battered earrings she's had since I was a child jangling against her neck.

'I may not be perfect, but I have made a lot of sacrifices for you two. And now you just take off on a holiday!'

'You could save up to take a holiday if you wanted to,' I say.

'Oh, could I?' She looks at me, eye twitching. 'Do you know how many times I've wanted to go somewhere and I haven't? In case we couldn't get to a hospital quick enough.'

My mouth drops open. 'Because of me?'

She frowns. 'Yes, because of you. What? You think it's easy watching you lie in hospital bleeding out?' She turns away and holds her face. I watch the slight tremble in her narrow shoulders; it's disorientating. 'And now you just decide you're seventeen, it's your body and if you want to destroy it then . . . that's fine?'

She turns back then so that we stand in a triangle, staring each other out.

'There's no more of you to cut away, Bea,' she says, and there's a tremble in her voice. 'They've taken everything they can without taking it all, and it's still creeping through you.'

'I know that. You think I don't know that?'

'What if you're in the middle of nowhere and you get sick?' She does this weird gasp like something just occurred to her, and she presses her knuckles against her mouth, like she's seen something.

Whatever else Joella is, she has this crazy ability to see things that haven't yet happened. She told me Jam's grandmother was dead hours before someone called from Syria to tell us. And so both of us just stand there petrified into stillness while she says, 'You'll hold her lifeless body in your arms, Joram.'

Jam frowns, 'Joella, don't say that.'

'And then you'll come back to me without her. You'll come back to me alone and say you're sorry. But don't bother, OK? Don't bother because I won't forgive you. I won't forgive either of you.'

The front door opens, then slams.

'Hello?' Ianto shouts.

I glare at Joella. 'You gave him a key?'

She stares at the floor.

He appears behind Jam and looks around at us all. 'Blimey, who died?' He pulls off his layers of coats and scarves and jumpers and leaves them on the floor, just on the threshold of my room. Every one of them is filthy. 'Did anyone change that light bulb in the bathroom yet?' He wanders through to the kitchen and I hear the fridge opening.

I look at Joella, but she won't meet my eye.

'We're going out in a minute,' I tell her.

'Where to?' She looks up, eyes narrowed.

'To see my dad,' says Jam. 'Remember? I told you I was using the visitors' passes this week.'

'Fine,' she says, turning to leave, but I take hold of her wrist. It must be longer than I thought since I last touched her, because she jolts a little, stares down at my hand. 'What?' she says.

'We won't be back until late, so we might not get a chance to say goodbye before you go to Fleece in the morning.'

'Goodbye?'

'Before we go on our trip.' I step into her space, look into the pale blue eyes I didn't inherit, before pulling her into a hug she tenses against.

She taps my back a couple of times before stepping back and looking at me. 'Well, if there's nothing I can say

73

to stop you, then enjoy it,' she says, then frowns. 'Is there something you're not telling me?'

I laugh, amazed at the way she can always do this, then say, 'Of course not!'

'Don't suppose you're going to hug me too, are you?' she says then, turning to Jam, hands on hips, as he slides his forearms on to her shoulders and she taps a couple of times at his back, his chin on her head and her face pressed sideways against his chest while she makes all these surprised noises and then says, 'Well, now I've seen it all,' and shakes her head before leaving.

Aphelion

'Ventura run the inmate calling service, don't they?'

'Hmmm?' God, I hadn't even realised I was falling asleep against the rain-streaked window until Jam said that and brought me reeling back to the surface, my neck muscles spasming.

'The inmate calling service. That automated message thing that plays when Dad calls asking us to accept the charges.' He glances at me before holding his nose and doing a pretty good impression of it. 'This is a Ventura Communications call from an inmate in the United Kingdom's National Prisons Service. Do you wish to accept the charges for a call from RYAN REES?'

He says the last two words in the exact gruff, super-Welsh voice his dad uses to insert his name in the message, as required.

I laugh at the accuracy of his impersonation before I say, 'Remember when you wouldn't even speak to him?' Because hearing it just reminded me of the way, back when it was all still new, he would hand over the phone to me or Joella if he picked it up and heard that message.

'I was twelve, Bea. My dad going to prison was the last thing I needed.'

'I know that,' I say, softly, studying the side of his face, his eyes tracking across the lights of the Abertawe Prison's transport station as we pull in.

We walk along the edge of the road between the station and the prison, part of the half-familiar troupe of fellow visitors huddling into each other against the dark and the rain and the night. Up ahead the prison is a horrendous grey eight-floor bunker of a building squatting across wasteland, lit from below in greenish floodlights that spill their beams up on to the low cloud and illuminate the rain so that it looks like picture interference. Lambs are being herded along the edge of the road just beyond the fence. There's so many they're like a soggy, grey river of wool and stench. They must be freshly separated from their mothers because they still haven't given up calling for them.

We sit in the first waiting room staring at the other visitors until the alarm goes and we are buzzed through to the second area where we have to turn out our pockets, strip off our coats and shoes, have everything security scanned, step into the body scanner, and even then we still get patted down. Then we walk through a metal mesh tunnel before getting kicked out into this room full of white tables where twelve cameras and two guards watch us from either end of the room.

When they let the prisoners through, Ryan is third in line and once he sees us he smiles and picks up his pace, while Jam and I get to our feet and I try to arrange my face so that it isn't showing what I'm thinking, which is mainly that he looks so skinny, so old, a little bent over, scarier than usual with a shaggy biker beard and long dirty-looking hair, extra tattoos including one on his neck, all of this even though I was just here six weeks ago.

He's allowed to come round and hug us when he first gets in so he does, kissing me and squeezing my shoulders as he says, 'Hello, Bumblebee,' and then going to Jam and pulling his head against his, his hand on the back of his neck, his eyes closed, momentarily silent and still and sad, like somebody having a religious experience. Then he steps back and says, 'I think you grew again. Did you grow again? Is he taller than me now, Bumblebee? Who's taller?' And he makes Jam stand back-to-back with him, looks at me to judge, and I end up saying, 'I think he is actually.'

And Ryan turns back to Jam, takes his hand between both of his, overcome for a moment, even though he looks like he doesn't want to be, and then the guard is shouting at us to sit down.

As we do, Ryan says, 'Before I forget,' and holds a dirty-looking envelope in the air which he waves at the guard, getting a nod from him before sliding it across the table at Jam. 'Bit early,' he shrugs, 'but it's for your birthday. In case I don't see you before.'

I peer over Jam's shoulder as he thanks him and slides his finger under the unsticky flap, sliding the paper out. It's the most amazing pencil drawing, almost photo-realistic, but made even better by the gorgeously rich and subtle shading. It's Jam and me, copied immaculately from a photo Joella took last year.

'Did you do it?' I ask Ryan.

He laughs. 'No, I did a few trades with a guy I know. He's good, isn't he?'

'He's really good.' I smile, studying it again. I remember the photo pretty well; I think I kept it on my data key too, but I can't help thinking it was kind of an odd choice, what with the way Jam is only visible in side profile, half turned away, looking down at the top of my head while I grin at the camera.

Jam folds it back into threes and pushes it into the dirty, reused envelope as he says, 'Thanks, Dad, it's great. I really like it.'

'Well, you'll be seventeen, Jim-Jam. Nineteenth of August. I expect you to be queued up for your driving permit first thing that morning. Get learning straight away like Bea did a few months back. Didn't you, Bumblebee?'

I nod.

'I can start drivers' education when we go back to school in September,' says Jam.

Ryan shrugs. 'Well, OK, that's a new thing. All I'm saying is, you need to do everything you can to make sure you're employable when you finish school.'

'I know, Dad. We've talked about this before.'

'Don't run out of options and end up where I did.'

'I don't plan to.'

'It's a pretty crappy world you've been born into. Fat cats in charge, rural populations sold a hollow dream and shunted off the land, every drop of our own Welsh water exported for profit, and as for the Information Collapse ... I mean, who knew it would be so easy to bring the whole world crashing down around our ears. Everything just –' he snaps his fingers – 'gone.'

'I know, Dad,' Jam cuts across him, since he can get pretty worked up once he goes down this road.

'I haven't given you the start I wanted to.' He glances at me. 'Either of you.'

'It's OK, Ryan,' I say.

'It's better for you two than it was for me and Jojo – at least you never knew what you were missing – but still, that's not saying much.' He grins, revealing tooth gaps and cheap metal crowns. 'Gower Gate Children's Services is a crap start by anyone's standards. Then spending the whole of school learning to do everything using the Internet, only for the viruses to hit and there to suddenly

79

be no Internet.' He laughs, though I know of old that this actually isn't at all funny. 'But that's life, eh? Takes you places you could never have expected,' and he gestures around at the visiting room.

Talking about the world before the IC is always so abstract for us since we weren't even born when it happened, so Jam takes the opportunity to change the subject, leaning forward in his seat. 'We're going away on a trip to Spain, Dad, so we thought we'd come say goodbye.'

'Oh right. Where in Spain? I used to know it pretty well. Used to head down to Morocco that way.'

'Andalusia.'

'Mmm-hmm.' He nods, lets the silence grow, then a slow smile breaks out. 'You're volunteering for Ventura, right?' He is pinning Jam with his eyes. 'Right?'

'No,' says Jam, shifting in his seat. 'Not at all.'

'Yes, you are,' says Ryan. 'Why are you lying?'

'We're not,' I say.

'Oh, I get it,' he says. 'You don't want to tell Jojo, because she'd make a scene – am I right?'

We look at each other, squirm in our chairs a bit more.

'Well, I think it's great,' he says, leaning forward over the table towards us.

'You do?' says Jam.

'I do.' And he smiles, looks at Jam glassy-eyed. 'I've been watching it on the TV, of course. We all have. And at first I was thinking – who the hell would sign up to that crap? Sit in a tin can for the rest of your life and never see the sun again, never hear the wind in the trees, never feel the earth beneath your feet? And then I thought – what's the difference? When do we ever see the sun or hear the wind here anyway? And at least there you'd be *doing* something ... something that's important.'

Jam pushes his hair behind his ears. 'It was Bea's idea,' he says. 'But I'm starting to realise it's a pretty good one.'

Ryan nods, flicks his eyes to me, then back to Jam. 'And you're both going? Together?'

Jam nods.

'That's good. I'm glad you look out for each other.'

He nods again, and Ryan smiles, hides his smile for a minute, before studying Jam again, a little more wet-eyed than he was before.

'You have no idea how much like your mother you are sometimes,' he says.

Jam studies his knees.

'She was so brave. Always up for an adventure. When I met her she had just made it all the way to Tangiers from Damascus on buses. It was like finding a star and picking it up and holding it in your hand.' He cups his hands as if he's still holding her there. 'There were normal people and then there was Shay. This is exactly the kind of thing she would have loved. She had no fear; she just wanted to live life.'

When Ryan gets like this, when he talks about Shayma, I hardly recognise him. I certainly never heard him talk about Joella quite this way, even though he says nicer things about her than anyone else ever has.

He is wet-eyed while he adds, 'She was so gentle, so kind, so beautiful, so ... special. And you're just like her.'

'Thanks, Dad.' Jam messes with his hair awkwardly, pushing it over to the side.

I stand up. 'I'll leave you to it for a bit.' And even though they both say I don't have to, I say, 'Please. I want to. I'll wait outside.' But before I go, Ryan stands to hug me across the table, pulling me against him where I hear the air whistle in his nose and feel his beard prickling my earlobe and it makes tears burn in my eyes. He kisses the side of my head, drops his voice. 'Tell me how you're doing though, Bumblebee – are you doing OK? I heard from a friend that there's a new medication on the market that they're trying out for conditions like yours – I can speak to a few people ... '

I smile but shake my head. 'Ryan, that's the kind of thing that got you in here. Just you worry about keeping out of trouble. I'm fine.'

He looks unconvinced, but nods. 'Take care of yourself, Bumblebee, and of him. I'll call Jojo's in a couple of weeks to see how it went, OK?' And I nod, tell him bye and walk away, only turning just before I get to the door to look back at the way he is pulling on Jam's arm over the table, reaching to push his hair back off his face once he gets him close enough.

The waiting room is empty now, the television in the corner playing to nobody – images of a supply transfer shuttle docking with Ventura, cutting to shots of beaming, waving teenagers queuing along the side of a huge Ventura-branded tent, sweating under Spanish sun, waving at the camera as it passes them. It feels almost impossible to imagine myself there, covering the distance, and yet, in some ways, I feel like I'm already so far gone.

Arrow of Time

Someone knocking on my window wakes me deep in the heart of the night. I move the blind, swipe away the condensation on the inside – it's Mali, her face twisted into sadness. I gasp, and I'm already hauling the window open when I'm suddenly paralysed by it: she knows. She knows about the night I spent at Micah's.

I hardly dare ask, 'What's wrong?'

I watch in abject terror while she levers herself over the sill, wet-faced and sniffing as she falls on to my bed on her knees.

But then she says, 'It's Topper,' and she wraps her arms around my neck and speaks wetly against my shoulder. 'He's dying.'

Topper is her grandfather. Until he moved to Canada with his new wife last year, Mali went to his place most days after school just to talk over his TV shows and make him laugh. When we were kids, he was the one who picked her (and often me) up from school while her parents were at work at Research. He had all these stories from before we were born about Mali's parents when they were teenagers, about a world we never knew where people lived out in little farmhouses or villages, and computers were like windows through which you could see anything you wanted.

'God, Mals, I'm sorry.' I pull her even closer.

'I have to go to him.'

'Of course you do,' I say against her shoulder.

'I'm going in the morning.' She pulls back, strokes my hair flat against my ears. 'My parents got me my ticket just now. They don't know how long . . . ' She trails off, lies back against my pillow.

'We'll wait for you.' I lie down next to her.

She shakes her head. 'You can't, you'll miss the deadline, you have to go to Spain. Take the boys. And have some fun on the way there, get some sunshine, see some beauty. Please. I want to know you're doing that.'

'This sucks,' I say into her shoulder. 'I don't want to go without you.'

She threads her arm behind me. 'I know. It's the worst. I *finally* get you to stop working long enough to have some fun and this happens. But promise me you won't . . . if you get picked, you won't just go straight away, will you? I mean you'll . . . you'll be back, won't you? I'll see you?'

I say nothing and just hug her. Because the answer to this, in truth, is maybe not. Whatever happens, the fact

I'm not even admitting to myself is that we don't have the money for the return trip. Luckily she gets distracted just then.

'Man, you're so skinny,' she says in a shocked voice, pulling away from the hug and looking down at my scarred stomach where my vest has ridden up, before I yank it down. 'What the hell is going on, Bea? Is it getting bad again? How bad is it?'

'It's fine,' I say. 'I'm fine.'

'You need to make sure you're eating enough – are you eating enough?' The worry in her eyes makes me lay my hand on the side of her face, then stroke at her eyebrows with my thumbs in a way that makes her close her eyes and smile.

'Remember when you used to do that when I got migraines when we were kids?' she says. 'I used to ask my mum to call you to come over in the middle of the night because nothing else would do.'

I keep stroking her eyebrows while she keeps talking.

'I always wished I could make you better the way you made me better, but I guess it doesn't work that way with your thing, does it? No matter how much we might wish it did.' She opens her eyes and looks at me.

'Are you going to go and see Micah?' I ask, changing the subject.

'I just came from his place,' she says, sad-eyed. 'Wanted some time with my best girl, didn't I?'

She sits up for a moment and looks around the room, tidying her hair back from her face. I've always loved the sunset-yellow colour of it, the way gravity seems to act less on hers than it does on mine, meaning it bounds up into big flicks on either side of her face.

'It's like some part of you has always known,' she says, studying my poster of the rocket launching from Cape Canaveral, time-lapse trail marking its route to the sky. 'You always used to draw stars all over everything as well, remember?' She looks at me over her shoulder. 'You knew,' she says dreamily, as if from far away.

'Is there any chance of you shutting the hell up at some point?' Jam's voice comes through from the other side of the wall, muffled.

Mali breaks into a broad smile. 'Joram Rees, get your arse in here, I need to talk to you.'

He groans like it's the last thing he wants to do, but I hear his bed shift against the wall as he gets up. He moves my door open with a foot as Mali lies back next to me, and he leans in the doorway, hair sleep-tousled, squinting.

Mali bends a finger at him. 'Get over here, gorgeous,' she smirks. 'Wanna be the filling in the hottest girl sandwich the world has ever known?'

'Mali, I'm tired,' he sighs, turning to leave, but with a hint of a smile.

'No, Jam, wait, seriously,' she says, and he turns back. 'I have to tell you ... ' She's serious now, swallowing hard.

'I can't come with you to Spain. Bea will explain. It's just . . . ' She looks at me, pushes my head to the pillow and slams her hand over my ear, but I can still hear her as she says, 'I need you to look after her for me, OK? Make sure she eats and doesn't overdo it and . . . ' She turns to gaze down at me and then looks back at him. 'I know you will anyway, but . . . she's my girl, you know?'

And I watch Jam nod, shifting his eyes to me just before he closes the door.

When I wake up Mali's gone, and it almost seems like maybe it was all a dream. It's only slowly, as I blink up at the ceiling, that I realise it was real, and it falls on me lightly, like winter snow, that this makes everything different.

'Will Micah even still want to go?' I ask Jam, once I've explained everything, sitting down at the kitchen table to watch him putting bread in the toaster. 'I mean, he'll go for us. He'll feel like he has to. But will he want to?'

Jam turns and leans on the edge of the counter, folds his arms across his chest. 'He'll go, man. What else is he going to do for the next two weeks?'

That's when I have this sickening, plunging moment where all I do is think of Micah, think of being with him without Mali there. I don't even realise that it's made me pull my legs up on to my chair so that I am in a full foetal position with my hands over my ears until Jam says, 'I

88

know it sucks that Mali's not coming, but we'll still have fun.'

I manage to uncurl myself and look at him. He's standing there in the ratty, dark green hoody that he always wears in the mornings. It's too small for him – Ryan's right, he's grown so much recently – but buying new clothes isn't a luxury he can afford. I don't know what expression I have on my face, but he is frowning at me in silence, right up until the toaster pops behind him and he leaves the couple of photos he's just pulled off the fridge on the table and goes to grab the toast. The radio is quietly murmuring, a discussion panel about the escalating price of water, as I stare at the top photo on the table. It's a photo of me and Jam both aged eleven at our parents' wedding, standing stiffly side-by-side. I move it with my finger and look at the one underneath – me as a toddler on the beach.

Jam tips a piece of toast onto the plate in front of me.

'No thanks,' I say, suddenly realising how sick I feel.

'Eat it, Bea,' he says, before taking a bite out of his slice and then saying through a mouthful, 'You're setting off for another country today – you'll need your strength.'

So I'm grinning, but still feeling sick, when I take my first bite.

Escape Velocity

I'm in the front passenger seat, the one that Mali normally sits in, and the mist lies over everything so it's like we're flying through the sky. The only landmark I can see is the enormous dark barrier of Gower Gate, getting smaller in the wing mirror. For a moment I find it almost impossible to believe that we're really leaving. I've always feared the gravity of this place would keep me rooted here for ever; I've always doubted I'd ever get up enough speed to break away. And now, without gravity, we're flying, floating, falling.

'What's up, Karlo?' says Micah then, glancing at the side of my face before laughing uncertainly. 'Man, you look like you're about to hurl.'

'Yeah, well.' I swallow, forcing a smile. 'Your driving could do that to anyone.'

It makes me laugh how bad he is at driving. Like right now, when he's kind of leaning over to the side and looking at his feet on the pedals, talking to himself, though what about I have no idea.

'Bexley, do you want me to drive?' I ask him.

He laughs, but scratches his head, messing his hair. 'No, I'm fine, man.'

'I don't mind,' I say again. Since I turned seventeen last term and passed driver's education at school, I've been able to drive pretty well. It's probably the only thing I ever felt like a natural at. 'Let me drive,' I say again, watching him look back at me. 'Please.'

There's this couple of beats before he pulls over, clunks the door open and gets out, walks all the way around to my side before pulling my door open too.

'Switch with me,' he says.

'For real?'

'I have no doubt you're better at it than I am.'

He stands there holding my door and watching me get out while I can't stop smiling. I run around to his side and get into his still-warm seat, lay my hands on the ghost of his steering wheel grip. Then there's this moment when I am wondering if maybe I have actually forgotten how to do this, or maybe it's the fact that it's a bigger car than I learnt in. Then I realise what's wrong and reach under the seat, grab the lever and haul it forward, all the way to the front of the runners.

Micah laughs, pulls down the sunshade on his side. 'Short arse,' he says.

I let that slide, because it's him. I adjust the mirrors and try my feet on the pedals, turn the key.

'Oh man.' I grin, feeling it come to life.

Micah gazes at me with this growing smile. 'You should have just said, Karlo. I hate driving.'

I wind down the window a little, only because I like the way the wind feels in my hair. I swear I am smiling so hard it makes my head ache. I pick up speed, watch the straight hedges of the Agri-Tract's vast sheep-filled fields track by, one by one.

'Music, man,' I tell Micah.

'I'm on it,' he says, and I can see him connecting his data key to a complicated series of adaptors and cables in my peripheral vision. This car is old; it's a Tesla 13, so it predates the Information Collapse and is only set up to get music via the now non-existent Internet unless persuaded otherwise.

The music starts and Micah drums out the irregular rhythm of the opening bars on the dashboard before saying, '"Go Your Own Way", Fleetwood Mac – utter classic.'

And Jam says, 'OK,' not sounding convinced.

Micah turns it up and shouts over it. 'What people don't realise is that the nineteen-seventies was really the defining era for modern popular music. So experimental.'

'Last month you were saying that exact thing about the nineteen-nineties,' Jam says.

'No, I wasn't.'

'Yes, you were,' Jam and I both say simultaneously, before laughing.

'Well, I was wrong,' he says. 'And I plan to spend this trip showing you why.'

'You're off to a good start,' I tell him, and then I start shrugging, twisting my shoulders, shucking off my coat. Micah reaches across to help me, but ends up pulling my cardigan off too, the backs of his fingers trailing down my shoulder blade, raising goosebumps.

He turns round and throws my cardigan on to the back seat.

I peer into the rear view, but Jam is expressionless, hood up, unreadable as ever.

'Whose guitar is that?' asks Micah, seeing it in the back with Jam.

'It was Jam's dad's,' I say.

'Why would you bring a guitar that nobody can play?' Micah laughs.

'Because this is a road trip,' I say, laughing too, 'and you need a guitar on a road trip.'

'You do? Who says?'

'You just *do*, OK? And we can learn. We can sit around the campfire and learn.'

'I am already LOVING road-tripping with you, Karlo, for the record.'

'Thanks,' I say, but it comes out quiet, and I can feel Jam looking at me.

Micah checks his watch. 'We've got time to make a stop. Next left,' he says. 'I'll show you something weird.'

The road we turn onto travels straight between hedges, and we pass all the shepherds who are waiting at the water stations with empty eyes.

'Why are they all standing there like that?' I find myself asking.

'Drinking water ration,' says Micah. 'Mid-morning.'

Once the road hits the hillside it winds up and we end up in a cloud, so thick and white I have to slow right down.

'Keep going,' says Micah. 'There won't be anyone else up here, I'm telling you.'

'Nice one, Bexley – get me driving and then take me off on some weird mission.'

'It's cool, seriously. We're almost there. In fact –' he points at a rock – 'turn down there. Follow the tyre tracks next to that rock.'

'We're going to get stuck,' I say, feeling the wheels spin a little.

'We won't,' says Micah. 'Trust me.'

The blue-grey sheep call to each other and run ahead, like they're leading the way, red ear-tag trackers bouncing, double-G branding on their hindquarters. We can probably only see about three metres in any direction and all there is to see is tufts of dew-soaked grass, water held like pearls. A world so wet, and never any water when you need it.

'Here we are,' says Micah, just as we get to an open gate.

I pull in, stop, wrapping my cardigan back around my shoulders as I peer into the mist. Micah opens the door and jumps out. I glance back at Jam before I get out and follow him.

The house materialises, stone by mossy stone. Not that it's exactly a house any more since there's no actual roof, not beyond a few rotten-looking beams. It must be four hundred years old or something, at least, judging by the walls, which are layer upon layer of smooth, charcoal-coloured stone, woven across with moss and bright yellow lichen. I lay my hand on one for a moment as Micah goes to the door and pushes it open. Inside, under the sky, there's a room with a huge fireplace, one room still wallpapered with this print of squirrels chasing each other among studded daisies, peeling into flaps. There's a huge stone fireplace and a winding staircase that leads up to the second floor that's no longer there. Down a narrow passage there's a half collapsed kitchen with a cooker that's been eaten into a lacy shadow of itself by rust.

'What is this place?' asks Jam, touching the corner of a wooden chair, the only piece of furniture.

'My family lived here,' says Micah.

'Seriously?'

'Yeah for, like, hundreds of years. They worked the farm. My dad was born here.'

'No way,' I breathe. 'That's so cool.' I walk into the middle of the building and try to picture what it must have been like to live here. I pan back down to Micah. 'I can't imagine belonging to a place in that way, having a family home. How does it feel?'

He shrugs. 'Irrelevant, I guess,' he says. 'The hills are full of abandoned houses. Now all of this is just . . . a load of stories we'll never get to hear.'

'This is better than nothing though, isn't it?' I say, looking at Jam. 'I mean, take us as an example – Jam's mum came from Damascus and he knows literally zero about it. Ryan and Joella both grew up in the children's home.'

'And what about the other side?' asks Micah, quietly. 'What about Dylan's family? They're from around here, aren't they?'

I can feel Jam staring at me in alarm.

'I've never had the chance to ask,' I say. 'Come on, let's get going.'

On the outskirts of Abertawe we stop to charge the car and, while it's hooked up, we walk to the HyperPharm. What's funny about Abertawe is that they kept much of the old city intact and just built on top of it, so there are these old buildings slotted into the bottom of the new ones like mismatched puzzle pieces.

At the HyperPharm, Micah realises he's forgotten his toothbrush and goes to look for a new one while Jam and I wait for my prescription.

Micah's barely out of earshot when Jam says, 'You told him about Dylan?'

'Yeah, I don't know why I did that.'

'I thought you were taking that to the grave.'

'Well, now Micah is too.'

He looks up at where there are tiny brown birds that have become trapped in here, chasing each other along just under the ceiling, beyond the fluorescent strip bulbs. He has this look on his face like there are all these things he is thinking of saying but in the end all that comes out is:

'He's Mali's boyfriend. Don't forget that just because she's not here.'

'Jesus, Jam, I know,' I say, before I turn to pick up my stupidly large plastic bag of medications, but Jam's still going:

'He can't just become one of your conquests.'

'Conquests!' I laugh. 'Speaking of which ... I really want you to make the effort to get some action this trip.'

He looks away from me, but I take hold of his sleeve, pull on it so that he faces me.

'Oh man, Bea.' He cringes. 'Come on.'

'Seriously. If you tell girls you're moving to outer space and never coming back they'll be all over you.'

He just stares at me, unreadable, so I give up on it.

'Let's find the sunscreen,' I say. 'And did you bring a hat?'

He shakes his head at me, as if despairing, and walks away.

'What?' I shout after him, but he's gone. Which is how come once I meet them both outside again, I shove this ridiculous woven sun hat on Jam's head and say, 'Now don't say I never get you anything.'

'Yee-ha!' smirks Micah, and when I look again at Jam I realise why. The shape of the hat, combined with his flicked out long hair and checked shirt, means that suddenly there is more than a little cowboy about him. It's actually not a bad look on him, if I'm being honest.

'Come on, desperado, saddle up and let's head out,' I say, but he just rolls his eyes.

Resonance

The raised Trans-Southern highway takes us across England at such a height and speed that we don't see anything of it. Or I don't, anyway, since I'm mostly concentrating on being part of the traffic on a four-lane, high-speed road for the first time in my life, shifting lanes and daring myself to push down the accelerator pedal, fingers gripping the wheel.

We get quite close to Portsmouth and Jam and Micah are both leaning at their windows, noses pressed, so amazed by the huge sky-scraping buildings that they forget they're supposed to be directing me and it's only by some miracle that I make the right turn for the port. We show our tickets and ID and get waved into a lane and then another lane, until we are in this huge queuing system with the boat up ahead, sitting on the beaten-metal grey of the sea, lowering its huge ramp with a hum. I'm looking around at the ranks of other cars lined up around us, and I see nobody but teenagers hanging off open doors, sitting side-by-side on bonnets or roofs. Music flooding out of every window.

We're only probably a couple of kilometres out to sea when I find myself at the back of the boat, watching the churned water it kicks out behind, the southern coast of England turning into nothing more than a line of clouds on the horizon. I get stuck, standing there, watching, part of me knowing I'm never going back; wondering if Joella was right and I will die out here. There are fathoms of water beneath me and I start wondering if they are full of fish, or rocks, or whales, or whether they're just empty. The only thing I see is plastic bags and bottles, swirling past the side of the boat like dead animals.

'Look at all that crap.' Micah appears next to me.

'This is our great filter,' I say.

'Our what?'

'From the Fermi Paradox,' I sigh. 'There's a theory that the reason we've had such minimal contact with aliens is that there are great filters that life can't survive; that civilisations get to a certain level of development and then just ... destroy themselves. So they never get advanced enough to colonise space or even travel through much of it.' I look back down at the currents of junk in the sea. 'The way things are going ...'

He turns so that he's leaning with his back on the railing, watching me, an amused smile. 'It's only a bit of crazy weather, some litter and a few dead polar bears,' he says. 'I don't know what everyone has to get so worked up about.'

I punch him on the arm and say, 'Let's get a drink.'

We stand next to each other at the bar and feel a surge beneath us.

'This is the first time I've ever been on a boat,' I say.

'Serious?' He smiles.

'Why would I ever have been on a boat?' I say. 'How have you ever been on a boat?'

'Fishing trip with Dad once. Off Barry Island.'

'Did you catch anything?'

He taps his lips with a finger like he's thinking about it. 'I remember a squid that I wanted to keep as a pet.'

'That's pretty cool.'

'It was. Until my dad made me eat it later, for dinner.'

'What?'

'Yeah,' he laughs. 'Some kind of life lesson.'

I make a face. 'Teaching you what?'

He shrugs. 'Not sure. Circle of life?'

I can't think what to say to that, so I'm relieved that the barman lines up three matt red beer cans with the word *Estrella* on them in front of us right at that moment.

'Have you seen where we're supposed to sleep?' asks Jam, just arriving next to me.

Micah stays at the bar while Jam leads me into the centre of the boat and down a staircase, then another, each getting narrower and dirtier and barer in structure until the last one, which is basically a ladder. At the bottom of it we're in a vast, windowless, airless room of filthy bunks, most of which are occupied by people hunched over bags they're sorting through.

'Oh man, are we –' I swallow – 'underwater?'

Jam shrugs. 'I guess so.'

'You don't think it would be like this? On Ventura, I mean,' I say, a wave of claustrophobia burying me.

He leans against a girder and shifts his hat back on his head a little before looking around. 'Maybe,' he says, nodding. 'Except if something goes wrong here at least we have a chance of swimming away and surviving.'

I hit his arm. 'Jam, you're not helping,' I say, and I'm smiling even though there's a tightness in my throat. God, it's hot down here. I touch the nearest metal wall and my fingertips come away wet.

'It's all good,' says Jam, pulling at the back of my shirt as he turns to leave. 'It'll be much cooler in space, and anyway the view will be better.'

Which is why I'm smiling as I follow him back up the narrow steps.

When we get back up to the bar all the seats are taken, and there are these two girls sitting either side of Micah in a patch of sun on the carpet near the door. They're both in super-short jean shorts and hoodies.

'This is Fin,' says Micah, right in the middle of laughing. 'And this is Tara. They've been hitchhiking. Who even does that?'

'We do!' says Fin, revealing ridiculously white and strong teeth.

'I drank your beer,' says Tara, staring at me.

'That's OK,' I say. 'Just get me a fresh one.'

'Sure,' she says, jumping up and pulling me over to the bar with her, where she looms over me and talks into my hair. 'Which one of these is yours?'

'Which one of what?'

'Oh come on,' she laughs. 'You can't call dibs on both, girl – play fair.'

I arch my back so I can get far away enough to shoot her a look. 'Where the hell are you from?'

'Wisconsin, USA – why?'

'What are you doing on this boat?'

'Same as you.'

I frown and she laughs, filling my blank. 'All the direct flights to Spain were full.'

'All the flights were full?'

She shrugs. 'Of course! Now ...' she says, stepping closer again, 'don't change the subject.'

I blink for a few seconds while she watches me. 'I ... um ... Well, I don't "claim dibs" on either, but you should probably know that Micah is my best friend's boyfriend.'

'What about the cowboy?' She turns her back to the bar and leans against it, watching Jam closely, biting lightly on a thumbnail, the smile of an animal on the hunt, if animals could smile. I look over at Jam, and end up seeing him through her eyes for a moment in a way that's disorientating. Dark hair falling over half his face, moody mouthed, hat tipped forward, lowering his long body to the floor in a series of graceful stages.

I shake it off and say, 'I assume you're talking about Jam, and to be honest, you probably won't even ... ' But before I can quite figure out what I'm going to say, the barman comes over and sets up a line of beers.

Tara takes hold of one of the cans. 'I probably won't even what?'

I laugh. 'It's just that Jam isn't a big talker, so it's not like ... ' I trail off again.

She raises an eyebrow. 'Who said anything about talking, girl? These might be my last days on Earth. And anyway, I love the strong-and-silent type,' She nudges me with her elbow before she heads back and takes the spot by Jam, folding her long legs up next to him and asking, 'So what's your name, cowboy?'

I snort and Jam shoots me a look from under the brim of his hat that makes me smile and look away.

After a while I get bored of watching Micah letting Fin grab at his arm and lean all over him while she laughs too much at every single thing he says, so I head out onto the deck again, alone. I rest my chin on the lowest rung even though the vibrations rattle my teeth. Sea to all horizons, and an overarching bridge of sky; a between place. I try to decide if the feeling that flaps against my ribs is fear or excitement. Pain rattles in my stomach and I hear myself draw breath through my teeth.

'They'll make you cut your hair, Jam, you know they will!' I hear Micah say and I turn and watch them through the open doorway. 'In fact, we should probably shave it all off right now.'

Micah sounds drunk. In fact, I can see it in the slackness in the muscles of his face – he's forgetting how he usually smiles. He looks over and sees me watching him. I look away but sense him coming over. I take steadying breaths as I feel him squat behind me, one of his knees contacting the small of my back.

'What are you doing out here, Karlo?'

'Nothing. Just thinking. Go back inside.'

He says nothing for a moment, then, 'Now that's what I call a sunset,' and weirdly it's only then that I notice it, the hot pink streaks that sit along the edges of the thick clouds, reflected in the milky smoothness of the flat ocean.

'Weird how the sunset is better if there's clouds,' I say.

'I don't think that's weird,' says Micah. 'It's the usual way of things. The imperfections that improve the perfections.'

'That's not a thing,' I glance at him over my shoulder.

'Yes, it is,' he laughs.

'Don't you have to get back to Fin?'

He laughs. 'Well, Rees has got his hands full anyway, whether he likes it or not,' and we both look back at where Tara is leaning hard into Jam's side, speaking into his hair while he studies his beer can.

'Just to be clear,' I say. 'I was flagging up the fact that Fin's hot for you.'

'I get it.' He grins.

'So you should mention, probably sooner rather than later, that you have a girlfriend.'

'I'm on it, Karlo, I promise you. I'm used to having to let girls down gently.'

'Of all the many nauseatingly arrogant things I have ever heard you say, that one's right up there.' I look back to the horizon while he laughs.

'Harsh,' he says. 'But true.'

'It's spectacularly crap that Mali couldn't come.' I shift a little, twisting until I am part way turned to him.

'Yep.' He nods. 'Bad things happen, though. I've learned that over the years.'

'You've learned over the years that bad things happen?' I make a face. 'Wow, Bexley, you're *so* wise. I mean, you're like some kind of oracle.'

He laughs. 'Well, it certainly looks like you've got giving me crap covered in Mali's absence, so that's a relief.'

'Oh, I've got it more than covered. Mals goes way easier on you than I will.'

He watches me for a few beats then, as I turn back to the view of tracking waves.

'Everyone on this boat is volunteering for Ventura,' I say. 'Have you noticed that?'

'Yeah,' he says, laughing, and I feel his breath on the bare skin of my shoulder. 'Hardly surprising, given the crap prospects people our age face.'

'Don't you think there's something super-weird about the fact that this whole boat is filled with people prepared to leave everything they've ever known behind?' I ask him.

He glances around at the groups and pairs of teenagers, up and down the deck in the violet light.

'I think it's sad that one of them is you,' is all he says.

I lean my forehead on the nearest railing.

'Come on, Karlo,' he sighs, after what feels like for ever. 'I know what'll sort you out.'

'What?' I croak.

'Vodka shot.'

'Urgh, no.'

'I'm afraid I must insist. It's what you need.'

I have no idea how many shots I've already downed when Micah carries another round over and lays the tray on the floor in the middle of everyone's legs. I watch Tara pick two of them up and hand one to Jam before doing hers neatly and watching him do his. Then she decides there's some on his chin that needs licking off, dragging her tongue up towards his lower lip. It's such a lame come-on, I roll my eyes. Jam being Jam, he doesn't react right away, he just watches her, and I'm so proud of him in that moment. But it doesn't last, and a moment later I find I'm watching the movement of his jaw as this long, slow kiss unfolds, and I must be staring hard enough for Fin to notice my expression and laugh, and that's when I realise I'm going to be sick and I get up and stumble to the bathroom and heave up the entire contents of my stomach. And I don't know if it's the pitch and slow swerve of the boat that's brought it on at this point, or the vodka, or maybe both. Either way, the vomit contains a single crimson streak of blood that I stare at as it makes its way down the dirty bowl.

I lie on the sticky floor, curled around the base of the toilet, until I get it together enough to stand and then I'm back outside, stepping on people's legs in the dark, heading forward and forward, following the movement of the boat until I run out of deck, and then I'm leaning out over the dark, crawling on to this little place that seems like it was made for me to lie there and watch the stars spin above.

Tidal Force

I wake up with my face pressed against the leg of Jam's jeans.

'You OK?' he says, laying his hand on my head. 'We found you curled around the anchor, you know.'

I try to laugh but it hurts.

'I'm glad you think it's funny,' says Tara. 'Because I think it's stupid.' She levers herself up on her elbows and looks at me. 'They spent an hour looking for you last night, panicking.' She sits and slides her back against the wall. 'Talk about high maintenance.'

I get up and pull at the door fifty times before Jam leans forward and pushes it open for me. I get out into the fresh morning air and gulp at it. A few metres away, Micah is leaning over the railings, watching the line of land that is appearing out of a blue, hazy horizon. I stand next to him, elbow to elbow.

He studies the side of my face, then says, 'Karlo, you

scare the crap out of me. If you were mine I would be ... just ... terrified, every day.'

If you were mine ...

Jesus, that spins me out for a good few beats before I pick up the thread again.

'Terrified of what?'

'Terrified of the moment you'd come back to me in a box.'

I narrow my eyes. 'Don't give me that sick girl crap.'

He nods, looks away. 'It's my fault. Shouldn't have let you get so drunk. I know you need to be more careful. And I know how reckless you can be.'

'So because I've got faulty equipment, I shouldn't live my life? I shouldn't be me? I should be an entirely different person?'

'That's not what I mean,' he says. 'But you do understand that Mali would kill me if something happened to you?'

I kick at the bottom rung of the railings, aware that I'm pouting like a child but not able to stop it.

He sighs. 'We're getting pretty close, we should go find the car.'

He curls his arm around my shoulders to squeeze them while we walk, like it's the most casual thing in the world. It probably is, for him.

Down on the car deck, the engines are making the world vibrate. We find Jam sitting on the floor with his back against the car door, hat tipped forward and head down. We get in the car and I take hold of the steering wheel and stare at it. Micah watches me, letting a smile grow.

'Oh man, this is hilarious,' he says. 'Do we even know where we're going when we get off this thing?' He looks back at Jam, who is pulling a map out of his bag.

'This is our route,' Jam says, tracing a line diagonally down from the middle of Spain's north coast to some spot way down in the southwest. 'But let's just get to the first place we can camp. We can work out the rest from there.'

Just then, Fin and Tara walk past Micah's window and lean down to press fishy lips on it, leaving smears on the glass and laughing as they walk away leaning on each other. We watch them sliding between the cars until they get to where two guys are standing leaning on the roof of their black car, raising hands at them.

'Looks like they found themselves a lift then,' says Micah.

'Good for them,' I say, staring at the steering wheel. 'Because if I see them on a lonely road, I am driving right on by.'

Micah laughs. 'They weren't that bad.'

'Well, Mali will be so glad to hear that you're assuaging your loneliness.'

'Assuaging my loneliness!' He laughs. 'Rees was the only one assuaging. I was just drinking, man!'

'Well, I wouldn't know.'

'Your choice, Karlo. You were the one that decided you'd rather cuddle up to the anchor and get yourself reported as a suspected man overboard.' He shakes his head. 'Crazy girl.'

I shoot him a look, even though sliding my eyes his way makes my head threaten to come apart, layer by layer, like an onion.

At last the massive hatch door at the end of the boat is lowering, letting the sunlight in, and because of the angle we are at, it belts right in at us, full light and heat in a way that almost makes me want to puke, that makes me hold my hand up in front of my face to try and hide from it. 'Find my sunglasses, Jam.'

'Have mine,' says Micah, and he pulls his off and hands them to me. When I push them on, the bit that was on his nose is still warm, and they slide down my face. Too big.

He laughs, which makes me pull down the sunshade to check the mirror. They look ridiculous. Mirrored aviators are something that Micah can pull off while most people can't.

We wait our turn to drive off the ramp, and I can't stop thinking about steering a little wrong and plunging us into the sea. I'm concentrating so hard, I don't even realise I am talking to myself ... 'OK, you can do this. You can do this.'

'Ah man, Karlo, you're scaring me,' says Micah.

But then I am on the ramp and all the things I am worrying about going wrong are not happening and we are out over the water and then we are on land. On Spanish land. In a foreign country for the first time in my life.

I can't help it – I end up letting out this ridiculous whooping sound. We're here, out of Gower Gate, out of Wales, in Spain, driving on the wrong side of the road, me and two of my favourite people in the world. And I almost say all this to them but I don't, so this one noise has to say it all for me and I guess it does because they both smile and watch me bang out a rhythm on the steering wheel for a few seconds before I shout, 'Let's go viva ourselves some España amigos!'

Santander is a massive Spanish city with crazy, honking, multi-lane traffic and tall buildings hemming in either side of every street; skyscrapers that disappear into the heights rub shoulders with edifices of pale honey stone, some of which have been partly consumed by the mirrored glass and metal of newer structures, just like in Abertawe. Heat and humidity and the overwhelming aromas of garlic and incinerator smoke and seawater buffet my face through the open window. I try to look around as much as I can without taking my eyes off the road, but there's so much to see. Giant faces on bright, moving advertising billboards keep catching my eye and throwing me off. At one point we drive along the edge of a square and there is this church, or cathedral ... I don't know what, like a giant palace or castle, as if we accidentally just drove into a fairy tale.

'Wow!' I say, leaning low to look at it as we pass.

Jam spreads the map out in the back seat, the wind flapping it in his face. 'Follow signs for Torrelavega.'

'Torre-where?'

'There,' says Micah, pointing at a sign, and a moment later we find ourselves on the highway, heading south, cityscape turning into hulking suburban urbanisations that look just like Gower Gate, but covered in way more interesting graffiti. And then we are in what looks like a Spanish version of an Agri-Tract. Either side of us, row after perfectly straight row of short, gnarled olive trees stripe past the window.

I glance out at them quickly, 'I'm confused – I thought they hadn't done the whole Centralisation thing here?'

'They haven't,' says Micah, his head turning as he watches the rows pass. 'The Spanish government just turned all the land over to export products. That's why they've ended up losing all the people, I guess.'

'Losing people?'

'This country's, like, four times bigger than the UK, but has only about a quarter of the population.'

'How do you know this?'

'Don't you listen in European Macroeconomics, Miss Karlo?'

'Of course not,' I laugh.

Beyond the tract, a wall of mountains rises in front of us, under a cloudless blue sky. They're almost perfectly triangular and each capped with a topping of snow, even though down here it's hot. They're what I would have drawn, aged five, if you'd asked me to draw mountains, and within half an hour we are in there, part of the picture, winding through them – a wall of rock on either side, bouncing back at us the David Bowie album Micah's playing. Sometimes we pass an abandoned village tucked in amongst the rocks, ranged along the water that babbles through the valley bottom.

'Full-on *Lord of the Rings*,' says Micah, winding down his window and using the little camera he has on a cord round his neck to take pictures.

I laugh. 'I know, right?'

There are places where the cliffs look like they're crumbling, where vast wire nets have been drilled into the face to keep boulders from tumbling on to the road and crushing whoever happens to be there at the time, and these giant lumps of mountain are caught, held in suspended animation in their sickening death plunge. It's so like being in another world that I don't even think about how scary it is to drive under.

That's when we see it up ahead, propped on the side of the road – a hand painted sign that says *CAMPING 1km*.

'I'm giving that a swerve,' I hear myself say.

Micah laughs. 'Why? They probably have facilities and stuff.'

'Is it safe to stay around here though?' I ask. 'What with the falling rocks and whatever.' And as I say it, as if on cue, the sun appears between the walls of the valley up ahead and the land parts, like curtains, and we are suddenly in these widespread green and golden hillsides, and there's another sign, but this time with an arrow pointing in through a gate.

'OK, fine.' And I turn in, bump on to the grass, and find myself pulling to a halt just short of ploughing down a red tent, with this guy standing just the other side of it, looking horrified. I can't help laughing.

We step out of the car and Micah starts speaking to the guy in Spanish. It's the first time I've seen or heard him do it, so I spend a couple of seconds mesmerised by how easy he makes it seem when even deciphering another language seems as impossible to me as sprouting wings and flying.

Because I'm pretty sure this guy is mostly kicking off about me nearly running his tent over, I walk away into the middle of the field and look around. There are a bunch of tents pitched on the gently sloping hillside, with people our age sat out in front of them, or on the bonnets of their cars. The mountains we just came through guard the sky to the north, while ahead there is this broad, smooth river snaking off among olive groves.

'Wow,' I hear myself say.

'Yeah,' says Jam, from right behind me. I didn't realise he had followed me.

Right then is when a black four-by-four speeds along the road, straight past the gate, before backing up with a screech to turn in, with Fin and Tara waving at us from the back windows.

And I say, 'Well, ain't that just perfect?' as I kick my way back through the grass to the car.

Sidereal

'Ernesto says there's a charge station down there that has a shop,' says Micah, while I'm struggling with a tent pole.

'Who's Ernesto?' I ask him, before getting up and seeing the guy I nearly ran over standing next to Micah.

'Ernesto Suarez,' he says, offering me his hand.

'Bea.' I take it. 'Sorry about nearly hitting you, but you are camped kind of close to the gate. You realise that, right?'

He half smiles. 'You're funny,' he says.

'So they tell me,' I sigh.

'I hear you're on your way to Andalucía too, to volunteer for Ventura?' he says with an accent.

I nod, noticing the golden glow of his skin. He's not my type, but I can tell I'm probably in the minority.

'I drive down from San Sebastian,' he says. 'Expensive trip. I stay off the *peaje*, like you.'

'The what?'

'The toll roads,' clarifies Micah.

'*Mira*,' says Ernesto, pointing way down along the length of the valley, squinting against the sun. 'You see it?'

I follow the line of his arm and finger to where I can just about see a structure striding out across a gap between distant hills, spindly and delicate against the sunlight.

'*La Red*,' he says. '150 speed limit, get you from one end of Spain to the other in ten hours. Connects only the metropolitan areas. But costs *muuuuucha plata*,' he laughs, and even though I don't know exactly what that means, I get the picture. 'If you're like me, you'll have to take the small roads. Will take a little longer, but I need money to make it home again if I don't get picked.' He's still laughing, but I'm not. I can't think about not getting picked.

Tara has Jam basically pinned to the ground. I'm all for a rescue, but Micah convinces me to leave him there while we walk to the charge station to buy food. It feels like leaving him in the wild to get feasted on by lions, but I do it anyway. Micah and I walk along the edge of the road in the sunset light, him stopping to take pictures every five metres, including one of me sticking my tongue out, mountains as backdrop.

The shop at the station turns out to be this little hut with about three shelves in it, but one of the shelves happens to have a basket of freshly baked, still warm loaves of bread on it. Hanging from the ceiling there are these huge, red and amber streaked sinewy legs that probably belonged to pigs, hanging on greasy rope. They stink of death and decay, but Micah somehow still says, 'Oh yes, this is exactly what we need,' and gets the guy to understand what he wants. Which is, seemingly, to have this revolting piece of animal anatomy hefted over to a circular blade where paper-thin, translucent slices are produced and sandwiched between sheets of waxed paper.

We are back out in the sun, and I am swearing blind that there is no way I will ever eat such a thing when Micah says, 'I think you should try it first.' His eyes flick to mine. 'Seriously. My grandmother brought some of this over once. I'm pretty sure it's going to blow your mind.'

I don't know why I trust him, but I take a slice of the meat between my finger and thumb and put it in my mouth. It's salty and warm and melting and delicious, and I start to wonder how many other things in life I have been so completely wrong about.

Back at the campsite, the last of the daylight is fading fast, and there is a fire, and everyone is sitting around it, and I can see how all this deserved to become a cliché. I don't know how much ham I have eaten by this time, but enough to leave me with greasy hands and chin, and make Micah decide he has to hide it from me so there's some left for the morning. This involves him prising it out of my hands and holding it above my head while I pull on his arms to try and get it back within my reach and then it kind of ends up where we're basically wrestling over it and then we're on the ground and I'm lying on him and we're both laughing and then there's just this millisecond where we both get still and are looking at each other. It takes that for me to realise how completely out of order we are being, and I untangle myself from him and sit up.

'You can play?' Ernesto says, pointing to the guitar that is leant up against the back of our car.

'No,' I somehow manage to say. 'Can you?'

'*Claro*,' he says.

'Help yourself, man,' says Micah, straightening up his T-shirt in a way that makes me blush hard and look away.

Ernesto steps through the long grass to our car and picks the guitar up by the neck. 'Oof,' he says when he twangs the first string. He brings it back into the light by the fire and cradles it in his lap, tuning it.

The stars are coming out by now, just a few, way up in the highest, furthest parts of the sky and I end up lying back in the cooling grass, watching them appear, as Ernesto makes the guitar quietly come to life. It takes me a while to realise that Micah is lying back too, at right angles to me, turning his head slightly my way as he says, 'What do you think about, when you look up there?'

I just about dare to look along the glossy grass at him, at the way he hasn't closed his mouth after speaking, so that his top teeth are resting just lightly on his lower lip, at the way he looks different when he's lying on his back.

'Does it scare you when you think about being up there?' he says. 'Or is it exciting?'

I look back to the sky and I'm aware of my heartbeat in my ears.

'What I think is –' I swallow – 'that Epsilon Eridani looks pretty far away.'

'You seriously know which star it is you're going to?'

I nod.

'Which one is it then?' He moves closer to me, staring up. 'Show me.'

I shift in closer, point up. 'See that one there, next to the really twinkly one, that's close to that formation that kind of looks like a seahorse ... there ... you see it?'

'Ummm, I think ...'

'So follow the line of stars that runs right along – see it? There's the Western Cross and just a little to the ... Bexley, you know I'm completely making this up, right?'

'Jesus, Karlo.' He shakes his head at himself.

'You're way too easy, man,' I laugh.

'Looks that way,' he says, grinning, and somehow we end up looking at each other again, spending too long on it so that I'm the one to break it.

Ernesto stops playing to say, 'Whose guitar is this?' and I point at Jam, over on the other side of the fire.

'Can you play?' asks Ernesto.

Jam doesn't say no, like I expect him to. Instead he reaches for the neck that Ernesto offers him, manoeuvres himself out of Tara's grip a little, settles the guitar in his lap, and to my amazement, starts to play. A few chords at first, then a tune, something I almost recognise.

'What the ...? Why didn't you say you could play?' I stammer out, stunned.

He raises his eyes to me for a second, keeps playing. 'You never asked.'

'You know, you don't even look a little bit like brother and sister,' says Fin.

I look away from Jam for a split second to make a face at her. 'Maybe that's because we're not.'

'Oh.' She frowns. 'Micah said ...'

'Jam's dad is married to my mum.'

'That is so weird,' she says, taking another pull on the bottle of wine she has in her lap, and shaking her head.

'Why is it weird?' I feel my face twisting up again. But suddenly I am completely distracted, because there is something familiar in what Jam is playing, especially now that Ernesto is humming the vocal melody over the top of his halting chord sequence. 'Oh my God,' I grin.

Jam doesn't respond at all.

'That's um –' I snap my fingers – 'that's ...' Jam glances up at me as I finally get it. 'Oh my God, that's "Creep". That's Radiohead.'

He barely responds, but I know I'm right.

'Man,' I say, 'we used to be so into them.'

'Oh, you're just so cool and alternative, aren't you?' says

123

Tara, and she's doing this big toothy grin at me through the darkness, but it is way more like a snarl than anything else. 'With your nineteen-nineties references and your go-to-hell attitude and your death wish.'

Suddenly Jam messes up, plays a wrong chord, stops to scratch his head, and everything goes quiet.

Into the silence I manage to say, 'I haven't got any more of a death wish than anyone else here.'

'That's probably true. You just make damn sure everybody knows about it.'

I can't help laughing at that. 'What is your problem?'

'Nothing at all. I just call BS when I see it.' And she widens her eyes at me.

Fin laughs.

'I think one spaceship's going to be way too small for the two of you,' says Micah, still lying flat, grinning at the sky.

I get to my feet, unsteady, grab Micah's wine bottle by the neck and take it with me, stumbling off through the grass, heading downhill, and talking to myself as I go. At some point I realise it's just me and the stars and the earth beneath my feet, and then there isn't even that any more, because I am at the river, and it is murmuring by, smooth and relentless, like an endless snake. I pull my trainers off and lower my feet into the cool water at the river's edge, sit swigging at the wine, watching the whispers of starlight on the water. The sound of the insects around me has changed; they are now loud and filling every inch of the silence, punctuated by a percussion section of frogs. All of that, and the warmth that sits on my skin in a sheen even though the night has fallen, makes me feel so far from home, makes me feel afraid, makes me feel like maybe I am just now coming to life for the first time.

Micah arrives next to me, and sits. 'Thought I'd better check you didn't fall in the river.'

'Well, I didn't,' I say flatly, refusing to look at him.

'So mean and moody,' he says, reaching down and splashing me with water.

I catch him with a gentle kick in the ribs but he hams it up, half laughing, falling on to his side in the grass.

'That really hurt,' he says, muffled.

'Good,' I say, smirking.

When he sits back up, slowly, adjusting back into a sitting position by stages, I leave my wet foot where it is and it ends up in his lap. He lays his hand on my toes for a moment, and I jolt from the contact. Then I watch his other hand reaching for me, moving along the length of my legs just inches above them and I . . . can't breathe. But then his fingers come to rest on the book that's just about to fall out of my bag as it sits on my hip. It's Shayma's copy of *Tender is the Night*, which I've been reading at every opportunity, falling pretty deeply in love with and going on about to Jam whenever I get the chance.

'OK, what's so good about this book then?' He leans forward over it, flips it so he is studying the back jacket.

'It's ...' I shrug. I'm always like this when it comes to justifying my feelings for something I love. I can feel it; I just can't talk about it. 'It's ... incredibly sad and incredibly beautiful. Both equally.'

He nods at the book for a few seconds before looking up at me again. 'Like its reader,' he says, handing it back.

He's holding it out for a few seconds before I take it. 'I'm not ...' I manage.

'You are. Both equally.' He smiles. 'I don't mean you're a downer or anything. You don't *act* sad. But it still seems like you are. Inside.'

I look out across the river and the silence goes on too long.

'I think you have good reason to be,' he says eventually, shifting in the edge of my vision.

I look back at him. 'What does that mean?'

He is wide-eyed. 'Just that you have a lot of crap to put up with. It would make anyone sad.'

I narrow my eyes. 'You and Mals sit around discussing my sad life, do you?' I pull my foot out of his lap and get up. 'I'm going to bed.'

'Don't be like that,' he says, laughing.

'I don't want your pity.'

He stands up too and lays his hands on my shoulders. 'Nobody pities you.' He sighs and I feel it on my lower lip. 'We've been good friends for what – three years? You think I don't know you by now?'

I turn to go, mostly because I can't be this close to him without feeling like I'm going to die from it. Die from the disease of him. Die from the disease of completely impossible love.

'I also said you were beautiful, Karlo,' he says to my back. 'For the record.'

It steals down across my skin, under my clothes. I don't stop, even though it seems like I should, or maybe at least say thank you to the first and only person who has ever said that to me. Instead I keep walking, under the diamond mine of infinite space above, the stars that seem to hum at me now, calling me to come get lost among them.

It's dawn when I wake up. There is a gentle light outside and I stumble over to the outhouse, looking up at the sky, the way it is this pale, watery colour just before the sun comes out. Birds have taken over from the frogs and crickets, filling the silence with eerie whoops and tweets I've never heard before. I get to the outhouse and the door is locked so I stand and wait, gazing up, unable to stop smiling at it all. After a minute it opens and Jam steps out.

'Dawns are different here,' I say before he sees me, and it makes him jump.

'Jesus, you scared the crap out of me.'

'Different dawns,' I say again, ignoring him. 'Different skies.'

He finishes clipping his belt closed; his T-shirt is draped over his bare shoulder.

'Did you sleep with her?' I ask him.

He doesn't answer, but he looks around the field once and then back at me, and I know.

'Gross,' I say.

'Why gross?' he says. 'Bea, you're the one who told me to get out there. You're the one who said we have this end of the world scenario ...'

'It's not an end of the world scenario with them – there's every chance you'll spend the rest of your life trapped in a spaceship with them.'

He concentrates on easing the outhouse door closed with his foot.

'Well, you know, it is how it is,' he says.

'It is how it is? Jam, Tara is horrible. I hope you're at least being careful.'

He rolls his eyes. 'Man, Bea, I'm not a kid any more you know.'

'I know.'

'Do you, though?'

He looks right at me, his dark eyes questioning, his face for once not obscured by a hood or a hat or hair. His hair is wet at the front and pushed back, his chest bare and already slightly darkened by the Spanish sun. I notice the line of dark, perfectly circular moles that run across it, and then the angry-looking, pink mosquito bites on his shoulder.

128

'You've been bitten,' I tell him. 'I have cream if you want some.'

'I'm fine,' he says with a sigh.

I follow his gaze as he looks up at the mountains behind me, where they are hiding in morning mist.

'You're flirting pretty heavily with Bexley,' he says then.

I reach for the door behind him, pull it open.

'I'm not,' I say, into the darkness within.

'OK, Bea,' he says, but like it's not OK.

'Even if I was – it's the end of the world, remember?'

'Only for us,' he says, and walks back to his tent.

Ultraviolet

It's later in the morning that the sound of people striking camp wakes me; also it is oven-like in my tent, thrumming with an intense, head-addling heat. I hear Jam then, talking to Micah.

'I'm going to collapse it with her in there soon,' he says.

'I'll take her some coffee,' says Micah.

I panic. I don't want Micah in here when I've just woken up and my mouth is dry and sour and disgusting and my hair is wet with sweat. Or do I? Because at the very same time there is a part of me that does want him here, right here, when I am only in my underwear. Which I am well aware is every kind of wrong. So as I watch the morning sunlight chase his shadow across the blue wall of the tent, I work out how to tell him I'm awake and end up doing this ridiculous fake yawn and stretch thing just as he is pulling open the zip.

'I'm awake,' I end up saying. 'I'll be out in a minute.'

I pull on my jean shorts and kind of spend a few

seconds looking for the hand mirror in my bag before I decide I couldn't actually care less and push on my sunglasses before crawling out into the sun, staggering a little before I stand because I am light-headed with the heat; my brain cooked.

They are both sitting in the long grass nearby, watching me.

'Morning,' says Jam, from under his hat. 'Coffee?'

It's Micah who holds it out to me though, smiling.

I look down at the brown dishwater in the battered green plastic cup and wrinkle my nose. 'Well this is definitely *not* what I had in mind.'

While we're pulling the tent pegs out, Tara comes over and stands close to Jam. She slides one of her feet around the back of his legs, takes hold of the back of his neck and talks into his collarbone. Micah and I are spreading his tent out flat and getting it ready to fold and so we aren't really listening, right up to the point where Jam says, 'Nah, I'm going to stay with these guys. But we'll definitely catch up with you along the way, OK?'

She says something else that I don't catch, and then she is leaning into him and they are kissing goodbye and something makes me stare at the way she pulls his face down to her level, her fingers in his hair, until they break away from each other and as Jam turns he catches me looking, and so I get back to shoving the tent into its bag.

*

We are some way out along the road when they overtake us, blaring past in Ernesto's car, music up and ragging the horn. Those girls are clearly going to car-hop their way down the country with whoever the hottest guy in the vicinity happens to be.

'Man, I don't have any clothes for this weather,' says Micah, blowing his hair up off his forehead and pulling another popper open on his shirt in a way that makes me forget my line of thought.

'I'm not sure there *are* clothes for this weather,' I say, yanking at my bra where it is sawing into my ribs. 'I don't even particularly want to have my skin on right now. Does this thing have AC or not?'

Micah laughs as he watches me wind my window down. 'It doesn't work if you open the windows.'

'Jesus,' I pant. 'I'm dying here.'

'That's because it's –' he leans over to look at the dashboard and in the process gets right in my space, so that I catch the warm sweet smell of his sweaty skin – 'thirty-six degrees.'

'Thirty-six?' Jam leans between the seats. 'Is that even possible?'

'Well, clearly,' says Micah, then, 'and since we're headed south it's probably only going to get hotter.'

'Hotter?' My voice fries out. 'Hotter? There is no hotter.'

'You should make the most of it,' says Micah. 'You may be heading for the vacuum of space, where I would imagine it's going to be pretty damn chilly.' And he turns Bruce Springsteen up and leans his foot on the dashboard, rolling his head back like he's made his point.

When we come to the turn-off for a town about twenty minutes later, Jam says, 'Can we stop? I could do with stretching my legs.'

I take the turn-off, but after a few minutes of driving through we realise there is something weird about Santa Clarita. The streets are empty, every shop is boarded up, there is graffiti sprayed in these long sentences over windows and doors and across crumbling bridges. There are dry riverbeds and disused storm drains populated with abandoned sofas.

'It's a ghost town,' says Micah.

They both look around, out of the windows, while I focus on the straight road ahead, the fading white line down the middle of it, dodging the tree saplings that have forced their way up through the tarmac, crumbling it like it was nothing.

'How long does it take for nature to just take a place back? Until it all becomes forest again?' I ask.

'I saw a TV show about that once,' says Jam. 'It actually takes a surprisingly small amount of time. Like months, rather than years. Weeks even. Without humans around, the power goes off in hours, then the water, and from there on in, it's full zombie apocalypse.'

'I need to stop anyway,' says Jam. 'Can you pull over

here?' So I ditch the car in the weeds next to the storm drain and Jam shoulders his door open, gets out and walks across the road to a wall where creepers, thick with orange flowers, have covered the entire surface. Micah basically does the same, opening his door and walking down into the storm drain, jumping across the bottom of it and striding up the other side, to where the pavement is just a collection of cracked lumps of concrete. I watch him while he stands there with his back to me in that weird position guys get into when they're doing this, hips thrown forward, hands out of sight.

I get out of the car too and walk up the melting, shimmery heat of the road to where it bends and goes out of sight, touching the tops of the sapling trees that I pass.

When I look around the corner, there's an abandoned car parked, the door open, like the driver left in a hurry. Beyond it, the plain stretches away, but it is armour-plated by a blanket of thousands of blue and silver solar panels, stretching as far as the eye can see.

Someone appears at my side and instinctively I know it's Micah.

'That's why they call it the battery of Europe,' he muses, snapping a picture of it.

'Jesus,' I say. It's epic, boundless, awful.

There's a long sentence sprayed in blue across the rock on the left.

'What does that say?' I ask him, pointing to the graffiti.

He's silent so long I end up looking at him, watching the way his lips are moving just slightly, like saying it to himself might help him work it out. He laughs a little.

'I'm not actually sure,' he says in the end. 'Something about people, power and possibility.'

I nod. 'Makes sense.' And I face him and smile.

He shrugs, half-smiles back, but mostly with his eyes. The whole move is achingly beautiful.

'What's the matter?' he says. 'You look flushed.'

'Nothing.' I shake it off. 'It's hot, that's all. Let's get out of here.'

Solar Flare

On the drive through the seemingly endless rows of solar panels, the temperature rises to thirty-nine degrees. Pylons are the only figures we see, marching from horizon to horizon, carrying the electricity away, and I swear every single one is topped by a huge bird's nest, most of them occupied by giant storks in ones or twos, cone-beaked and gazing across the landscape. We pass through two more ghost towns, like desert islands in a sea of humming power. The featureless landscape, added to the fact that we can't use the main highways, is leading to some seriously challenging map reading on Jam's part every time we hit a junction.

We only realise we're passing Madrid when the solar panels take a brief pause to make way for this enormous retail estate made up of shops the size of aircraft hangars. Poligono del Oeste has what looks like a thousand acres of car park, shaded by a roof of yet more solar panels. We pull in.

*

We buy burgers in the most intensely noisy fast-food place I've ever been in and eat them sitting on the shaded roof of the car, gazing out at the view of Madrid in the distance. It's a forest of skyscrapers, the *La Red* highway swooping in from the sky. Several million privileged lives are being led within it, the like of which I will never know.

'This is where my mum grew up,' says Micah, through a mouthful.

We both study him for a minute, before I say, 'Do you want to go there? Is there anyone you want to visit?'

We watch him shake his head. 'They're all dead, or gone away,' he laughs, even though it doesn't seem like it should be funny. His laugh dies as he looks back out at the cityscape.

'My dad used to say he sold just as much TCA to city types who'd drive out from Caerdydd as he did to Gower Gate no-hopes,' Jam says. We both look at him because he never talks about that stuff. 'They're just as bored as poor people.' He shrugs. 'Trapped in a different way, I guess.'

'It's a lot easier to escape if you have money, though,' I say.

'Maybe, maybe not.' He takes another bite of his burger. Just then I notice that right between the giant furniture store and the gargantuan supermarket there is a church, clearly old and spared from demolition. It has the most crazy-tall pillar coming out of its roof, heading straight for the sky. Jesus, or maybe God, or maybe just a saint, is standing way up there, arms held out to the side. I point him out, and Micah takes a picture, showing me a close-up of the statue's face.

'What do you reckon he makes of this crap?' he asks.

I study the saint's curled lip and say, 'I guess he's seen it all by now. He's probably past caring.'

I've been driving for another five hours, sweating through my clothes and into the seat, and we are still adrift in the ocean of humming panels, heat-shimmering dust and not much else.

'Want me to take over for a bit?' Micah asks.

I don't even slightly want to be driven by him, but I am aching with the need to stop.

'Thanks. We need to find a charge station soon too,' I tell him.

I sit in the passenger seat and feel every muscle release a little. Behind my shades my eyes close irresistibly and I drop into a series of mini-sleeps, complete with dreams, that I keep jolting awake from. But then I end up watching Micah drive, watching his hands on the wheel, his feet on the pedals, the way he shifts his hips in the seat.

The charge point station we pull into an hour later is called *Galp*. I watch Micah getting blasted by the hot, sand-laden wind while he hooks up the car.

I go to the vast empty bathroom and the mirrors

are set up facing each other in such a way that I stand suspended in the infinity of them. I splash my face with water that I wish was colder and lean across to look at myself closer: no make-up, hair in a messy ponytail, face and arms browner than they've ever been, hair beginning to streak into blonde at the front, nose dotted with the freckles I never knew I had. I've barely left the house without my eyeliner on since I was twelve, but right now it's lying forgotten at the bottom of my bag, crusting up in the heat. The sun is turning me into a different person.

I find them in the station shop, sitting at a long polished bar, on high stools, drinking glasses of coffee, a third on the bar in front of the empty stool between them.

'They don't do takeaway coffee,' says Jam, sliding mine to me on its saucer while I'm climbing on to the stool. He's watching the TV behind the counter.

'Look,' he says, nodding up at it.

An aerial shot, swooping over the sea. A white sand beach, dunes beyond and then thousands of tents, covering the land as it unfolds beneath, occasional groups waving up, just like old footage of music festivals. As the drone banks right and the camera moves, we see it – La Verdad – Ventura's facility, all high metal perimeter walls and the giant dishes of the radio telescope and the towering structures that mark out the space port.

'What's it saying?' I look at Micah.

He frowns at the screen, head tilted like it might help him hear better. 'I can't understand,' he says. 'It's too fast.' He turns to the guy behind the bar who is just pouring frothy milk into glasses lined up in front of him, the milk misting through the coffee in pale clouds. '*Que dice?*'

He glances up at the screen and says something that makes them both laugh and which Micah translates as: 'He says there are thirty-five thousand crazy teenagers camping outside La Verdad waiting for the first round selection.'

'Thirty-five thousand?' I hear myself say.

'I think that's what he said,' says Micah, suddenly unsure. He looks back at the guy. '*Treinta y cinco mil, verdad?*'

'*Si, treinta y cinco mil locos y creciendo*,' he says, shaking his head. I get the gist.

'Thirty-five thousand people already for three hundred places?' I look at Jam but he stays blank. 'I mean . . . wow. We have literally no chance of getting through, do we?' I laugh, but not like it's funny. 'Like, zero chance.'

Micah pushes his sunglasses into his hair. 'Well, I reckon it still looks like a lot of fun.' He raises his eyebrows at me, but I let my face fall forwards on to my hands and keep it there, in the dark, even when I feel his hand between my shoulder blades.

'Don't stress, Karlo. It'll be cool,' he says.

'This isn't a joke for me, Bexley,' I say, sitting up again

to glare at him. 'It's my life. It's our lives.' I only dare glance at Jam quickly. 'This is the only thing I've ever really wanted and now it turns out *thirty-five thousand* other people want the exact same thing.' I get off the stool, would fall off it really except for the fact that Jam takes my arm to steady me from behind just before I do, and I am struggling to breathe, lunging for the door because I need air, realising too late that there's even less outside than there is in. I am pulling hot air into my lungs, holding it, letting it out slowly, trying to blink back the water that is burning in my eyes, watching the way the blue sky and the one single vapour trail bisecting it seem to shrink away from me, and when I look back down Jam and Micah are standing watching me, each a couple of metres away, as if I am a wild animal that's about to bolt.

'I used to think they were called paper trails,' I say, pointing up.

Micah smiles. 'Seems reasonable,' he says. 'Come on, let's go.'

'What's that up ahead?' Micah squints through the windscreen at the intertwining multi-coloured plastic of what would seem to be enormous children's slides. Water slides, judging from the just-visible queues of people wearing swimwear. There's a gap in the solar panels here to accommodate a sudden uprising of rocky hills, ancient trees clinging to their crests.

It's only when we get close that we realise.

'It's a campsite,' I say, reading the sign. 'Pull in, let's check it out.'

We walk into the vast, glossy reception area where I feel ridiculously damp and dusty and out of place, and Micah talks to the woman behind the desk. I listen to the distant squeals and splashes of the pool.

When he translates the nightly price, I cough.

'How much?' I almost shriek, because it's about three times as much as I have in the world. 'For what? For a patch of dirt to put a tent on?'

'It's OK, Bea, we'll just keep going,' Micah says, shooting an embarrassed smile at the girl behind the desk. 'I thought this would probably cost too much.'

'And all these people can afford to pay that?' I'm still too loud as Jam starts to pull me towards the door. 'For one night on a patch of ground? That's stupid. That's just stupid,' I say as I storm back to the car.

Micah drives for another hour while I rant.

'Back home we pay through the nose just to get enough water on the meter to take a shower, while they're using it to lubricate their slides!' I seethe. 'I've always known this was a stupid world, but I guess I underestimated the depths of it.'

They let me go on monologuing while Jam keeps messing with the map, until he finally manages to cut in to say, 'Listen, I should probably tell you that I think I've got us lost.'

The sun is dropping and I've been staring out of the window at the passing solar panels for so long that my eyes hurt when I turn to stare at him.

'Not a big deal,' says Micah, bouncing over a pothole. 'We'll just stick the tent up here. You know, a night in the wild is probably just what we need.'

We've pulled the car in under a huge humming solar panel and Jam is looking through the mess in the boot for the tents while I stand on the road and try not to think about the fact that, even though I know that photo-voltaic cells are harmless, there's something about the idea of sleeping under one that makes me feel like we'll be pulverised into the dust that seems to be the only thing that can live beneath them. Instead I look up at the uninterrupted sky, at the way it fades from red bruised with purple in the west to a deep inky blue in the east, the stars just arriving. When it's like this, I can see why the first scientists took a while to work out it wasn't just a pretty dome that was decorated and put there by a higher power just for us.

When music suddenly blares out of the open car doors, I look back to where Micah is standing.

'I've been making a playlist for you,' he says, shouting a little over it. 'For both of you. For when you get to space.' He holds his finger up. 'Notice I said *when* not *if*,

143

because I have no doubt they'll want you. They'd be nuts not to.'

'Bexley ... ' I watch him through my fingers because he's just started doing the cheesiest dancing imaginable, pretend-lassoing me closer.

'Anyway there I am making this playlist, and I listen to this song and I'm like: it's perfect. Because this song is *so* you. You know you need a spark to start a fire. You're staying hungry, you're shaking this world off your shoulders. You're two of the only thirty-five thousand people in the world brave enough to leave it all behind. And that is so unbelievably cool.'

He looks over at where Jam is now lying on his back on the bonnet of the car, goes over to him and pulls on his leg until he gets kicked away. Then he comes back to me and takes my hand and pulls me into dancing with him even though I'm resisting, laughing, totally dizzied by the closeness, by the warm sweet smell of him, by the fact that even lame dancing is insanely sexy when it's him doing it.

He catches my eye and holds it, as he sings along with the lyrics of the song, and I think about how much I love his half-flat singing voice while I let my eyes drop to his throat and the open top buttons of his shirt as he raises his arm to make me twirl under it.

Because of the music, we don't hear the car approaching, so it's only when they pull up just next to us that we notice the Australians at all.

'Is this a private dance party or can anyone join in?' grins the one driving. 'Love a bit of Springsteen.'

'We're lost,' I tell him, breathless.

'No you're not,' he says, pointing at the screen of the Ventura Com Navigation System in their new rental car and then straight out the front windshield. 'Lejillo should be two kilometres that way. Follow us.'

Lejillo turns out to be this little fortress village on a hill, another island in this strange metal ocean. The makeshift campsite has been set up just outside its walls, and when we get there there's just us and the Australians we followed here and some fairy lights in what turns out to be an almond tree. The girl that's running the place is hardly any older than us, this tiny little Spanish girl called Carmen who speaks perfect English in this accent I can't get enough of. She only wants five euros from us, but we give her ten because her family basically owns a patch of dirt that's sandwiched so hard between the solar panels that it can't even be farmed any more. Her house is this little one-storey stone box with a saint painted on a huge tile by the front door, with coloured pots full of pretty plants nailed to the wall. She tells us she'll take us for a tour of the town once we've set up our tents.

'Does anyone actually live there?' asks Jam, taking a break from banging at a tent peg with a rock to stand and squint at the ghostly pale stone of the defensive walls.

'There are a few of us still,' Carmen says, setting her shoulders back a little, like it's a matter of personal pride. 'My cousin has a bar in town. There's not much else.' She shrugs. 'Apart from the Parador.'

'The Parador?' Jam frowns.

'I work there part time. The hotel. They made the *monasterio* into a state-run hotel, for tourists.' She shrugs again. 'When you're ready I show you, *vale*?'

'*Vale*,' says Jam, smiling at her as she walks away, adding once she's out of earshot, 'She's cool.'

'Better than Tara,' I say.

'Oh, you approve this time?' He raises an eyebrow.

'Oh, Jam, come on, Tara was *horrible*. Did you hear the things she said about me? Didn't that bother you?'

'Of course it did,' he says, squatting back down. 'But there was a certain element of truth in it too. I mean, you *are* a pain in the ass.'

I kick him on the hip but he grabs my foot and lifts it until I fall over next to him. 'See, this is exactly what I meant,' he says, making a big show of ignoring my struggle to get away as he sits on my ankle and goes back to hammering at the tent peg. 'A pain in the ass.'

Once the tent is up, we sit in the dust and watch a fat orange moon crest the horizon, listening to Micah talking Spanish to the guys sitting outside a tent that was here when we arrived. It's only then I realise that they're Ernesto and his friend, from the last place, having seemingly (and thankfully) lost Tara and Fin somewhere along the way.

'I'm sorry,' I end up saying to Jam, without planning it.

'For what?' he says, turning to me.

'For bringing us all the way down here and spending all our money and not thinking through the fact that we would be up against tens of thousands of other people and would have no chance of actually making it.'

He looks at the side of my face for so long, I can't help but turn to him, even though I don't want to, and when I do he says, 'We have as much chance as anybody else. And even if we didn't, there's no way I'd ever regret any of this. I already feel like I've visited another planet, don't you?' he adds.

'I do,' I say, and it's true, but I have to blink back tears a little; I have to physically swallow the fear of what will happen if it all comes to nothing.

He's just about to speak again when I get up.

'I need a shower,' I say, looking down at him in the half-light.

So he just says, 'OK,' and then watches me as I smile, but I can tell from the way he looks at me that it must seem as fragile and intangible as it feels.

Wavelength

The bathroom is this little brick outhouse that looks like it's been here a million years judging from the way it is tiled in orange and has a little square window that looks out across the plain. There isn't a shower, since this place just has the one tap that is connected to a bore-hole that draws direct from the water table, and so I just have to fill a bucket up and then use this little plastic scoop thing to dump water over my head a few times. It sounds terrible, but I'm so hot and dusty it feels like medicine.

When I get out, Ernesto is giving guitar lessons in the glow from the lights in the trees, moving Micah's fingers on the frets. I smile to myself a little watching Micah's face as he concentrates – the frown, the way he bites his bottom lip. The chords he eventually manages to make sound flat and twangy, so that in the end Ernesto takes the guitar back off him and starts to retune it, as if that might be the reason he's failing to get a single decent note out. Ernesto tries again, shifting Micah's fingers around, murmuring a few encouragements, but it isn't long before he sighs and sits back, brushing dust off his jeans as he says, '*Mira, hombre*, not everyone in this world is musical.'

Which makes me laugh.

We walk up the hill to the town. The cobbled road has these two deep grooves in it and Carmen tells us it's from where the horse-drawn cartwheels used to run. I look out across the plain to where the army of solar panels are reflecting the moonlight and I try to imagine what it was like when animals and plants and the rhythms of nature filled this place with people and life and possibility.

We get inside the city walls and wander through the narrow alleyways. Pretty much every house looks abandoned. Carmen tells us, or mainly tells Jam in fact, about how Lejillo was actually the hometown of many of the conquistadors, who were the first Europeans to travel to the Americas.

I stop and peer into a darkened, empty doorway. Micah stops beside me and I say, 'Can you imagine how hardcore you had to be to even conceive of doing that? I mean, how long do you think that journey took back then? Months? Years? And how many people would die along the way? You had to be some kind of badass to head off into the complete unknown like that.'

'The same kind of badass who would think it was a

good idea to go into space and never come back, I guess,' he says, and there is something in his eyes I can't read.

The Australian guys are mainly interested in drinking so we come to the main square where there is a massive crumbling church on one corner, a statue of a guy on a horse in another and this one little bar where a waiter is laying out tables and chairs. It's Carmen's cousin's bar.

The Australian guys head over, turning as they leave: '*Cerveza*?' they call back to us.

'Sure,' says Micah, and follows them.

'I was going to show you the *monasterio* first,' says Carmen.

'You two go,' says Micah. 'Monasteries aren't really our thing, are they Karlo?'

'I . . . ' It takes me a few seconds to catch on, but when I look at Micah and he is winking at me I get it and so I'm like, 'No, yeah, no, you two go,' and I am watching the embarrassment dawn all over Jam's face as he pinches the bridge of his nose and Carmen says, 'OK, well, tell Ramiro I sent you, and we meet you back here, OK?'

They leave and I watch them walk away, Jam more than a head taller than her. I'm still standing watching when Jam looks back at me, and it's a beat before I look away again and go and join Micah.

'So what's the deal with you guys then?' says Dev, one of the Australian guys, once we're sitting at a table. 'Threesome situation?'

I make a face. 'And if it was like that, you honestly think I would open up to you about it?'

'I'm hoping so,' he says. 'Because I'd be up for hearing some details, to be honest, freckles.' And he leans right into my space.

'Freckles?'

'Just let me know what you'd rather be called,' he says. 'I'm easy.'

'If you need to call me anything, why not try my actual name?'

'Which is?'

'Beacon.'

'Beacon?' he laughs. 'That's not a name.'

'Wow, did you go to charm school or . . . ?'

'Why do you ask? Is it working?' He's wolfish when he smiles, but not in a good way.

Micah's been distracted by talking to the waiter, but I'm relieved when he stops and slides my beer, which has just arrived, in front of me and so I pick it up and take a drink. It is so awesomely cold, the glass so thin, condensation running down the side, and I nearly sigh in pleasure.

'I was just asking Beacon –' Dev the Australian says my name like it's in quotes – 'about your little love triangle here.'

Micah laughs, shifts in his seat.

A plateful of discs of hot sausage arrive at the table

and I'm the first to take one and eat it. It is smoky and sweet and chewy and everything good, and I reach for a second while I'm still chewing.

'Who ordered this?' asks Dev.

'No one,' says Ernesto, leaning in with a smile. 'This *tapa* comes when you order drinks. It's free. That's what they do in this region.'

'It's amazing,' I say, just before I put the second disc in my mouth.

Dev is watching me and I glare back, expecting him to look away, but he doesn't until his friend starts pointing something out to him on the other side of the square.

'Did you like your bucket shower?' asks Micah then.

'I did,' I say, turning to him, trying not to wonder why he would ask that. Trying not to wonder if it made him think about me naked. He's getting this beautiful tan across his cheekbones, his hair turning lighter along his front hairline. Damn it, I'm just staring again.

'I guess you've realised by now that I stole your book,' he says, letting me stare, staring back.

'You did?'

He laughs. 'You didn't notice? I like it. It's beautiful. The bit where they've been out all night and they sit on the back of the milk truck to come home at dawn ... '

'I know.' I grin. 'I love that part.'

'Remember when we did that?'

I nod, when what I'm really thinking is: *I'll never*

forget. Mali and Jam always thought The Mixed Feelings were too whiny, so the night they played the Abertawe Bayside, Micah and I went alone. I became utterly terrified in the hours before we met at the external transport line. We'd already spent so much time together, and we usually talked non-stop, but suddenly I was agonisingly shy with him, deaf to the music I loved so much, the only details left clear being the ones that directly related to him – the sweet smell of him as he leaned down to shout in my ear from behind, the pliant feeling of his hand as he pulled me through the crowd, the shine in his eye when he squared up to someone for pushing me – and those moments got tattooed on my brain, woven through the fabric of me, indelibly, for ever, like permanent bruises.

'Walking all the way home from Abertawe …' He shakes his head, stirring me out of the memory. 'We were mad.'

'I think that lambing truck only stopped because they saw you giving me a piggyback and felt sorry for you.'

He laughs. 'That gig was so worth it though.' He frowns just quickly and then it goes. It's one of his many beautiful tics. 'Super memorable night.'

'Yeah, for *me*,' I say, letting the icy bubbles run down my throat. I don't know why I admit how much more significant it would have been for me than for him; I must be a bit drunk, but I don't even realise I've done it until he says, 'Why just for you?' With that fleeting frown again.

Luckily Dev saves me. In no world did I ever think I would be thankful for him. 'So tell us what takes you to space, Beacon? Are you running away, deluded or clueless?'

I empty my glass. 'Why do I have to be one of those things?'

'Everybody bound for Ventura is,' he says loudly. 'And you're about to ask which one I am.'

'I wasn't actually, but I'm guessing you're going to tell me anyway.'

He laughs and says, 'She's great,' to his friend, not even that subtly, then he turns back to me. 'I fall into deluded. I always dreamed about going to space. Wasn't getting the grades for astronaut training. Started thinking about haulage. Then this came up. It's perfect.'

'But why does any of that make you deluded?' I frown, tracing my finger down the condensation on my glass.

'Well, here I am, labouring under the illusion that Mission Ventura's going to be this amazing, meaningful adventure, when in reality it's far more likely to be a giant, hyperdrive-powered prison where our only function is manual labour and occasional breeding.'

Micah laughs. 'You're the ones that came to the other side of the planet to try out for it!'

'Like I said –' Dev grins, prodding at his forehead with his finger – 'deluded. Now which are you, Beacon?'

'Runaway,' I say. 'No question.'

He carries on smiling but there's a hint of wariness in the dark eyes behind his thick-rimmed geek glasses. 'And what are you running away from?' he asks.

'How long have you got?' I say, and he laughs again, picks up my empty glass and waves it at the waiter, spreading his fingers.

'And which are you, Micah?' he asks, then downs his beer.

'None of the above,' he says. 'I'm just along for the ride. I'm actually starting to get into the idea of going, but I don't think my girlfriend would be happy. We have plans. Well ... as much as anyone from an agricultural urbanisation can.'

Dev raises his eyebrow. 'Oh, so you don't see a long term future in this love triangle here?'

'Oh I didn't say that,' says Micah, sharing a look with me.

'Micah's the boyfriend of my best friend, and Jam's my step brother,' I clarify.

He smiles. 'Leaving you single.'

'That's right,' I say. 'Shall we throw me a pity party?'

'On the contrary ... ' He leans back to let Carmen's cousin leave fresh beers on the table. 'I think it's excellent news.'

He looks at me heavily then, but I look around the square, watching the way the dim light from the bar picks up the patterns on the front of the old stone buildings. I know this game, but I'm not up for playing it.

Carmen and Jam get back just then, both of them smiling and sheened with sweat. Jam sits down with us while Carmen goes to talk to her cousin.

'Monastery good?' asks Micah, shoving back his chair while Jam collects two more from a neighbouring table. 'Looking pretty sweaty there, Rees. What were you doing? Going at it up against the wall?'

'Jesus, Bexley.' Jam shakes his head, and wipes his face on the hem of his T-shirt.

'What?' Micah laughs. 'It's what everyone's thinking.'

'Well, it is now,' says Jam.

'Yeah, it's quite an image,' says Dev, blinking.

'If you must know, it's a bit of a hike up the last bit,' says Jam. 'And the temperature gauge up there said it was thirty-eight degrees. I'm Welsh, OK? I'm not used to it.'

Carmen comes to join us, followed by a waiter with two more beers. Jam touches his glass to hers and almost chugs his in one, then watches, baffled, when this plate of beautiful curls of ham on bread arrives out of nowhere.

'We were just getting to know each other a little

better, Jam,' says Dev. 'We need to know which category of Ventura hopeful you are – runaway, deluded or clueless.'

Jam laughs. 'I don't want to be any of those.'

'Exactly what Beacon said.' Dev shows his big teeth and slides his eyes my way. 'But we've yet to meet anyone Ventura-bound that didn't fit into one of these categories, unless you're suggesting you're the first of your kind?'

Jam picks up one of the little bits of bread and ham and holds it just in front of him like it might be whispering him an answer. Then flicking a quick look in my direction, he says, 'Clueless, probably.'

'I have no idea how you can think of doing such a thing,' says Carmen, suddenly. 'I think it's awful. Just –' she looks a little like she might cry – 'awful.'

'What's so awful about it?' Dev asks.

'You're never coming back! You are *never* coming back. You leave your home. The Earth. The place that's in your blood. You know?' Her eyes are wide in the dark, looking around at everyone and then settling on Jam. 'And anyway, Ventura Com – I don't like what they're doing – recruiting only young people who don't know what they are doing. It's . . . not moral.'

'I feel like I'm making a free choice,' says Dev.

'Why did you set up the camp if you hate it all so much?' I ask her.

'My sister was the one who set it up,' she said. 'She left a week ago. To go to La Verdad.'

I almost laugh, until I realise how sad she is about it.

We spend the whole night drinking beer, eating whatever food arrives and having circular debates. Later on, someone turns the music up and we watch Ernesto and Carmen dance in this effortless, moody way that looks like they were born knowing how to do it; like an instinct that only Spanish people have. Carmen tries to teach Jam some of the steps, but it is mostly a mess that the rest of us laugh at. And I guess they don't even care because at some point I notice they've left without saying goodbye. I suddenly notice the air is cooler.

We shouldn't drink any more, but Ernesto keeps telling us how this area is famous for its sherry and how we have to try it and it's actually a whole lot better than I thought it would be – kind of savoury and nutty and also at the same time a little sweet. And by then I realise I am kind of drunk and so I shove my chair back and stand and everyone looks at me and Micah says, 'Where you going, Karlo?'

'Home,' I tell him. 'The tent.'

He laughs and stands next to me. 'I'll take you.'

'I can,' says Dev. 'I was headed down there anyway.'

'That's OK,' I say, hearing the slur in my voice. 'I want him to take me,' and I point to Micah, before adding, 'but thanks.'

I stagger off and I feel Micah following me. We weave down the wrong alleyway and end up winding up through town when we should be going down. Neither of us seem to care that much though, and we just keep laughing. There's no warning before the alley we're on kicks us out into a courtyard in front of this huge edifice, lit in orange and carved into a thousand gargoyles and figures and faces, light in almost every window, city types sitting drinking under umbrellas on a patio out front.

'The monastery hotel,' says Micah.

'It's beautiful,' I sigh.

Micah slides his arm around my shoulders, his camera at arm's length. 'Proof we were here,' he says, both of us holding our breath when he presses the button. Then he turns round and squats down a little. 'OK, hop on. Let me give you a piggyback, for old times' sake.'

I go to him, slowly, and when I feel his hands on my legs I jump, wrap them around his hips, settle my face against the side of his head.

'You OK?' he says, and when I nod, he starts walking.

His hipbones hurt immediately against my thighs, but all I do is link my ankles and tighten my grip on him.

'I ended up with bruises last time, you know, on my inner thighs,' I tell him.

'You did?'

I nod.

'I'm sorry I'm not more comfortable, madam.'

I laugh, and, without thinking, I say, 'Don't be sorry. I loved those bruises.'

'You did?'

I nod as he goes down a stone step at the top of an alley and I bite my tongue a little.

And then there's silence, and after a few seconds he stops, is suddenly still, and we are right under this low archway in the city wall and I feel him loosen his grip so that I unhook my ankles and drop my feet to the ground, step away from him until I feel the hot stone wall behind my back and from there I watch him turn to me, watch him take a step closer.

'Why did you ... why would you love bruises?' He frowns, lips parted, almost taking another step towards me, then not doing it.

And it is so much, too much, everything, but somehow I don't look away, somehow I stay looking back at him while he looks at me, even though there is no answer coming, and there never will be. All I do is try to breathe, even though it's getting harder, and I watch him take it in, take it all in, the way my chest is heaving, heaving, heaving, my head dropped back against the wall behind me, and every part of me knowing that if he kisses me I will die and if he doesn't I will too. God, it's hard when you feel someone the way I feel him; so hard to spend every day for years close enough to feel the heat from him, knowing that what fills your heart is something you can never, never, never show, let alone act upon. And suddenly being here is like standing on the edge of a cliff, knowing I can't fly but some part of me wanting to do it anyway, knowing it all comes down to making the one move you know you shouldn't, mustn't, cannot make.

'Karlo, don't do this to me,' he whispers.

'Don't do what?' I manage to whisper back.

'You know what,' he says, and shakes his head, but at the same time he takes the step towards me that he didn't take before.

And I don't say anything else. I can't. Not while he's this close to me, not while he's looking at me like this. All I can do is stay alive. All I can do is breathe. There are so many things I could say. I could tell him that sex only makes sense when I think about doing it with him. I could say that every time I've done it has felt like pretending but I know that with him it would feel real. Even standing here now feels more real than anything I've known.

But I don't say any of that, I just watch the long transit of his Adam's apple while he swallows; watch the movement of his chest up and down as he breathes, heavier every moment. Then his hand is on my shoulder, so hot there it burns, his thumb on my collarbone, moving along it. A soft sound escapes my throat that I don't manage to stop. My hands stay on the warm stone behind me, gripping it so hard it hurts my palms. I let my head drop back a little more but keep watching him along my nose.

'I want to,' he says, swallowing again, shaking his head, just barely, 'so much.'

Silence again. Both of us breathing hard. *I want to so much*. Just like that, after all these years, he knows. Just like that, after all these years, we are standing here wanting each other. Wanting to *so much*. I am staring at his beautiful mouth, just like I have done a million times before, only now I am looking at it knowing he wants to kiss me. I unstick my hand from the wall behind me and it moves through the space between us and then it's on his hip, taking a handful of his shirt to steady itself, pulling on him just a little.

'Karlo, don't.' He shakes his head. 'We can't do this.' But at the same moment he closes the space between us and his mouth is inches from mine, so close we are breathing the same air and I can feel his heat, all of it, everywhere, in every part of me. And all I can think is that it's a different world out here, way out here, and I'm so tired of wanting things I can never have.

But then there are voices, close to us in the darkness. They have probably been getting closer for a while, but we haven't noticed them. It's the others, stumbling over the cobbles. He steps away from me, steps back, with difficulty, like someone resisting an irresistible force, his eyes not leaving mine.

'Hey,' says Dev. 'There you guys are! We are so lost!'

There's a beat of awkwardness while I watch his eyes shift between us, almost like he catches on, and then I'm saying, 'I'm pretty sure it's this way,' even though really I have no idea and I am just plunging off down the rocks outside the walls, but I want to walk ahead, I want to be alone in the dark while I get my heart to stop thundering in my chest. Right now it's so loud I bet everyone in the world can hear it.

Eventually we spot the fairy lights in Carmen's row of almond trees, and as I walk into the circle of tents, Dev says, 'Before you go to bed, lend me your guitar, let me show you my skills.'

And at the same time Micah says, 'I'm going to bed,' and even though I hardly dare to look at him, I do anyway and he isn't looking back, doesn't until he is almost at his tent. And, after a beat, he crouches down to crawl inside it.

There's this alternate universe where I follow him, where I go to his tent with him and crawl in next to him and maybe we lie face to face for a minute, or several long ones, before we kiss. But in this one I stay with Dev. I get the guitar and listen to him murder Pink Floyd on it while the others go to bed, and when he kisses me I let him, and it is more like pretending than ever. We are lying in the grass when he says, 'Wouldn't it be awesome if we both got picked?'

And I say, 'Shut up, you idiot,' and kiss him again, because it's easier to imagine he's Micah when I can't see or hear him.

Sometimes I take my own breath away with how messed up I am.

Supernova

In the morning, it's so hot so early that I have to get out of the tent before I've even got dressed. Once I'm out, I notice the guitar left on the ground and it reminds me of last night. I groan and lie flat in the dew-damp dirt, look up at the high blue sky, which is so clear. I guess I fall back asleep because the next thing I know Jam is sitting near my head, halfway through saying something I missed the start of.

'Is that OK?' he says. 'I mean, I know final enrolment day is in two days but we can get there tomorrow – it won't take long from here, so it's not like one more day makes much difference.'

'Jam, what are you talking about?' I lean up on one elbow and squint at him in the sun. He has his sunglasses on and I'm so jealous of him that I hook them off with my index finger and slide them up my own nose.

'I just . . .' He looks off across the plain. 'Carmen's really cool and . . . what difference does it make if we stay here one more day?'

I lie back down. 'Yeah, OK, we can stay. I'm knackered anyway.'

He laughs. 'Hungover you mean.'

I slide the glasses down my nose and look at him over them. 'This is really working out for you, isn't it? This last lay on Earth thing.'

'Shut up, Bea.'

'Don't you think you should be nice to me right now?'

He reaches for the sunglasses and takes them back. 'I am being nice.' And as he gets up to go, he leaves something so cold against my arm that it makes me gasp. It's a little bottle of orange juice and I swear I basically rip the top off and chug the whole thing down in one.

I'm eating crisps, the kind that are thick and hard like cardboard and leave orange cheese dust all over your hands, when Micah appears and stands next to me so that I am looking at his legs, battered jeans coated in pale dust. I don't look up.

'Jam wants to stay another day,' I tell him.

'OK,' he says. 'Well, then, I need to go to that town today, to call Mali.'

'What town?'

'La Herida or something. It has another one of those state hotels, but it also has a public Coms office. You don't mind me taking the car?'

I'm just about to say I don't when Dev unzips his tent

and crawls out, pushing his hair back and meeting my eye once, surreptitiously.

'I'll come with you,' I say to Micah. 'When are we leaving? Now? I'll just get my stuff.'

I drive to La Herida and we mostly just listen to Peter Gabriel. Though neither of us is talking, I am pretty sure both of us are thinking about last night. I can almost hear it rattling around our heads.

We see the solar farm long before we get to it; twenty towers beaming a light so hard and bright it is hard to believe it's of this world. We even stop the car to take a look.

'Wow,' says Micah, sitting on the bonnet next to me. 'How do they work?'

'Parabolic mirrors,' I tell him, squinting at them.

'Para what now?'

'A series of parabolic mirrors reflect the sunlight on to those towers so that it's massively concentrated and the heat is converted into power and stored in a battery.' I notice the way he's watching me with this smile on his face. 'What?'

'You know I love it when you come over all science geek.' He shakes his head, half winks.

'Shut up, Bexley.'

He laughs. 'What? I mean it!'

But there's this moment of awkwardness then, because it doesn't feel the same. There's an extra layer to it now that probably means it never will.

We get into the town and leave the car on the side of the road, find our way through the shady alleyways, passing nobody, and out on to a walkway that takes us to a bridge. Once we're standing on it we realise we are over this deep gorge, a bright blue river snaking along the distant floor, the cliff walls to either side so steep they're almost vertical, the old buildings of the town clinging to either side. There's a sign nailed to the keystone and Micah reads it.

'The Spanish Inquisition used to throw people in here,' he paraphrases, and we both lean over the edge again, look down.

We get to the other side and sit on a table outside a bar.

'What do you want?' he asks me, when the waiter appears.

'I'm driving so I guess it better be Coke, but you have beer if you like.'

'No, I'd better not,' he says, ordering two Cokes before turning back to me.

'You'd better not?' I raise an eyebrow.

He sighs, leans forward over his spread knees and chafes his palms together. 'I was pretty drunk last night and that's what I'm blaming for ... well, you know.'

I tilt my head. 'Do I?'

He's inscrutable for a minute behind his aviators, but then he says, 'I should apologise, you know. It's totally my fault.'

'What is?'

He looks at me steadily. 'Come on, Karlo, is that really how you want to play it?'

And he looks at me and, just like that, cuts through my BS. Only he can do that. Well, him and Jam.

'The thing is . . . ' he starts, then sighs again.

'I know what the thing is, Bexley, you don't have to explain.'

'I want you to know that . . . it's not like . . . I mean, I want to. I want to just as much as you do.' He makes a face, like he's sheepish. 'As much as I think you do, anyway. But we can't. We never can. Never.'

I laugh and roll my eyes. 'Jesus, tell me something I don't know.'

'I could never cheat on Mali. I would never forgive myself.' He shakes his head, looks off into the gorge. I study him while he's turned away. It's so hard to explain why I want him as much as I do. He has plenty of flaws: a slight overbite that even makes him lisp a little when he talks; so many freckles that they are merging into patches on his cheekbones. I know that behind his sunglasses he has one permanently bloodshot eye from a ridiculous accident with an aerosol can. But then . . . like he said about the sunset on the boat, somehow all the imperfections are what make him even more perfect. The way the overbite stops his beautiful lips from closing means that I just can't stop thinking about them; his freckles beg to be touched; the red on that side of his eye only makes the blue of them even more like the sky just before dawn.

I watch his hands, where he is still rubbing them together between his knees. That's another thing: his hands are beautiful. They are the kind of big, clean, short-nailed boy hands that make me think about having them on my body. I can't help it. I look at the one nearest me and I want to reach for it and take hold of it, pull it into my lap. I imagine sandwiching his hand between both of mine, comparing the size, our fingers interlocking, linked. But I don't do it.

Our Cokes arrive and Micah thanks the waiter.

'This trip's working out pretty well for Jam, right?' he says, changing the subject, as if we aren't sitting there thinking about what almost happened last night. 'He couldn't get play to save his life back home and now he's everybody's favourite drink of water.'

I recalibrate for a second, and think about Jam – glancing back as he walked away with Carmen last night, smiling while Tara dragged her tongue along his lower lip on the ferry, squinting in the morning sun outside the outhouse with his T-shirt slung over his shoulder and his hair pushed back.

'I guess back home nobody realised he'd grown up,' I hear myself say. 'His mum dying messed him up for so long. Then his dad went to prison and he was just ...

paralysed by it for years. I guess we all forgot to notice that he isn't that weird, stuck little kid any more.'

He nods, then says, 'It's because of you.'

'Because of me?'

The sun flares off his glasses, making me notice my reflection in them.

He shrugs. 'That he got unstuck. You were there to show him how to come back to life. How to put other people's crap in the rear-view mirror and do whatever you can to make the kind of life you want.'

I smile and say, 'More Springsteen lyrics?'

'No.' He smiles back. 'Just an observation.'

Maybe that's the thing I love about Micah Bexley the most. He sees me. I don't feel like anybody in this world sees me except him.

He sighs, and pulls some wrinkled euros from his pocket. 'Come on,' he says. 'Let's find this Coms office.'

We walk back across the bridge, stopping to watch an arrow of white birds fly underneath us.

'It looks like you can go down there,' I say, pointing out some people moving along the valley floor like dots on a map.

'We'll go check it out after,' he says.

After. After he phones Mali. His girlfriend. My best friend. The girl we both love most in the world.

The Coms Office is in the main square. It has a huge yellow sign with a phone on it, in case you could miss it.

It's opposite the church, which I point to and say, 'I'll go in there and wait for you.'

'You're not coming?'

I'm standing close and it makes me super aware of our height difference. It's not that big; it's just about what you would want it to be. I shake it off.

'I'd better not,' I say.

'Don't you want to say hello to her?'

'She'll want to talk to you, Bexley. I'll see you in a minute, OK?' And I walk over to the church before he can stop me. I don't add that I can't bear the thought of watching him speak to her, watching him light up at the sound of her voice the way I know he will.

Inside the church it is so dark that for a while I can't see at all; I am utterly blind. Once my eyes do recover, I realise that every wall is covered with statues and gold and whatever else. The Jesus on the cross at the front is huge and lifelike and painted with lurid streaks of blood.

Way sooner than I expected, Micah is sliding on to the bench next to me, his breathing irregular.

'You OK?' I say.

'She wasn't there,' he says. 'She's out horse riding. The housekeeper said to call back in two hours.' He lets out a breath of laughter, which sounds a bit like relief. 'Let's go find a way down into the gorge.'

The path is steep, in some places made into stone steps of irregular depths so that they are hard to walk down.

172

Crickets are setting up a steady whirr that's almost a scream as we descend past doorways built into the rock and trees clinging in the cracks.

It surprises me when Micah says, 'Why did you kiss that guy last night? You didn't even like him.'

I glance at him over my shoulder, but he is watching his feet as he takes a deep step.

'You don't know whether I liked him or not,' I say.

'He was a tool,' he says, and then laughs. 'But when it comes to guys, you're pretty inclusive as a general rule.'

I stop for a second in pure shock, almost like he just punched me in the stomach, and he fetches up close behind me so that for a second we are standing close, side-on to each other, his expression fading from a smirk into something completely different as he reads the hurt I can't keep off my face.

I narrow my eyes and shake my head, watch him open his mouth to speak and I go to take off down the steps before he can, but he grabs me, won't let me. I elbow him in the stomach, getting him just under the ribs so that he winces.

'I'm sorry,' he says. 'Really, I'm sorry. I didn't mean it.'

'Yes, you did.'

'Seriously, I didn't. I was kidding.'

'No, you weren't.' I can't look at him so I end up yelling into the canyon. 'I know that's how people see me. Just because I'm not too scared to go out there and live my life.

173

Just because I'm not sat alone in my room waiting for the world to happen to me.'

'And I love that about you,' he says. 'I mean it. All of those things. I love them.'

Right then he is still holding me, holding me while I am half turned away, but he takes hold of my wrist and moves my arm, twisting me round until we are facing each other, facing each other and looking at each other and breathing like there's not enough air.

I start to speak, but I have no idea what I was going to say, and I will never find out, because he kisses me, and my whole life turns into a before and after of this moment. This moment when we are closed-mouthed and nose-breathing noisily because it is all too much, way too much to even believe. And as soon as I do believe it, I am opening my mouth and so is he, and I am sliding my hands on to his shoulders and his are on my hips. And I was right; we are the perfect height for each other. And he tastes like salted caramel, just like I always knew he would.

Once upon a time he was nearly mine. This is how I justify it; this and the fact that if these are my last days on Earth, then this is my final chance to live my own truths, the ones I've spent too long ignoring while they literally eat away at me.

Like he can hear my thoughts, Micah pulls back just a little and looks at me.

'I knew I wouldn't get through this day without doing that,' he says, staying close. 'And I already want to do it again.' He's frowning in such a way that it breaks something open in me.

'Do it again then,' I tell him.

So he does.

Cosmic String

We try to stop; try to leave, so many times. We get some way up the path and then slow our steps to look at the view, then we forget to look at it and look at each other instead, and looking at each other pulls us back into it, like something inevitable. Now I've kissed him it feels like it's all I want to do in the world. Now I've slid my hand along the waistband of his shorts, into the sweat that's pooling in the small of his back, all I can think about is doing it again, doing something else, doing more. When he puts his hand under my top at the back, grazing his fingers along the edge of my bra, all I can do is push myself closer so that I feel him against me. At the halfway stop, at the *mirador*, he backs me against the rock face and I wrap my legs around his hips, sigh against him, arch into him, even though it's almost unbearable. For now, in this moment, he's mine and I'm his, and I can't bear to spend a second not showing him that.

Eventually we pull apart and watch each other's faces

while we think the same thing. 'What time were you supposed to –' I swallow – 'call Mali back?'

'Yeah, I guess I'm late with … that,' he says, and his smile fades.

We climb the last three steps in slow motion, fingers linked together tight.

Once we're standing back at street level, I feel his hand loosen in mine. He sighs. So do I. I can't tell if he's looking at me or not because of his sunglasses.

He starts walking, doesn't drop my hand, and I watch his back, watch the way his shirt hangs off his shoulder blades. He pulls on my hand, my arm, pulls me in next to him, moves his arm around my neck so that his hand, still holding mine, is over my shoulder. God, why does it feel so good? Why does he fit me so perfectly? He kisses my hairline, speaks into it. 'Karlo,' he says, nothing else.

'Bexley,' I say, but more like a question.

In the main square there are more people around, tables full of rich tourists. I only realise now that there are orange trees around the perimeter of the square. We weave through them on our way to the Coms office.

'Come in with me?' he says, once we get there.

I shake my head.

'Man, I don't think I can do this now.' He forces a joyless smile.

'You have to,' I say. 'You said you were going to call her back.'

177

'I know.' He makes a face. 'But I just can't.'

'She'll be expecting your call,' I say quietly. 'Please don't let her down.' But how can I say that after what I've just done? The pain of it pools in my stomach, turns hard. 'I'll ... I'll wait outside for you, OK?' I manage to say.

It's less than a minute later that he comes out and joins me under the orange tree where I've been waiting.

'She's still out.'

I study him through half closed eyes before I say, 'You didn't call, did you?'

And he shakes his head, watching me steadily.

We're probably halfway back to the campsite, solar panels striping past the door, music up and dust blowing in on us, when I realise what's about to happen and pull over, ditching the car and flinging the door open, running for it. I heave up the contents of my stomach, then follow it with several lumps of dark blood, which I end up coughing out so that it spatters on my chin and legs before I manage to hide it. Micah stands a metre away and watches in horror as I straighten back up and wipe my chin on the back of my hand. My eyes are watering and I'm out of breath with it but I manage to say, 'Come on, let's go,' like it's nothing.

He takes my arm as I pass him, but he's looking at the blood in the dirt behind me. 'Karlo, tell me what's happening. Tell me what I can do.'

I wipe my mouth. 'Nothing is what you can do. You can do nothing.' I go round and open the driver's door.

'You should let me drive at least,' he says, but I shake my head and get in.

'I'm fine,' I tell him.

We're moving again and the wind feels good on the new layer of sweat I have on my face.

'I'm sorry, Karlo,' Micah says, staring at his lap. 'I always forget. And then today's been so crazy. Shouldn't we get you checked out by a doctor or something?'

'Don't do that.' I hold up my hand. 'Seriously. Don't do that. Don't look at me that way. Don't say those things.'

'I'm sorry,' he says. 'It's just that it scares me. But I guess not half as much as it scares you.'

'It doesn't scare me any more.'

'Really?' he asks.

'No,' I say, laughing. 'It annoys me, but it doesn't scare me. Maybe it should, but it doesn't. One day it'll kill me, but there's not a lot I can do about it. It's me, my own immune system, turning on itself. What can I do?'

I feel him watch the side of my face. I reach to turn the music up; Kate Bush.

'You're so brave, you know,' he says.

'I told you not to do that, OK?'

'OK,' he says. And we both listen to the music, the wind, all the things we aren't saying.

*

179

Back at the camp everybody has left and there's only footprints in the dust and a couple of bags of rubbish in a pile next to the gatepost. Our two tents look lonely. In the outhouse I break the dusty surface of the water in the bucket to gargle and splash my face with shaking hands, and then try not to meet my own eye in the mirror. Back outside I kick my trainers off and lie down on a blanket in the shade, my face pressed against my forearm. I feel Micah sit near my legs, then his hand on my ankle. I hold my breath; it seems like the only way to keep from screaming.

'Don't touch me,' I say into the blanket, my voice hardly there, so that he says, 'What?'

And I say again, 'I said – don't touch me. Please.'

I hear him sigh; feel him lie on the blanket next to me on his back. I turn my face to the side and open one eye to watch him. He has his hands in his hair at the front, gripping it.

'I'm sorry, Karlo, for what it's worth,' he says. 'You don't have to feel bad, OK? It's on me.'

'How is it on you?'

'I'm the one that's cheated on my girlfriend.'

'And your girlfriend happens to be my best friend.' I press my face against my arm again. 'What I've done is worse.'

'How is it worse?'

'Boyfriends and girlfriends do things like this to each other. Best friends aren't supposed to.'

'Oh man,' he groans, rolls on to his side so that he's facing me, pokes one finger into my ribs. 'It's OK. Let's just ... we don't even have to own it, you know. We can just forget it ever happened. I think that's for the best, right?'

I nod, face still hidden, which is a good thing because I have a sudden urge to cry.

That's when he touches me just like I told him not to, moves my hair behind my ear, strand by strand, so gentle. Tears burn, but I shift my eyes to meet his, and we are both so sad.

'You don't have to feel bad,' I tell him. 'This is the kind of crap I pull. I mean, it's even in my genes. I'm not a good person.' I blink and a tear spills, out on to the blanket.

'That's not how it was,' he says.

'I was so close.' I almost laugh.

'So close to what?'

'So close to getting away from you without ever letting it happen.'

I shift on to my side and watch his eyes – fathomless blue, dark eyelashes that are longer in the outer corners – shifting focus from one of mine to the other, then to my mouth, his fingers on the side of my face, his thumb on my chin, then on my lower lip. I swear I am liquefying. Nobody has ever obliterated me the way he can. I reach for him, tracing his freckles, and when my fingers reach his lips he parts them. I slide my thumb across his mouth and find the edge of his teeth.

'I love your teeth,' I manage to say.

He raises his eyebrows a little in surprise. 'They're a mess,' he says. 'Mali wants me to get them fixed.'

'Please don't,' I say. 'Don't change anything.'

When we kiss then I fall apart, open to my centre pages like a book. How good it feels outweighs how bad it is that we are doing this, by a hundred to one.

We don't even hear the car when it pulls in. Or maybe we don't care. Either way gravel popping under tyres and car doors slamming doesn't register with me at all until a voice says, 'Sorry to crash your party.'

And it's this girl with long dark hair, glasses, tight smile, looming over us while we sit up like two people waking from a dream.

'Are you running this place?' She tilts her head at us.

'No,' says Micah, getting it together quicker than me. 'Carmen is. She's . . . somewhere.' He gestures at the house. 'If you want to pitch your tent, I'm sure it'll be fine and you can catch her later.'

Kristina and Arianna, sisters, both have long, black hair that waves in the wind, and have driven down from Madrid, having flown in from Kuala Lumpur. We watch them put their tent up as the sun begins to set and then they walk up the hill to visit Carmen's cousin's bar.

We're on the rocks looking at the view when the sun is

just about to drop beyond the armoured landscape and the crickets are changing, the ones that chirp through the night taking over from the ones that shriek all day. Right now it is all of them, together, heralding the night in a deafening buzz. I'm still in shorts and I can already feel the mosquitoes coming for me, but right now, with Micah's fingers on my thigh, I couldn't care less. We are looking into each other's eyes like we are reading something there. I am trying so hard not to kiss him. I think he must be trying too.

'It doesn't ... ' I shake my head. 'We should never let it happen again ... I mean, you know that, right?'

Suddenly he hides his face in his hands, groans there. It's another tic of his; one I've only just started seeing, but now seem to be seeing a lot of. 'But the fact that this happened – it must mean something, right?' he says into his hands. 'It must mean that something's wrong with me and Mals.'

I shake my head. 'No, I don't ... I really don't think it does. I just think it means you're a human. I mean, it's not like you're never going to want anyone else. I don't think it works that way. It's animal instinct, Bexley, that's all.' I shrug as if shrugging will make him believe that none of this matters; shrug like it'll make me believe it.

'Really?' he says, letting his hands drop. 'Is that all it is for you?'

It takes me a while to respond, because the way he's

looking at me makes it almost impossible to speak. 'No,' I admit, before sighing and adding. 'But it's irrelevant.'

'It is?'

'Whatever happens at La Verdad, I'm ... I'm never coming back to Wales.' This is the first time I've said this outright, but suddenly I know it's true. Apart from anything else, how can I ever look at Mali again now? I let it settle in me for a moment before I say it again. 'I'm never coming back to Wales, so you and Mals will be together, and I won't be there, and you'll both be way better off without me around.'

Just at that moment a hundred solar panels flare in a ray of sunset sun, and I half-close my eyes against the brightness.

'I don't feel like we'll be better off without you,' he says.

And I say, 'You will.'

And he says, 'We'll be missing you.'

And I say, 'You won't.'

And he says, 'Don't go.'

And I say, 'I'm already gone.'

And he says, 'No, you're not.'

And I don't say anything.

Supernova Remnant

'Bexley?'

It's Jam. It wakes us both up with a jolt, but Micah thinks faster than me.

'Morning mate, what's up?'

'You know where Bea is?' His voice is literally just on the other side of the tent material; I can hear him breathing. Micah has his hand laid on my head, leaning up on one elbow, his eyes shifting to meet mine.

'Yeah, she . . . um . . . she went for a walk, an early walk.'

'She did?' He sounds as surprised as I would be.

Micah cringes. 'Yeah,' he says, then seems to think of something, most probably the fact that this is Jam's tent too so he could unzip it and crawl in at any moment. 'Give me a second and I'll come with you. We'll go look for her.'

'OK,' says Jam, still sounding baffled.

Micah and I look into each other's eyes for a minute, but we can't speak with Jam just there. I watch him as he raises his hips to pull his jeans on. I watch the muscles shift in his bare shoulders and back as he hunts for his shirt, finds it just under my right hip and then twists to pull it on. He runs a hand through his hair but it's a mess, all fanning up like a parrot. I'm smiling about that when he turns to me and, even though he shouldn't, he leans down and silently presses his parted lips to mine. I lay my hand on his jaw and frown against him, keeping him there as long as I dare, and then he is gone.

I wait to hear their voices fade and then look for my clothes. My pink bra is under his pillow, my jean shorts in a corner. Every inch of my skin smells like him, like his bed. Just as I'm about to climb out, I notice my copy of *Tender is the Night* just under the corner of the air mattress; he's using a ferry ticket as a bookmark.

I'm in the shower by the time they get back. I knew if I didn't wash last night away, I would spend all day thinking about it. Thinking about how we told each other that we were only going into his tent because we wanted to keep talking and there were too many mosquitoes outside. Thinking about how we started out kissing slow and soft and gentle, like it might cause less damage that way. Thinking about how long we managed to keep our underwear on before, at almost dawn, we didn't any more. Thinking about how he whispered against the damp skin of my collarbone: 'So beautiful.' Thinking about the way he looked when he held himself above me, still for a moment, watching me, touching my lips with his fingers, that slight frown, looking like he might be about to say something that I was scared of hearing, but then just kissed me. It felt just as beautiful and real as I knew it would, maybe more so, but at the same time I kept wondering if he was the same with me as he is with Mali, the shadow of that always there, casting shade over all of it, the way it is with something stolen, no matter how precious it is.

When I get out there, wet haired, Micah and Jam have collapsed the tents and are just pushing theirs into its bag. Carmen is under the tree, folding Jam's shirts. Kristina, one of the sisters, is sitting in the open door of her car, looking at a map.

'Where were you?' asks Jam, and suddenly they are all looking at me.

'In the shower.'

'No, before.'

'Just ... um ... I couldn't sleep so I was, you know, walking.' I shrug.

Jam frowns and says, 'What happened to your face?'

I touch it, feeling my stomach sink, realising it's probably beard burn. 'I'm not sure, maybe I got sunburnt.'

'On your mouth?' He puts a hand on a hip while I shove things in my bag.

'Look, guys,' says Micah, clearly panicking, 'we really need to go if we're going to get there on time.'

We get in the car while Jam says goodbye to Carmen.

She looks so sad. I stare for a while at the way she is holding his hand in both of hers, examining it.

Just then Kristina appears at my window. 'Want to follow us?' she says, pushing her glasses up her nose. 'We've got a Ventura Com Navigation System in the hire car so ...'

'No,' I say hastily, without even thinking up an excuse. I can't risk them giving us away.

'No?' She frowns.

'Thanks,' says Micah from next to me. 'Thanks, but we'll be fine.'

'Up to you, but it's not easy on these small roads, and we've only got until three to get there.' She shrugs, walks away, raises a hand. 'See you down there I guess.'

Jam gets in the back seat at that moment. 'We should follow them down,' he says. 'They've got one of those Ventura Com—'

'We'll be fine,' I cut in. In the silence that follows, I start the car and mess with my wing mirror, wiping a layer of dust off it with my sweaty fingers.

'Why wouldn't you want to follow them?' says Jam, and I glance at him in the rear-view.

'They're weird,' I say. 'I'll explain later.'

We're on the long straight road that heads directly south when we first smell them; an intense, beautiful, floral smell that couldn't be anything other than exactly what it is – a blanket of orange trees as far as the eye can see, rows to every horizon, passing the car windows in rank after rank, the fruit hanging off the branches so abundantly it's almost ridiculous. In the end it's too much and I have to stop the car just to look at them, just to breathe their air.

Micah gets out and walks to the fence, gripping it with his fingers.

'Come on, Rees,' he says. 'Give me a boost.'

'That's stealing,' says Jam, but he opens his door anyway.

'Does it count as stealing when there's a million of them and they belong to a multinational conglomerate?'

'Good point,' concedes Jam.

I open my door and step out. A hot wind kicks sand at us while Jam cradles his hands together for Micah, who steps on them and scrambles up the side of the fence so that it rattles all along its length.

'Where's the camera?' I ask. 'Seriously, I could make an instructional video right now of how not to climb fences.'

Once Micah finally gets his leg over at the top, he peers down at the ground on the other side while he brings his other leg over and drops down what must be about three metres, squatting to absorb the impact.

'How are you planning to get back over?' I call through to him.

'Not sure,' he says, laughing. 'I'll figure something out.'

He goes to the first tree we can see and reaches up between

the leaves, pulling at a huge fruit, causing another three to fall at his feet. He lobs them up over the fence one at a time; I catch the first and Jam catches the following three.

'How many more do we want?' he calls, tossing a few more, some of which we miss and end up chasing across the road as they roll away.

'OK, that's enough,' yells Jam.

Micah struggles to get back over the fence initially, getting about a metre up and then falling again.

'Guess we'll just have to leave you here,' says Jam, sitting in the dirt with his back against the front tyre. 'Nice knowing you, Bexley.'

I sit next to Jam and watch Micah scrambling for purchase again before falling. I'm holding one of the oranges in my hand and I push my thumbs through its waxy skin, pulling it apart, bursting it, the smell almost unbearably beautiful. I notice Jam watching me.

'What?' I ask him, but when I look at him I realise. For a second we are reading it, all of it, in each other's eyes; I've never been able to hide anything from him. 'What?' I ask him again, trying to laugh it off.

'Nothing,' he says, looking away. 'Nothing at all.'

In the end Micah only gets over at all because he backs all the way up to take a long run at the fence and uses the momentum to defy gravity, running up the fence and snatching hold of the top of it. While he is rattling it to pieces and monkeying over the top, I am pulling an orange segment out and handing it to Jam, pulling out another and bringing it to my lips, biting at it gently, then sucking.

'Oh my God,' says Jam, through a mouthful, just as I am thinking almost exactly the same thing.

It's so intense, so sweet; so strong that to taste it almost feels like pain. I let my head fall back against the hot body of the car.

Micah drops to the ground in front of us, disturbing a cloud of dust and brushing off his jeans.

'Enjoying my ill-gotten gains?' He takes one out of my lap and starts to peel it, sending a zesty spray into the air.

'Why don't they taste like this at home?' I ask, as Jam gets up and walks to the other side of the road to gaze up into the heat shimmers in the distance. 'I've never had one like this before.'

Micah laughs just faintly through his nose, and we watch each other for a moment as he pulls off a section and lifts it to his lips.

'This place,' says Jam from across the road.

I peer around the bumper at him. He's looking up at the blue sky, arms slack by his sides. 'Everything's better here.'

'Is it though?' says Micah. 'Cities have got all the money, the countryside's been sold off by the state to the highest bidder to produce whatever on a massive scale. It's worse here than Wales, in a way, because ninety per cent of it is for export. Didn't Carmen tell you that, or were you too busy to do any talking?'

'Her father was fighting the forced land sale when he died,' Jam says, staring up the road again. 'Then it was seized because of some legal loophole to do with inheritance.'

'Exactly,' says Micah, like this proves his point. 'Same problems, different country. All that's different here is the weather.'

'Yeah,' says Jam, still gazing up at the dome of perfect blue above. 'That does make quite a difference though, doesn't it?'

We stop at a charge station and when I come out of the bathroom Micah is standing at the bar with three little cups of coffee in front of him.

'How are you?' he says as I stand in next to him.

'I don't know,' I say.

He reads the side of my face for a second before he says, 'Don't worry about it, Karlo.'

Don't worry about it? I'm about to get annoyed when I am derailed, because I look up at him and remember the way he sighed when I kissed his neck, when I painted a line of kisses all the way down to just over his heart before he scooped me back up, his mouth to my mouth. God, why did it all feel so easy?

Jam gets back and I stare down into my coffee. He says, 'They have a Coms Office here, you know, if you need to call anyone.'

'You should try Mali again,' I tell Micah, my voice more full of meaning than I want it to be.

'I thought you called her yesterday,' says Jam, frowning.

'Yeah, I ... she wasn't there,' he says, looking at me, biting his lip. 'I'd better try again.'

'OK, but make it fairly quick,' Jam says. He turns to me as Micah is walking away. 'Aren't you going too? I thought you might want to speak to her.'

I shake my head and swallow, while he raises his eyebrows, and the untruths sit in the silence between us again, like something tangible.

'I ...' It comes out of my mouth before I've planned the rest, and both of us hold our breath, waiting to see what I will say. But I can't give physical form to what I've done by saying it out loud, and even if I could, I know all I would want is for Jam to say it's all OK, to make it better, to forgive me. And now it comes to it, I'm pretty sure he won't do any of those things. I know I wouldn't, if I were him.

I can tell he's still waiting for me to speak, even though he's finishing his coffee and then pushing his hair over to the side before putting his hat back on.

'I ...' I start again, and he is still, waiting, one hand on the bar beside me, watching me, but then I only say, 'How much further is it?'

A missed beat, then, 'Maybe four hours.'

'So close,' I sigh.

'Having second thoughts?'

I narrow my eyes at him, wondering if there's a double meaning in his words. 'No, I suppose I've just spent so long thinking about it and it's weird that it's about to be real. But no, I want this more than ever.'

He watches me the way he does, still and unreadable.

'Any second thoughts from you?' I ask.

'Thinking's a waste of time,' he says.

Outside we walk across miles of scalding hot car park and nearly get run over by three massive juggernauts, whose horns scream at us as we jog out of their way.

'What's with all the road-trains?' I ask.

'Europe's salad bowl,' says Jam.

'What?'

'Andalusia, where we are now, just about, gets called Europe's salad bowl.'

'Oh my God,' I say, suddenly remembering. 'Staff Ed at AcePrice. I can't believe you actually remember any of that crap.'

'I only remember because they said they were visible from space.'

I frown. 'What were?'

'You'll see,' he says.

We're only just getting the AC going when Micah's door opens and he sits in his seat, stiff and staring like a crash-test dummy with both of us watching him.

'She's arriving tomorrow,' he says.

'What?' It's out of my mouth before I can stop it. 'Arriving where?'

'Here,' he says, still dummy-like. 'Well, Seville. Her grandfather got a little better apparently, and he found out about the trip and told her to go. She's just about to leave for the airport.'

'Seriously?' says Jam, smiling. 'That's awesome!' He is leaning between the seats looking from Micah to me and then back again. 'Isn't it? What am I missing?'

'Nothing,' I manage to say, pulling off the handbrake. 'Bexley's just worried about her grandfather, aren't you?'

And Micah says, 'What? Oh . . . yeah,' before pulling his sunglasses down and staring out of the window.

It's no more than twenty minutes until we are lost among an epic, endless shantytown of greenhouses. So big and so many, they stretch further than we can see, coating the land in shining reinforced plastic sheeting that bounces the sunlight so hard that most of the time I am blinded, even in my sunglasses. The road makes its way down a tight space between them.

'Visible from space?' I ask Jam, watching him nod in the rear-view.

We see people sometimes, workers, lined up along the side of one, huddling into a tiny patch of shade, passing a bottle of water between them.

The greenhouses only end when we reach the mountain range that has been looming in front of us for half the day. The road is carved out of the rock itself, winding up, through canyons, clinging to the side of the mountains. This is one of the only places we've seen that has stayed a wilderness. It's just too steep, too rocky, too wild to be tamed into Europe's dishwasher or Europe's bag of crisps or whatever other kind of service they might choose to offer.

I'm too busy concentrating on driving to catch any of the views that are making the boys murmur periodically, but I do notice the bunches of flowers by the side of the road, just about every few kilometres, every time the road does some sharp swoop around a shoulder of rock where you could go slamming headlong into someone without any warning. Or maybe swerve to avoid them and end up sailing into the abyss.

'I'm going to have to stop,' I hear myself say.

'Where?' says Micah, studying my profile. 'There's nowhere.'

'I'm freaking out,' I tell him, cutting to the chase.

'You're fine,' he says, but I see the fear on his face too.

I swallow. 'I bet all these people thought they were fine too. Oh God, I'm going to get us all killed.'

We pass another bunch of flowers tied to the crash barrier, just where the road cuts into the shoulder of a mountain.

Jam leans forward between the seats. 'Bea, you are an excellent driver, you're the best I know. There's nobody I'd rather have behind the wheel right now.'

And suddenly, just like that, I am calmed, and then I hear Micah say, 'Oh man.'

And when I look to see what he is looking at, it is the sea. Our first sight of the Mediterranean, and it is blue and glimmering, like crystallised sky.

'We're OK, Bea,' says Jam, from behind me. 'We're almost there.'

We're down in the foothills, heading seaward, when we start to see the drones, circling and low.

'La Verdad,' says Micah. 'Has to be.'

That's when we hit traffic for the first time in the whole trip. It's actually disorientating for a moment to have to pull up behind another car, to have to stop after a thousand kilometres of open road.

Micah strains in his seat to see what the hold-up is, then opens his door and steps out on to the road.

'Well?' I call to him.

He gets back in, leaving his door open. 'Some kind of checkpoint thing,' he says. 'We're not that far away from it. Ten cars or something, I guess.'

Being stationary, we start to heat up. There is a wind

but it's hot, like a hairdryer blasting at us from down off the brown mountains we just left behind. The temperature on the gauge reads forty-one. I feel the sweat in my hair form into drops that roll down the side of my face.

Once we are one car from the front, we watch a guy in a grey uniform come to the driver's window of the car ahead and lean in, talking to the guys before waving them on, waving us forward. I pull up and he leans low, peers at me from under the Ventura-branded baseball cap he's wearing.

'Good afternoon,' he says, glancing at each of us. 'Welcome to Ventura Com's La Verdad Space Research Facility.' He is disorientatingly American. 'All recruits?'

'Just these two,' says Micah. 'I'm only along for the ride.'

The guy presses something on the handheld device in his hand that makes it beep twice. 'Two recruits, one *acompañante*. Please park over there in the overflow camping area. Recruits to proceed on foot to the green-flagged area for initial screening. Thank you.' And he stands back, waves us on with an odd circular motion that he's obviously done a million times.

'That's intense,' says Micah, looking across at another guy in uniform, wearing a gun strapped across his front that he is holding super casually.

We bump over shrubs and ditches and come to a slight

rise, and as we go down the other side we get a view across the site, across thousands of multi-coloured tents, a sea of them, and beyond that, the real sea. People our age, coated in dust, slow-limbed and sweaty, a disproportionately high number in white T-shirts. We see a woman in a grey uniform and Ventura cap, who waves us into a space next to another car that's just parking up.

'Leave your vehicle here,' she says, without making eye contact. 'Make camp in the overflow field – straight over there and to your right. Welcome to Ventura Com's La Verdad Space Research Facility, and good luck in the recruitment process.' She walks behind us and starts waving to the next car.

I unfold myself from the driver's seat and stretch, meet Micah's eye over the car's dusty roof.

It seems like we have ten times more stuff now we suddenly need to carry it. We're weighed down by sleeping bags, backpacks and even Jam's guitar, which he refused to leave behind. We straggle across the sand in the heat, strung out in a line, buffeted by the hot wind. This place looks different to the way it did on the news; busier. Now that I'm here, it's suddenly all too real. And terrifying.

Only one corner of the overflow field has any space at all, almost like we are the very last people to arrive, which I guess we are. Amazingly, because it's right on the edge, the one remaining spot has this epic ocean view. I've never seen water so blue, shading out from turquoise to a rich jade, flecked with golden sun.

'How cool is this?' says Micah.

Camping in the spot next to us, there's this middle-aged couple sitting in camp chairs, side-by-side, clasping plastic wineglasses and watching us pull our tents out flat on to the ground. They're watching us so hard, smiles in place, that in the end Micah goes over to them and shakes hands.

'Micah Bexley,' he says. 'This is Beacon and Jam.'

They don't speak any English at all, but somehow, mostly through sign language and patchy Spanish, they seem to get across that they're from Brazil and that they're here with their son, who's over at the first round phase of testing.

Jam's standing next to me watching it all play out. He hands me his water bottle as he says under his breath, 'Who the hell would bring their parents on this trip? I mean, man, it could be your last few weeks on Earth. You wouldn't want to spend them with your parents.'

I'm in the tent, changing my sweat-soaked vest, when I hear voices. It's Kristina and Arianna, and they spend these few minutes talking to Jam and Micah about how they actually ended up getting lost and how they should have followed us.

'Our parents are ex-military – they'd be so disappointed

in us,' says Kristina. Then she asks, 'Where's your girlfriend?'

And I hear Micah force out this super-fake laugh. 'Bea? Bea's not my girlfriend.'

'Really?' she says. 'Um, OK. You've got a funny way of showing it.'

Super fake laugh again. 'We're friends is all.'

I finish pulling on my top and dive for the door.

I struggle out, stand up into the middle of them and look around. 'Hey,' I say to Kristina. I glance at Jam, who doesn't meet my eye, and then back at Micah, who is staring at the ground. 'We're just leaving. Going to initial recruitment. You coming?'

They need to pick up a couple of things and Jam needs to visit the *servicios*, so they say they'll meet us over there. I'm waiting in the queue with Jam when he says, 'What was all that about?'

'All what?'

'Actually, forget it.' He pushes his hair over to the side, wipes sweat off his forehead with his wrist before putting his hat back on. 'I don't want to talk about Bexley. Not even a little bit.'

I laugh, but even I can hear it comes out nervous as I say, 'Why do you say that?'

He looks at me like I just said the stupidest thing he ever heard. 'Oh come on, Bea, whatever,' is all he says, and I notice the way the heat has brought blood to the surface of his skin and he is flushed along his jawline as he sighs hard to mark the change of subject. 'So this is it,' he says, raising his eyebrows.

'This is it,' I agree, nodding, unsure what to feel or what to say.

We get to the front of the line and Jam goes to the nearest unit, and when he comes out again Kristina and Arianna are just arriving, Kristina carrying this huge lever-arch file in her arms.

'What's that?' I ask her as we walk.

'Our paperwork.'

'I thought it was just school and medical records.'

'I brought everything I had, just in case,' she says.

I look sideways at the file and think about my records, all three or four crumpled sheets, folded into quarters and pushed into my back pocket with my ID card.

'I don't think there's enough evidence of me or my life to even populate a twentieth of that space,' I say, and she laughs.

'Don't worry,' she says. 'The initial recruitment is just about medical wellness.'

'It is?' I feel my steps slow.

'Yeah.' She shrugs. 'Like, whether you have any pre-existing conditions.'

Obvious, really. I don't know why it hadn't occurred to me before. I only realise I have stopped walking when she stops too, stares back at me, Jam fetching up beside me.

'They're going to reject me right away, aren't they?' I say to him. 'I'm never even going to get to see the facility. They're just going to see the pre-existing on my record and count me out instantly. Why didn't I think of that?'

Jam shakes his head. 'That would be discrimination.'

I laugh. 'I think they probably get to discriminate.' Something inside me is sinking into my feet, through them, into the ground.

Up ahead, in the green-flagged field, there is a queue snaking around an enormous grey tent so that it looks like the world's most popular theme park attraction. I swallow fear, ignoring the voice inside me that asks if maybe I want to be counted out straight away so I don't have to go through all of this. So I don't have to care. Maybe it was easier when I *didn't* care about anything. That's the problem with wanting something – suddenly you have something to lose.

Kristina says, 'To be honest, I think they're only interested in one thing anyway.'

We both look at her.

'Your fertility,' she says, like it was obvious.

Jam curls his lip at her. 'Our fertility?'

She almost laughs. 'You know what you're being recruited for, right?'

We both watch her in silence.

'Their breeding program,' she says. 'I mean, you knew that, right?'

'So if we're picked, we're going to be expected to –' I swallow – 'make babies for them?'

Kristina laughs. 'It's not *The Handmaid's Tale*. We'll only be expected to have two. It's a structured society with assigned partnerships and ...' She frowns. 'Didn't you do *any* research?'

I look up at Jam and he looks down at me, pulls the brim of his hat a little lower over his eyes.

'You guys are hilarious,' says Kristina.

Magnetic Field

Once we get into the main entrance area of the tent, there is a screen on the wall, playing a video – tracking shots of the Ventura itself, then library images of happy couples kissing their baby so that I can only assume it's some kind of propaganda movie to convince us that this isn't weird at all, when it is becoming increasingly clear to me that it actually is pretty weird.

'We're the next batch,' says Kristina, as if we're products in a factory, which I guess, right now, we are.

The woman at the front is wearing the same uniform as the guys outside, but with a white coat over the top, like someone pretending to be a doctor.

'Females to this side, males to this.' She points to two areas that are marked off with retractable barriers that basically look exactly like pens for cattle. Something makes me panic then, and I'm suddenly short of breath, but when I turn to Jam he just says, 'Don't worry,

Bea, you'll be fine. Just breathe,' like he sensed it already.

And I do breathe, in and out, and feel the panic start to ebb away.

He watches me for a minute before he says, 'Well, I'll see you in a bit I guess.'

I grab a handful of his shirt and pull him close, lay my ear against his chest. I feel him tense up in surprise, since hugging isn't something we do all that often, but then his hand is on my back and when I pull away he looks at me, eyes narrowed.

'Sure you're OK?' he says, watching me.

And I nod my head and force a smile. I take a step away from him, even though it feels hard and we watch each other the whole time.

When Jam has gone through the barrier, Kristina turns to me and asks, 'So what's the deal with you and him then?'

'Our parents are married.'

'So ... he's your brother?'

'No.'

'A boyfriend that's not actually your boyfriend, and a brother that's not actually your brother?' She raises an eyebrow. 'Do you have any other fictionalised relationships in your life or just those two?'

'Just those two,' I say, smiling. 'Look, about Micah ... the thing is, I kind of need you to ... ' And I'm just about to ask her if she can arrange some amnesia for herself before Mali gets here, when the woman in the white coat appears next to us and hands us each a dog-tag. Mine is oddly cold in my palm.

'Put this around your neck,' she announces to the world in general. 'Keep it on at all times and memorise the number. If you are ejected from the process, you will surrender it.'

I look at mine: B-37-37.

'Move through here and wait to be seen,' she says, ushering us through a doorway where we stand against the wall of the tent, feeling the heat that comes through it from the sun beating on the outside. Five uniformed Ventura employees are sitting at terminals with chairs in front of them.

Right at that moment my number appears, in red dot matrix, on one of the little screens in front of the terminals. I sit down on a chair and the woman behind the screen looks up at me.

'Your paperwork?' she says in a Spanish accent, watching me closely as I hand over my few wrinkled pages.

'My school records are OK,' I say, 'but my medical ... I have a pre-existing ...'

'What is it?' she asks, without looking away from her screen, without slowing her fingers as they fly across her keys.

'It's an ulcerating DTD, an autoimmune ...'

'Not a problem,' she says.

'What?'

'We find that long-term space travel tends to reset the immune system, so autoimmune conditions aren't a consideration for us.' She keeps typing, having said something I never thought I'd hear in my life. I sit back in the chair.

'So I'd be ... cured?'

'Essentially.' She nods. 'There are other complications associated with long-term space travel, but they tend to be unpredictable. All we're looking for in your medical notes is whether you have something terminal or infectious. You don't, so you can pass through to the examination area behind me and see my *compañera*. Thank you.'

I'm dazed, but I manage to get up and walk past her, out through a flap in the tent's wall to find myself in a narrow roofless compartment where there is another woman wearing a white coat, standing next to a bench and a machine, holding something flat and grey in her hand, not even glancing at me as she says, 'Lie here on this bench, and try to relax. This is a scan to assess your fertility. We're really only looking for those who have optimum fertility.'

I take a deep breath, go to the bench, sit on it, swing my legs up.

'Just pull your shirt up a little for me and unbutton your shorts, please.'

'How many times have you done this over the past few days?' I ask her, studying her face as she stands next to me, double-taking at my stomach as she notices the huge puckered surgery scars across it.

'A lot,' she says, and smears a handful of gel just above my pants. She places the warm metal of the paddle against me, pressing it as she moves it and looks at her screen with half-closed eyes.

I clamp my teeth together tight, not because it hurts but just because there's something so awful about letting a stranger look at my insides in a tent in a field in a foreign country, and I have a feeling I just might scream in horror. With all the time I've spent at hospitals, I should be used to this kind of thing by now, but somehow it's never lost its impact. I watch shifting shapes on her screen, but I can't make anything out, and suddenly she says, 'You're done. Please wait in the next room, and check the screens for your number. Thank you,' and she hands me this single paper towel before she turns her back and busies herself with wiping off her paddle, ready for the next victim.

I stand and wipe at my sticky stomach before heading through the door, dumping the damp paper towel in the big, almost overflowing bin next to it on the way. I come through to find Arianna sitting in the middle of a long, meandering line of empty chairs.

'Hey,' I say, on an exhale, sitting next to her.

'Hey,' she says, and I realise I have barely heard her voice.

Up in front of us, there is another dot matrix screen.

All it says at the moment, at the top, is 'Room One' and 'Room Two'. We stare at it in silence while another two girls come in and give us blank smiles before sitting down. My number is the first to appear, right under 'Room One'. I check it a couple of times before I say, 'I guess that's me,' and get up. Just as I do that, Arianna's name appears in the other column and she stands, and for a moment we are looking at each other, wondering which future belongs to whom, trying to read it in each other's eyes.

I step through the next door and find a guy there, staring at a handheld device for a while, before he convinces himself to stand and acknowledge me. 'Here,' he says, handing me a Ventura branded T-shirt that has 'RECRUIT' written on the back. 'Welcome to Phase Two. Put this on and keep it on for the remainder of the process. Report to Main Gate at oh-nine-hundred hours. Thank you.'

I can't help but laugh as I'm pulling the T-shirt on over my vest-top. 'Oh-nine-hundred?'

'Yes,' he says, making a face. 'Is anything about that unclear, recruit?'

'Sir, no, sir,' I say, pulling a mock salute before stepping out into the sun.

I am almost blinded. Then I turn and see Arianna. She isn't wearing a T-shirt. I got picked and she didn't.

I walk over and she speaks before I do.

'It's fine,' she says. 'I've always had mixed feelings about it anyway. I've got a college place next year. It's just a little bit worrying, you know? I mean, does this mean I'm infertile?'

'No.' I shake my head. 'I'm sure it doesn't mean that.'

She looks up at the sky.

'Didn't they tell you anything?' I ask. 'Didn't they explain?'

She shakes her head. Kristina comes out then, behind me, wearing a white T-shirt. She looks at Arianna for a minute, smile faltering, and then goes to her, pulls her into her arms.

I look along the back length of the tent to the boys' side, but there's nobody appearing out of the doorways. It takes an agonising few minutes until a boy finally steps out, no white T-shirt, not Jam. I'm swallowing fear now, head pounding with it. What if . . . ? And then he's there, just easing his hat back on, wearing a white T-shirt, looking along towards me as I run to him and take his hand, wrapping myself around his arm as we walk together.

'God, I was so scared,' I say against his T-shirt sleeve. 'Arianna didn't get through and suddenly I started thinking maybe you wouldn't . . . I guess I never really thought that part of it through.'

'There's a lot about this whole thing that we didn't think through,' he says.

Red Shift

We hear Micah's music before we get there, overlaid with him extolling the virtues of Dire Straits' early albums. When we get closer to the tent, we see him lounging on the sand in the late sunlight with four people in white T-shirts we've never seen before.

'Yes!' he yells out when he sees us. 'You made it. Nice one!' It's only as he gets up that he sees Arianna walking with us and says, 'Oh,' and nothing more.

'It's OK,' says Arianna, holding a hand up as she passes through on her way to the tent. 'I am perfectly fine about it,' and then she's gone, with Kristina following her.

'Who are your friends?' I ask, peering over his shoulder just as they stand up. They're two guys and two girls, all ridiculously tall and pale and utterly unsmiling. The guy nearest me offers me his hand and I take it. He grips it so hard it makes me wince.

'Kazimir Sherbakov,' he says in a thick accent that could only be Russian.

He stares so hard at me that I (infuriatingly) fumble my words when I introduce myself.

'Get this,' says Micah. 'These guys grew up, like, actually *grew up* in space. They're the kids of haulers.'

'I didn't know haulers took their families with them,' I say.

'Some do, some don't,' says Kazimir. 'It's not a life everybody would choose. We only came back to Earth two times.'

'A year?' says Jam.

'No,' Kazimir says, 'two times in my life.' He shrugs. 'Including now.'

Jam laughs.

One of the girls says something in Russian.

'You will excuse us,' says Kazimir. 'We go to cook.' And just before they leave he turns again and says, 'We see you at phase two.'

'Wow,' I say, once they're out of earshot.

Micah laughs. 'Yeah they're really interesting.' He's popping open a tin of beans. 'But come on, tell me what happened. How was it?'

'Weird,' says Jam.

'Weird how?'

Jam looks at me. 'It was pretty, I don't know, biological. I mean, it was a fertility test, basically.'

Micah lets his mouth drop open. 'The Russians said it was a medical suitability test.'

'Look, I get it. The mission is hundreds of years long, which means they need babies to make up a future generation of crew,' says Jam. 'What would even be the point in taking volunteers if we can't fulfil that function? We don't have any specialist knowledge at all – no experience. All we have is ...'

I watch Micah taking this in before he says, 'I mean, would they want you to, like, have babies right away?'

'No.' I shake my head. 'I don't think so.'

'And do you choose who you have the kids with or ...?'

I look across at Jam, but he's just staring at the ground in front of him.

'Here.' Micah breaks the heavy silence by handing me a piece of white bread. 'We lost our plates somewhere, so make yourself a beans sandwich.'

'Wow,' I smirk. 'How will I ever leave all this behind?' But when I meet his eye, I see something sad there, even though he's smiling.

After we eat, Jam drinks two beers and falls asleep in the sand, on his side, hands tucked into his armpits, slight frown. Micah and I watch him for a minute. Then Micah reaches for my hand. His fingertips have hardly touched my skin when I pull my hand away.

'Don't,' I say.

'Karlo ...'

'Mali gets here tomorrow.' I shake my head. 'And we've got enough problems as it is.'

'Talk to me, though.'

I shake my head.

'Please.'

I point across at Jam and say, 'Well, not here.'

'Where then? The beach?'

'No.' It comes out of my mouth too loud and I know why – it's because it's me I'm trying to convince. 'I'm not going to the beach with you.'

'Come on,' he says, in that soft voice. 'I want you to see it anyway.'

'It's dark, Bexley,' I say, still not daring to look at him.

'There's moonlight,' he says.

Oh God.

But somehow, before I can do anything about it, I am walking over the dunes with him.

'Kristina thinks you're my boyfriend,' I sigh, but it hurts.

He flaps a hand. 'She's just jumping to conclusions.'

'She saw us making out, Bexley. She spent the night in a tent three metres away from where we ... It was probably a pretty logical conclusion to jump to. And now, when Mali arrives ... ' I can't even finish that sentence so I just shake my head.

'So ask her to keep quiet about it.'

I shake my head. 'I already tried. I can't do it.'

'Why?'

I walk ahead of him, up to the top of the dune we're on.

From the top I can see all along the beach, the moonlit crescent of sand and the tops of the gentle waves pulsing in like something inevitable. My hair blows across my eyes in a warm gust from off the land. It's so amazing, so beautiful, I'm momentarily afraid my heart will explode, or cave in, or both.

'Because,' I say into the wind, 'as soon as I start asking people to lie for me about it, it will feel real.' I turn back to him. 'But right now, I'm still hoping that when she arrives tomorrow it can just ... evaporate.'

He laughs. 'I'll be honest.' I watch as he takes a deep breath, in then out. 'I kind of hope it will. But I'm not sure.'

I look away, back out at the beach, heart rattling out a million beats per second, stomach roiling.

I feel him step closer to me. 'I'm scared,' he says. 'Terrified, in fact ... that it won't.'

I dare to look up at him, then wish I hadn't. 'Don't,' is all I say before I walk off towards the sea, feeling him follow me. I spin round and shout again, 'Don't!'

'Don't what?' he asks again, to my back.

'Don't ...' I look for the words. 'Don't be you. Don't be here. Don't remind me every single time I look at you how good it feels to kiss you. Don't be the boy who has been on my mind for almost every second of the last three years. Don't be my best friend's boyfriend.' There are so many more things I could say, but none of them are helpful. I stop and let the wind move my hair, feel his hands on my shoulders.

'OK, I won't do those things,' he says. 'As long as you stop doing what you do to me. Don't be so funny and cool and sexy and sweet that I can't believe you'll never be mine. Don't be Mali's best friend. Be someone else. Because if you were ...'

I turn to him. 'Don't say that.'

He bites his lip. 'So many things you don't want me to do.'

And I'm thinking: *And so many things I do want you to do*. And I swear he must hear my thoughts, because something shifts, and suddenly standing there and looking at each other without kissing is torture. I break away, walk away, even though I have no idea how I manage it.

'The only reason that any of this even happened is because I thought I was never going to see Mali again,' I say, my voice cracking on her name. 'I have no idea how I'm going to look at her now. How will I ever look at the girl I love most in the world after what I've done? At least I'm one step closer to being a million light-years away, and neither of you will ever have to think about me again.'

'You're not actually ...?' He leaves the question hanging.

I turn to face him. 'I'm not actually what?'

'You're not actually going to leave? After today ... It's all pretty horrible, Karlo – don't you think? I mean, you're

217

going to sit in a spaceship for the rest of your life churning out babies? What part of that is working for you?'

'That's just the way it has to be.' I gape at him in amazement. 'It's a multigenerational mission – it makes perfect sense. Having children is essential to the mission because it's about creating the future crew. The point is I get to be part of the most important scientific project in the history of humanity – that's what's working for me, Bexley.'

He is wide-eyed in the moonlight, watching me, both of us a little breathless.

'Plus they said I'd be cured,' I add. 'That being in space would most likely reset my immune system and I just . . . wouldn't be sick any more. I've spent my whole life knowing I was on borrowed time and suddenly they're telling me I could live a normal life. A long life.'

'What?' He blinks, recalibrating. 'I mean, if that's true it's . . . amazing. But can they say it for sure?'

'They seemed pretty sure.'

I look up at the sky then, mostly because I'm a little lost for words, and there they are: the stars. Thousands upon thousands of them, more vivid and bluer and closer and truer than I have ever seen them, and I hear myself draw breath.

'Look at that,' I breathe.

I walk up to where the sand is drier and sit in it. After a few moments Micah comes and sits next to me. He sits with his knees up, arms across the top of them, looking up. 'I guess this is why they put the facility here in the first place,' he says. 'Clear skies, no light pollution.'

I gaze and gaze without any hope of really taking it in. The more I stare, the more stars seem to appear; it's as close to understanding the vastness of the universe as a human brain can get. From down here, anyway.

'I mean, seriously, look at it,' I hear myself say. 'I guess, when it comes down to it, I just want to be a part of something beautiful.'

He watches me, mouth slightly open, almost in disbelief. 'I get what you mean,' he says, 'but maybe you're idealising it. You're not thinking about what it would really be like. And all the things you'd be giving up.'

'Such as?' I say. 'Gower Gate? AcePrice?'

He lets his face drop against his arms for a moment before sitting back up. 'I was thinking more like, I don't know, dancing, summer rain ... Spending the whole rest of your life cooped up in a grey, metal flying prison doesn't seem like your style.'

'What do you know about my style, Bexley? I don't even know what my style is.'

'I know you're not the kind of person who should be partnered with someone in some weird child-rearing business arrangement. You're the kind of person who should ... fall in love, for real.'

I watch my hand pushing into the sand; watch it falling through my fingers.

'Falling in love for real is overrated,' I say, my voice quiet.

We happen to look at each other at the same moment then, and it's only because it could be the last time, that it *will* be the last time, that this is goodbye, that I lay my hand on the side of his face and lean into him, press my lips against his.

'Seriously?'

We move apart at the sound of the voice and look up. It's Jam.

'Hey, Rees, it's not ... um ... it's not ...' says Micah, fading out because there really isn't anything he can say to make this OK.

I'm so busy feeling the world drop away beneath me that I can't speak, can barely even breathe. Jam's gaze shifts to me, the stars his backdrop. I want to say something to explain, but nothing comes out. He shakes his head at me, walks past us and off down the beach.

I get up and run after him. 'Jam!'

He spins. 'Do *not* follow me, Bea. I mean it.'

'Don't be like that,' I plead, touching his wrist.

But he shakes me off and then he's gone, striding down the beach, kicking sand up behind him, shaking his head at whatever his internal monologue is.

Micah's standing behind me when I turn back towards camp.

'He won't say anything,' he says.

'I know he won't,' I sigh. 'That's not the point.' And I push at the sides of my head, trying to prevent it from breaking apart. 'I need to be alone,' I say then. 'Please.'

And when he doesn't move, I leave him there and stride out along the beach without looking back, even though he says my name more than once as I go. I walk for maybe a minute in the same direction that Jam went, before I stop and bend double to cough blood into the sand.

I keep walking, scanning the dark sands for Jam, occasionally calling for him. Eventually I give up and sit under the stars, listening to the waves while I try, and fail, to swallow the hard onset of tears. In the end, he almost walks into me before I see him and quickly jump to my feet.

'Jam, I . . . '

'I don't want to hear it, Bea,' he says, without stopping.

'Why are you being like this?' I run after him, my feet sinking in the soft sand.

He turns to me as I get level with him, disappointment and anger mingling on his face in a way I've never seen before. 'How do you expect me to be?'

'I thought you'd be on my side.'

'I am on your side. I always have been. That is exactly why I am so angry with you right now.'

'That makes no sense.'

He shakes his head. 'It makes perfect sense. That's what being on your side is like. Because *you* are your own worst enemy. You know you are.'

He double-takes at me then, notices the tears I haven't fully managed to wipe away, softens a little. 'I guess I just never really thought you would do it, Bea. I thought you would stop yourself, stop him, before it went that far.'

My throat gets tight, but I manage to say, 'I tried.'

'Well, that makes it OK then,' he says, heavy with sarcasm.

He storms off and leaves me behind, music and laughter from the camp coming to me from so far away, it's like I'm part of a different story, one about how it feels to disappoint the only person who ever truly believed in me.

Planemo

Jam still isn't talking to me in the morning when I climb out of the tent. Instead he stares at the kettle of water, getting hot on the stove.

Micah stands up out of his tent a few minutes later and says, 'I'm heading out now. I need to be in Seville for eleven. To collect Mali.' He looks at me, but only quickly, like he hardly dares to. Then he looks at Jam and says, 'Rees, look—'

'Save it,' says Jam, tight-lipped with the anger he's barely keeping in. 'Seriously. Why would you want to talk about something that we all need to pretend never happened?'

Once he's gone, Jam and I head over to the research facility in an almost unbearable silence. I sneak looks at the side of his face and open my mouth to speak many times without ever being able to think of the right thing to say.

Along the way, we are being joined by more and more people in white T-shirts until over the last open stretch we are walking along like some kind of army on the move, the wind whipping across the causeway and flinging sand in our eyes.

'Please don't be angry with me,' I say to Jam eventually.

He sighs. 'It's a truly horrible thing to do to your best friend, Bea.'

'I know that, but ...' I search for the words. 'It felt like it had to happen.'

He sighs again. 'It felt like you wanted it to happen.'

'OK.' I hold my hands up. 'OK, yes, I wanted it to happen. But I tried really hard for it not to. I've been trying really hard for a long time. And maybe, out here, it just all got too much. I thought I was never going to see Mali again and I've had feelings for Micah from the moment I met him. You know I have.'

'That doesn't excuse what you've done,' he says.

I feel him watching the side of my face, looking straight through me at everything I'm hiding, just like he always can.

'I know.' I nod. 'You're right.' I dare to meet his eyes briefly and then take his forearm in both my hands. 'Just, please ... please don't be angry with me. Isn't it bad enough that I have to live with what I've done? That I have to ... lose him?'

'You can't lose something you never had,' he says. But

then he softens. 'I'm angrier at him than I am at you. He knows how much you . . . ' And then he checks himself.

I blink. 'He knows how much I what?'

'Never mind.'

'How much I what, Jam? Tell me!'

'Just . . . leave it, Bea. I really don't want to talk about it any more.'

We get to the tarmac road that leads up to La Verdad and find there are TV vans parked everywhere and people in high-visibility vests that say PRESS on the back standing in front of expensive-looking cameras, talking into them, pointing them in our faces as we pass, drones circling to film us from the air. As we get closer to the gate, the buzz intensifies, with hordes of reporters stopping people, firing questions at them like bullets. I shift away from the edge until I'm safely in the middle of the pack, but their questions reach me anyway.

'What made you decide to volunteer?'

'What have they told you so far about the mission?'

'What have you had to do?'

'Do you know what's happening today?'

As we get closer to the big sliding gate ahead, I see them – the famous giant brushed chrome letters that are fixed across the sweeping lawn to the left of the entrance to the facility: *Every day a little closer to the stars.* My heart starts banging in my chest, breath catching. It doesn't feel real that I'm standing here; that I'm standing here in front of something I've only ever seen in photographs and I'm a part of it, about to go in.

The gate starts to wheel open on its runners as soon as the first people get there.

'It's like *Charlie and the Chocolate Factory*,' I say to Jam, just about getting the words out.

'I was thinking the exact same thing,' he says, double taking at me and then squeezing my wrist when he sees how overwhelmed I am.

There isn't really much to see along the first stretch, just a flawless tarmac road that runs in a bizarrely perfect straight line ahead of us so that it's almost like an optical illusion. There are people in uniform every forty metres or so, with big intimidating guns strapped across their front. It's weird how much scarier it is to be in the presence of an actual gun, compared to just seeing them on the TV.

Every large building we pass is low and squat and square and concrete. There are a couple of roads leading off that have smaller buildings spaced at regular intervals; clearly residential.

'People live here,' I say, only just realising.

'Yeah,' says Jam, 'I guess most of the people who work here have to live here. We're in the middle of nowhere.'

The giant satellite dishes have been visible since we first arrived at the facility, but it's the sheer number of them that isn't clear until we're walking right alongside. Each one is five storeys high, looking at the sky at the same angle as the other thirty or forty that are ranged across the sand.

'Wow,' says Jam. 'They're serious about getting their cable channels.'

I give him a look. 'It's the LVA.'

'The LVA?'

'The La Verdad Array. It's a radio telescope. This is how they discovered the signal.' I stare out across it, walk through the shadow of one of the giant dishes, straining my neck to look up at it without any hope of taking it in. 'I've always wanted to see it; never dreamed I would.' I'm still smiling when I look back down at Jam, and he's watching me.

We end up in this weird square, like one of the plazas we've been seeing in the towns on the way down here but totally fabricated and fake, like a film set. There are no clues as to what will happen next apart from the fact that everything is draped in Ventura logo banners and flags, and there is a raised stage area with a line of chairs and a lectern. Taking up one entire side of the plaza, watching all of us, is a line of fully uniformed guards – legs planted wide in big black boots, not a single smile among them.

Jam is straining to look around, across the crowd; because he's tall, he can do that.

'Looks like they already cut our numbers quite a bit,' he

says. 'There can only be two thousand of us here. But they had another batch in here yesterday and the day before too, so let's say seven or eight thousand in total.'

'Jesus,' I end up saying. 'We never really had a real chance of making it through, did we?'

'That's a lot less than thirty-five thousand,' says Jam. And I have to concede he's right. But that just makes it worse. I never should have come here; I should have walked away yesterday before the stakes were so high. How is it going to feel to lose out now? On my dream? On my only chance of being well? I wonder if I'll even survive it.

I look over at Jam and realise he is still studying me with a frown. I'm just opening my mouth to speak when someone walks up on to the stage. He's in the same uniform as the guards, but is older, fatter, sporting this huge combed moustache. Next is a woman in full Ventura uniform, bobbed hair, mumsy and scary at the same time. Next, a guy in a grey Ventura-branded jumpsuit and buzzcut. I vaguely recognise the last guy from the TV without being able to quite place him, but he's obviously pretty important, judging from the suit and the super-waxed hair and the way he stands at the lectern and looks around with this smile and expects everyone to shut up for him.

'Good morning, recruits,' he says, in a thick Spanish accent, but because everyone's still talking he has to say it again. 'GOOD MORNING, RECRUITS.'

And then there is silence.

'For those of you who don't know, I am Luca Torres Gallego, CEO of Ventura Com. May I please introduce my colleagues, General Vazquez, who manages security for us here at La Verdad; Veronica Rojas Moreno, the European Space Agency's Director of Operations; and Lieutenant Kolbasenko, Supervisor of Off-Planet Operations. Firstly, we would like to thank you for coming all this way and for volunteering for the Ventura mission. If you are one of the lucky three hundred who are selected, we know you will not regret your decision.

'Since its inception, La Verdad facility has been leading the world in working to realise the dream of making contact. Eighteen years ago, in the years immediately following one of our planet's greatest setbacks, the Information Collapse, and when most of you were just being born, the Epsilon Eridani alien communication signal was discovered and identified. This is why, when the opportunity came to become the sponsors of this amazing facility and the mission it was designing, it seemed the perfect fit for Ventura Communications. We have been at the cutting edge of communication for over thirty years, and we remain so. Our latest product, the Pod –' as he says this, pictures of one appear on the screen behind him – 're-establishes instant text, audio and video communication between users in a post-Information society. This device avoids all of the hazards that brought about the Information Collapse by utilising our secure, virus-proof global intranet. We don't believe that information and communication should be just for the privileged few, so we are bringing it back to the people of this planet, starting today.'

He's grinning away and all super smooth, until he looks round and notices that most people are pretty indifferent. For people our age, who've never known any different, these kinds of promises are pretty abstract. He gets serious again.

'But our commitment to realising the dream of contact runs far deeper than that.'

New video footage of the Ventura spaceship starts running on the screen now. I always think it's kind of ugly, like a giant, several-kilometre-long cruise liner.

'As we all know, environmental changes and global resource shortages have made space travel into an economic and practical enterprise over the past decades, with the vast majority of funding and sponsorship being focused on short-term hauling to bring back valuable ore and resources from our nearest neighbouring planets, or the construction of long-term Pioneer vessels seeking to colonise habitable planets in more distant systems. But Ventura is a First Contact vessel. She does not seek to abandon our planet but rather to connect her, for the first time, with her universe. We believe that the possibility of exchanging knowledge with another species, possibly one far more advanced than our own, could be the key to overcoming the challenges we currently face and finding a future for ourselves. And in the coming days, her mission to seek out intelligent life will begin.'

Total surge of talking and looking around, while Luca Torres side-steps and manoeuvres Veronica Rojas in front of him.

'On this momentous morning,' she begins, 'ninth of August 2050, let me start by welcoming you all to the La Verdad Space Research Facility. Hopefully while you are here you will get a chance to see a little of the facility that is the driving force behind Mission Ventura. Around half the crew of the mission will be made up of scientists from this base, most of whom have lived here for many years in what is a very close-knit community. The Ventura project will be a lifetime commitment, but one in which the ties of community, that have been so essential in our success up until now, will sustain us into the future and beyond. What we hope to assess over the next three days is your suitability to leave your former community behind and integrate fully and wholeheartedly with this new one.'

She steps back from the microphone and glances back at Lieutenant Kolbasenko, who steps up to the podium like he's about to take it on in a fist fight.

'Now, lucky me, I get to be bad cop,' he says, booming, too close to the microphone. 'It is my job today to assess your physical ability to withstand the stresses and pressures of space travel, and I have to tell you now that less than a quarter of you will make the cut. Please will you all proceed to the Training Centre where you have been divided into groups for today's activities, and you will receive a full briefing from our colleagues. I wish you all the best of luck.'

People look at each other then, all open mouthed and muttering as they start to file out of the plaza.

'What the hell kind of test are they going to do to assess our ability to withstand the ... what was it? Stresses of space travel?' I ask Jam.

'Sounds like simulators, which I hate. I'm definitely getting cut today.'

'Not necessarily,' I tell him. 'It's not going to be like the crappy simulators at Abertawe Bridge Entertainment Village.'

He nods up at the structures we can see just beyond the squat building of the training centre – towering cranes with what look like passenger pods attached to the arms.

'Are you sure?' he says.

Just then he gets ambushed by a crazy person. All I see is this grinning girl with a ridiculously deep tan leap on to his back, wrapping him in bare arms and legs.

'JAAAAAAAM!' she yells in his ear, which is when I realise who it is. Tara. Tara from the ferry. Fin appears next to her, laughing, all teeth.

'It's you guys!' she says. 'Well, I'll be damned.' And she shakes her head.

Tara, still on Jam's back and talking in his ear, says, 'What group are you in, sexy?' and I find myself fighting an urge to wrench her off onto the ground.

'I don't know yet,' he says, cringing away and easing her off him.

'Well, go and find out,' she says, pushing at his hip. 'And make sure you're in mine.'

We edge though the crowd towards the screens that show the groupings, and once we get close enough we both study them in silence and end up saying, at the same time:

'We're not in the same group,' and looking at each other with a fear neither of us manage to hide in time.

I sigh, and force a smile. 'Never mind, *sexy*. Maybe you'll be with Tara.'

A smile fleets across his face. 'Yeah, great,' he says, super sarcastic.

It turns out he's not in the same group as Tara either, but I am in the same one as Fin. We find our way to Room 22 and, all the way there, she is going on about how wasted they've managed to get every night since they got here. Room 22 has three lines of terminals each with a chair and a woman sitting at the front staring at her computer. I sit near the back and Fin sits next to me.

'So have you made out with Micah yet?'

I reel back in shock before I manage to say, 'What? No! Of course not!' but I am so stuttery and lame that she nails me right away.

'I thought that might happen.' She nods, wisely. Then she adds, 'Wait, didn't you say he had a girlfriend?'

I nod, but my face is burning; I can feel it. 'She arrives today,' I manage to squeak out.

'Bummer,' she says, before yawning theatrically. 'Don't worry – she'll probably turn out to be some loser and he'll dump her.'

I'm flinching as I say, 'She's my best friend actually.'

She laughs. 'Seriously? Wow, you are COLD.' And she shakes her head at me and laughs again. 'I'm actually quite impressed at how stone cold you are.'

I'm about to try and deny everything, but right then the door slides open again and Kazimir and the three other Russians are standing there. The four of them are so tall, so pale, so completely and utterly unsmiling, that the whole room is suddenly silent and staring at them. They walk in like they own the place and find chairs, sitting in them languorously with spread legs, before starting to chat pretty loud in Russian.

'Who are *they*?' gasps Fin.

'They're the Russians,' I say.

'The *hot* Russians,' she says, looking at Kazimir. I don't see whatever it is Fin sees, except that he is broad across his shoulders and that he, I don't know, owns it I suppose.

234

He must feel us looking because he slides this glance over his shoulder at us, which is when I notice his eyes again, pale and grey, like every bit of colour has been leached out of him.

'I think he's like some kind of space vampire,' I tell Fin, probably a little too loud.

'A *hot* space vampire,' says Fin, motionless and smiling vaguely in awe.

'I'm Lieutenant Marisol Dean,' says the woman at the front. 'Welcome. We will participate in two computer tests this morning, followed this afternoon by exercises in our training craft.'

She then goes on to explain for ever about what these computer tests are for and how they work and how long we have for each section, but what it comes down to is they are the most boring set of multiple choice questions that don't seem to be related to anything at all, so it becomes completely obvious that this is some kind of psychological profiling.

If you found a genie in a lamp that was going to grant you three wishes, what would you wish for first?

A. *World peace*
B. *To be extremely rich*
C. *Ultimate power*
D. *To be invisible*

And a whole bunch of other things like that. I mean, literally hundreds of pointless what ifs, enough to keep us clicking answers like a room full of sighing zombies until lunchtime.

We get taken to their canteen and it's disappointingly identical to the one at school. I look around for Jam but he's nowhere.

'I don't see Jam,' I say, and feel the panic rising.

Fin scans around. 'Taz isn't here either.'

The blond guy opposite us overhears. 'They're probably in the other *fase* –' he says it the Spanish way – 'they did the craft tests this morning; we swap after lunch.'

He double takes at the way we are staring at him, then offers his hand across the table. 'Caleb Lomax,' he says. 'I live here, so I have a little of the inside track.'

'You live here?' says Tara. 'What's that like?'

He looks up at the ceiling, like he's thinking as he finishes his mouthful of food. 'I never lived anywhere else, so it's difficult to say.' He has this weird hybrid American accent that sounds like he learned it off the TV, like the Malaysian girls. 'My mom used to be one of the research scientists at the Array. She's up there now.' He points at the ceiling.

'Dead?' gasps Fin.

'No,' he laughs. 'On Ventura. She went off-planet a week ago.'

'There are people up there already?'

He nods. 'Of course. There's been people up there for years.'

'So, if your mother is one of the top brass, you must be a shoo-in for this,' I say, narrowing my eyes at him.

He shakes his head. 'No, I'm the same as anyone. Just hoping not to get cut. Apparently they cut two thirds of this morning's *fase.*'

I feel my eyes widen. 'They did?'

'Yeah,' he snorts. 'Panic attacks in the sims. Puke everywhere, apparently.'

I swallow, thinking of Jam after the sim at Abertawe Bridge, so bad he couldn't even stand, regurgitated popcorn and candyfloss in a hot puddle between his knees.

A tannoy announcement beeps on, and I realise it is the same computerised female voice Ventura use for all their communications systems, including the prison telephone service that we've heard once a week for years. It tells us that if our number appears on the screens in the canteen then we didn't pass the psychological profiling. I stare up at them while they change from the Ventura logo into a list of numbers and realise I am holding my breath. Considering the number of times I've been told about my bad attitude, I'm amazed when my number isn't there. *Every day a little close to the stars.* It pops straight into my head and makes me smile.

*

After lunch, we're taken back outside into the brutal heat.

'I'm Lieutenant Cristobal Sanchez, and welcome to our flight training centre,' says this guy as he presses a button on the crane structure that we're standing close to and it starts to retract, squealing and clunking. A simulator pod lowers to the ground. 'First ten come forward please – let's get started.'

Once everyone's inside and the door is securely shut, the crane starts to rise up into the air and we follow the guy to the base of the next one. While he's getting another ten to stand forward and lowering the cabin, I turn and watch the previous one over my shoulder lurching and dipping on its suspension.

I'm in the fourth. We sit in two rows and pull on seatbelts while the screen starts up. I try not to think about how hot it feels, how little air there is. The screen shows a surprisingly lame space simulation and we start almost immediately to swoop and list. I mainly focus on trying to ignore it, but it gets pretty hard when Fin leans all the way forward and clamps her head between her knees. I lay my hand on her shoulder and haul her back up to a sitting position.

'That won't help,' I tell her. 'I used to get car sick. You have to look out the window.'

'There are no windows,' she says through her teeth.

This is when I look over and see Caleb, the guy from lunch, leaning against the far wall and watching us, smiling.

The first pukers start shortly after that. One of them goes for the door and presses desperately at the button before collapsing to the floor and chucking up right there. The second does it between their legs so that when we bank left it flows on to our feet before we get a chance to lift them.

'You think it would really be like this on Ventura?' asks Fin.

By the time we're being lowered back down and the door hisses open, we are all partially coated in sick.

'Nice job,' says Lieutenant Sanchez as we clunk to the ground. 'Can the following recruits step to one side please –' he consults the handheld he supports on his arm – 'C-45-67, C-85-41 . . .' and so on until I watch both the guy from the door and the between-the-knees girl get called and asked to hand over their dog tags, before walking away aimlessly, cut adrift.

'The rest of you please follow me for the aquatic training exercise,' beams Lieutenant Sanchez.

On the walk over to the giant hangar at the end of the field, I watch my sick-soaked trainers taking me another step closer, and wish my stomach didn't feel so tight. Inside the hangar is a space so huge the end of it is lost in darkness. Once my eyes adjust, I notice that to my left there are about ten illuminated tunnels, each containing a narrow vehicle on rails.

'These are our submarine vessels,' says Lieutenant

Sanchez. 'They are the closest thing we have, bar the real thing, to space shuttles. These travel from right here in our training hangar, all the way out to the Atlantic Ocean, where they mimic the conditions of deep space. You will simply be required to pilot it unguided, cope with the claustrophobia and return unharmed. Ten at a time, please.'

The first one fills quickly and we watch it shoot off down the long tunnel with a hiss.

'Next ten,' says Lieutenant Sanchez, and Fin and I step forward, clambering into a ridiculously tight space filled with seats.

I watch Fin click her seatbelt in.

'Just stay calm,' I tell her.

'I am calm,' she says. 'Or I was until you said that.'

We feel ourselves lurch forward on the rails.

'Oh God,' I hear myself say, while Fin looks at me.

'Oh God indeed,' she says. 'Under the Atlantic without anyone who has any idea what we're doing.' She dodges her eyes around then while she thinks about it. 'Oh my God,' she says then. 'What are we doing?'

We judder along, watching each other's flesh vibrate against our bones.

'This can't be legal,' says Fin, screwing her eyes shut. 'Why did we agree to get in here?'

That's when the vibration stops, and suddenly there is silence.

'What now?' asks Fin, then louder, 'What now?'

The Chinese guys sitting up front are pulling on the featureless levers in front of them.

'Can you drive it?' she yells at them. 'Do you know what you're doing?'

'No way to see out,' we hear one of them say. 'No windscreen.'

I remember something from a movie and look around inside the cramped cockpit for some kind of periscope, but there's only riveted metal and struts and ... down around my feet there's water. Was that there before? I slosh my trainers around in it.

Fin glances down at the noise. 'We're taking on water!' she yells and suddenly a guy a row forward starts shouting too. 'Press the emergency abort button or something – there must be one!'

'No button!' the guy at the front yells back. 'Just steering.'

The water is still rising, and by now it's almost up to my knees.

'We're going to die here!' someone says, horribly emotionless.

That's when I decide this is not how and where the story of me ends. So I close my eyes and try to tune it all out. I tune out everything until I can only hear my own breathing. I picture us, out at sea. I feel the weight of the ocean that surrounds us, presses in on us. I look down through the rising water at my feet, and this is when I notice my laces waving like underwater weeds, moving in an invisible current; a current coming from behind me. I get up on my chair and try to rend it away from the wall. I can't so I climb off it, into the narrow space next to it and into the cold water that is now so high that it has covered the seats. I plunge my hand in and feel for where the water is getting in.

'The leak's here!' I shout, before taking a breath and plunging underwater again, feeling it out with my fingers. The weirdest part is the way it feels, like it's coming through some kind of narrow pipe. By the time I get up again, I realise the cabin is now pretty much half full of water. 'We need to stop the water getting in.'

I look at the others, most of them stood up in their seats, bracing off the ceiling, watching the water level climbing. The guys in front are still pulling and pushing at the controls. I can't get Fin to stop yelling long enough to listen to me, let alone to help.

I pull my T-shirt off and duck under the water with it balled in my hands and feel for the hole. I run out of breath and stand back up, up to where there is only about a foot of cabin space left above the water.

And this is when I realise. I look around at everybody's faces tilted up into the remaining airspace and I lick my lips, rub them, lick my lips again. 'It's fresh,' I say, too quiet. 'It's fresh,' I say, louder this time.

I watch the frowns that spread from one face to the next, the way people dip their heads so that they can taste it themselves. I turn to the door behind me, notice the red lever: Emergency Exit. I grab hold and yank it as hard as I can. The heavy metal door flies open and pours me out on to the concrete of the hangar floor where I lie in the draining water like a dying fish. Someone else falls out on top of me. We cough and look around, look up at Lieutenant Sanchez as he walks over, beaming hard. The others, soaked and coughing, are just climbing out of the sub behind me.

'We never even went anywhere,' I hear one of them say.

'Well done,' says Lieutenant Sanchez, picking up my dog tag and reading off it. 'Congratulations, B-37-37. You just earned your crew a pass through to the next round of recruitment. That's exactly the kind of lateral thinking we're looking for.'

'Are you crazy?' I ask him, struggling to my feet. 'That was a *horrible* thing to do! We thought we were going to die!'

He smiles. 'You were perfectly safe the whole time.' I watch his eyes track down to my bra for a second and I fold my arms across my chest, roll my eyes.

Just then, I hear a siren – a great big honk that fills the hangar – and one of the Ventura guys pulls open the door of the sub next to us, emptying the panicking recruits out on to the floor, coughing and terrified.

243

'You get a kick out of terrorising teenagers, do you?' I ask Lieutenant Sanchez.

He laughs, so I walk away in protest.

'See you tomorrow at oh-nine-hundred hours, recruit,' he yells at my back.

'Don't count on it,' I yell back.

Perpetual Motion

I don't even slow down until I'm all the way out of the gate, which is when a reporter starts asking me questions and sticks a camera in my face and I start to spiral into panic. But then I feel a hand on my elbow, pulling me out to safety, walking me away as I collapse into his side, hugging him around the ribs, because it's Jam, and he's still wearing his dog tag.

'How did you get through the sim?' I ask, once we're away from the reporters.

He shrugs. 'Don't know really. Mind over matter. Kept my eyes on the screen like you always told me.'

Hot wind gusts at us as, my T-shirt almost dry already.

'That's great,' I say, 'but I'm not sure I'm going back there.'

'What?' he laughs.

'They're sadistic, Jam! That submarine trick!'

'I know,' he says. 'Pretty low.'

'I thought I was going to die. We can't trust our lives to people who would do that.'

'That's one way of looking at it.'

'Is there another?'

He bites his lip like he's thinking. 'Well, you could say that they're just making sure that the people they take are brave and good in a crisis. That's a good thing, isn't it?'

I'm considering this when I hear a scream. It's Mali, tearing towards me, having obviously just spotted me. I'm terrified, frozen to my core for a moment, then she comes leaping through the tents at me like a gazelle, and grabs me. And I remember I'm not scared, I could never be scared, because this is Mali; this is my best friend Mali, who I have loved since I was eight years old when she used to let me ride her bike around the walkways of level twenty-two any time I wanted. And here she is, when for a while there I thought I would never see her again, and I pull her in against me and all I can do is focus on not bursting into tears and telling her everything. Now she's in my arms, I feel like I am breaking open, crumbling, shattering.

'Bea, you are so *tanned*!' she yells into my hair. 'You look so sexy! I hate you right now!'

I pull back a little and I try not to quail while we study each other up close. She's tanned too, freckles just across her nose, and she changed her hair, had shorter layers cut around the front. I want to say a lot of things but I only manage to say, 'I missed you.'

And she rubs a tear off my cheek with her thumb and kisses me on the same spot before twisting to look at Jam.

'Joram Rees,' she says, like a teacher telling him off. 'When the hell did you get so hot?' And she kisses him on the lips in a way that only Mali can make seem platonic.

I only notice Micah then, standing close by. He looks crazy beautiful just then in a way that physically hurts – tanned and sand-flecked, squinting slightly in the low sun.

'So?' he says. 'Did you both make it?'

I nod.

'Come and have a drink then,' he says. 'Tell us about it.'

We sit in the camp drinking beer, and listening to Todd Rundgren. Mali tells us about Canada, about how she went horse riding every day, to this place in the woods where she could sit surrounded by trees, where she didn't have to think about her grandpa, lying in his hospital bed, only able to recognise her once for about five minutes the whole time she was there.

'I think moving to Canada made his memory worse,' she says. 'Like he didn't have any landmarks of who he used to be and it just set him adrift. Anyway,' she says, like she's waking up from a dream, 'tell me more about space camp. And how was it getting down here? What did I miss?'

There's this missed beat then, this moment where Micah and I make fleeting eye contact before Jam says, 'Nothing much really. Just heat and dust and solar panels and giant greenhouses and ghost towns and monasteries.'

She makes a face. 'What? Are you serious? That sounds amazing.'

'Hey guys,' says a voice from behind the tent, but it's the one I've been dreading.

'Hey, Kristina.' Jam, unsuspecting, introduces her to Mali, but without mentioning that she's Micah's girlfriend. I wonder for a second if I can add it without looking weird, but then too much time passes and I'm stuck with things as they are, with waiting for the axe to fall. There's a huge knot in my stomach, tightening by the second.

I watch the light from the late sun bounce off Kristina's glasses.

'How did you do today?' she asks, sighing.

'It was horrible,' I say. 'But we got through.'

'You did?' She smiles. 'Really? How did you manage that?'

I shrug. 'Figured out that it was a fake. Busted out.'

She grins, looks at Jam. 'Were you in her sub too?'

'No. I just decided to open the door because I thought

it would be better to try my luck in the sea than die in that thing.'

'Oh wow.' She shakes her head. 'If only I'd gone with you when I saw you. I guess I must have ended up in the pessimist's sub, because we pretty much just accepted our fate.'

'You got cut?'

She nods.

'I'm sorry,' says Jam.

'No, it's for the best,' says Kristina. 'I need to get Ari home anyway. She's hated being here since she got cut. She's barely left the tent. We'll get going first thing.'

'Do you want a drink?' says Mali. 'Send off?'

'Sure,' she says. 'What have you got?'

Mali dives into Micah's tent and comes out with this weird pink bottle filled with clear liquid. 'Canadian maple syrup vodka!'

'Sounds disgusting,' says Jam.

'Eeyore –' she tilts her head – 'don't be so ungrateful.'

It does turn out to be pretty disgusting, as we discover, knocking it back in one burning shot. But it doesn't stop us pouring out another shot each, which is probably the reason that by the time I hear the next voice I should dread, it doesn't scare me that much.

'Heeeey.' Fin makes this one word last ten seconds. 'There she is. My hero.' And she comes to me and pulls me into a headlock so that I can't really see until I push her off and then notice Tara coming through the tents too, followed by the Russians.

'Has she told you how badass she is?' she says, beaming at everyone.

'I've always known she was badass,' says Jam, his words sliding together a little the way they do when he's on his way to being drunk.

'Have you been drinking already?' says Fin, like she's reading my mind. 'So have we. Taz and Ksenia got cut so they're drowning their sorrows. Kazimir, Oksana and I got through so we're celebrating.'

I notice Kazimir smiling, which is new.

'Similar situation here,' says Micah, holding up the bottle.

Fin looks at Mali. 'Wait, who's this? Are you ... are you the girlfriend?'

Mali smiles at her. 'That would be me, yes.'

Fin reaches for her hand and shakes it. 'Nice to meet you. I have heard absolutely nothing about you,' she laughs. 'Which is interesting, right?'

I watch Mali frown slightly, while I cringe in the awkward silence, which stretches until Kazimir, most unlikely saviour ever, says, 'You should all come with us. You don't need shoes. Bring alcohol.'

'Oh wow,' says Mali. 'How perfect does that sound?'

We walk along the beach towards the huge sand dune that marks the furthest point of the bay. The water in the bay is silky and opaque, like a puddle of spilt milk, but twinkling where the sun hits it. We set off up the incline of the dune. The sand is so fine, so white, collapsing under our feet. It becomes like a moonscape; like being lost on another planet, just sand and sky to all horizons. It could feel empty, but somehow there's something so relaxing about it. I'm walking along in someone else's tracks, increasing my stride to fit my feet into where their much bigger ones were, and as I look along I realise they are Jam's, which makes me smile.

'I heard about you,' says a voice, and when I turn it's Kazimir. The setting sun seems to have lent him some of its colour.

'What did you hear?' I ask, curiosity getting me.

'That you thought your way through the problem. In the sub.'

'I guess.' I shrug. It's making me out of breath, walking in the soft sand, so steeply uphill, but I try to hide it. 'How did you get out of it?'

He squints out at the setting sun. 'I've seen that kind of thing before so ... I knew.'

I nod. 'I still think it was an evil trick.'

He looks back at me. 'Maybe, but you understand what they're looking for.'

I snort. 'Fertility?'

'OK, sure,' he concedes. 'But mostly they're looking for courage. That's what you need, more than anything, to live in space.'

'Because it's scary?' I squint at him from behind my sunglasses.

'Yes,' he says, simply.

We get to the top of the dune and I turn on the spot, taking in the view of sea, white sand edging it, and then behind us the thinning tents and behind that La Verdad. From here the spiked fence that surrounds it looks even higher. Its squat grey buildings and endless huge telescope dishes cover the ground all the way to the open tarmac of the spaceport, which is when I notice it.

'A rocket launch,' I say, watching the squad of vehicles currently heading away from the vertical shuttle on the pad. 'How did you know?'

When I turn to Kazimir he is smiling. 'There's a schedule. It's not random.'

'I realise that.' I make a face at him and I'm about to point out that he's a patronising asshole when Fin takes his arm, pulling him away to the edge of the dune.

I watch Jam for a moment then, the way Tara is holding his hand and leading him to sit in some dune grass, even though I can see he doesn't want to. Then I pan over to Micah and Mali. He's standing behind her, arms wrapped across her chest while they both look out over the sea towards where the sun is sinking. I turn away, my skin crawling with how alone I suddenly feel, only to crash straight into Kristina.

'Looks like it's just you and me,' I say to her, smiling through the sadness that is blooming in me. 'And the good news is, I am still in possession of the maple syrup vodka.' I hold it up between us, and she grins.

We sit in the cooling sand and take brave swigs from the bottle while the shuttle's engines start up. The sound rumbles out along the ground and the flames are yellow and blue.

'I'm annoyed you didn't get through and Fin did,' I say, after a minute. 'I would much rather have hung out with you some more.'

Kristina smiles. 'I'm pretty annoyed about it too,' she says. 'I know now how Ari was feeling yesterday. She kept saying she felt like she was grieving and I thought she was seriously overreacting. Now I know *exactly* what she means.'

I hand her the bottle, watch her take a drink.

'I mean it's like –' she coughs and laughs, starts again – 'it's like you had this whole future mapped out ahead of you and then suddenly … it's gone. I mean, really, it's best that I go back and finish school, and if I'm honest, I really hated the idea of leaving my family behind. But still, it's just such a feeling of loss. That's the only way I can describe it. Loss.'

She pushes her hand into the sand between us; buries it.

'Or maybe it's a lucky escape,' I say, raising my eyebrows at her in the failing light.

Just then the engines get so loud we can feel the vibrations in our chests. Fire spreads out from the bottom of the shuttle and along the ground.

'This is it,' I hear myself say, and it is only a few seconds more before we hear the creak of it releasing from the support tower, the boom of the thrusters, then the oddly quiet moment where it first takes to the air. And then it is going, going, looping up into the sky on a great arcing trajectory, soaring up and over our heads, carrying supplies, off to find the Ventura, gliding in its invisible orbit.

'That's so ... ' But there aren't words, so I watch it soar. I have no idea why a tear slides out of the corner of my eye and down my cheek but it does. Must be the alcohol, making me stupid. I push the tear away quick but I think Kristina notices. She blinks slowly, wistful.

'I really think you'll make it, Beacon,' she says. 'I hope you do, if it's what you want.'

'If it's what I want?'

She shrugs. 'I ended up questioning it in the end; wondering if it was the kind of life I wanted – being told who to partner with, perhaps never experiencing love.'

'It's more important than that though, don't you think?' I hug my knees. 'It's a bigger picture. I get that it's a sacrifice, but I guess it's one worth making for something so important, something you believe in. And it's not like there's a whole lot of choice in love anyway.'

I notice Micah then, over her shoulder, his face pressed against the side of Mali's head. She is smiling and he isn't. I sense him feeling me looking, sense that he's about to look back. I know I won't be able to bear it if he does, so I shift my gaze over to Kazimir, to the way Fin straddles his lap and kisses him. It looks like the wettest kiss on Earth and I wonder if that's her or him. Tara and Jam are still watching the shuttle, or at least he is. She seems to be mostly looking at the side of his face. Mali and Micah sit down close to us.

'Finished the vodka?' asks Mali.

I hand it to her.

'How are we going to get down off here in the dark?' asks Jam, also arriving next to us.

'Oh, Eeyore,' says Mali, 'live a little.'

Tara laughs. 'That's what I was just telling him. These could be his last days on Earth.'

'He already knows that, Tara, he doesn't need you to show him the light,' I say, though I think I only meant to say it in my head. Mali saves me by laughing it off and changing the subject.

It's hours later by the time we stagger and slip down the dune back to the beach. Kazimir and Fin drop back and head down to the water.

The sand feels so cool and soft under my feet that it's hard to resist lying down in it. I look over at Jam and the way he looks back makes me take his hand and lean my face against his shoulder. 'Carry me,' I say.

I feel him press his mouth against the top of my head for a second before he puts his arm around my shoulders and helps me walk. He doesn't let me go until we're next to the tent. I drop on to my knees and climb in; lying in there, face down on my sleeping bag, has never felt so good. I feel Jam climb into the tent and lie next to me.

'You'll have to put up with me now Mali's back,' he says, shifting position, opening out his sleeping bag so that his stuff drops out, a book flapping open to its centre pages so that I lever myself up on to my elbows to pick it up and read off the cover – *Tender is the Night*.

'Bexley finished it?' I ask him.

'Bexley?' He makes a noise. 'He hates reading.'

I frown. 'We were talking about it.'

'I read him some of it a few days ago.' He shrugs. 'The bit where they come home at dawn. It reminded me of your story about your ride home in a lambing truck after that gig in Abertawe. He'd forgotten about it.'

I look from the book to his face.

'It was you that read it?' I say.

He nods.

'And you ...?' But I run out of words, end up just staring at him until he says, 'And I what?' and almost smiles.

Neil Young starts playing on Micah's speaker.

I shift close to him, and he adjusts his position, lifting his arm over until it is behind me, and I lay my head on his chest. I find myself relaxing there, relaxing completely for what feels like the first time in so long, feeling the long slow up and down as he breathes.

'Tell me what you thought of it,' I say, knowing he'll know what I mean.

I feel him tense up for a moment; feel him think about making an excuse not to open up, like he always does. Then he says, 'Um, OK ... Everybody's pretty messed up in it. Everybody's pretty sad and unfaithful and lost. It makes me think that that stuff maybe doesn't get any easier, even when you get older.'

I hold my breath, hoping he'll say more, and then he does.

'I guess it's about love really though, right? Messy, crazy love. Feeling it no matter what. Doing anything for that one person you can't live without.'

I swear it's the first time I've heard him talk like this in so long, maybe ever. I'm desperate not to break the spell, so I'm still practically holding my breath, but then he says, 'I wish you'd told me about Micah.'

'Why?' I recalibrate quickly. 'So you could get mad with me and tell me what a horrible thing I was doing? I already knew that.'

He sighs, and the outrush of air disturbs my hair. 'I never lie to you,' he says.

'I didn't lie to you exactly; it's just that I didn't tell you.'

'It's the same thing,' he says, then after a pause, 'Are there other things you're not telling me?'

'No.'

He watches me steadily until I say it again. 'No. I mean it.'

'I hope not,' he says, and because he is lying on his back, his dark hair is falling away from his face, and I can see it clearly for the first time in ages. Even though he always has a golden tone to his skin, the sun has made it darker, closer in shade to the honey brown of his eyes. He has this cleft in his chin, a kind of split in his lips too, almost like his face didn't quite finish fusing together when he was in the womb. It sounds awful, but it's actually always been quite lovely. Vulnerable. And lately he's grown into it, made it his own. It's so rare for him to smile but he does it now, and says, 'What?' because I've just been staring at him all this time.

Why does everything go so still then? Like time actually stops, or shifts, to give us time to look at each other, to look at each other like we never have before.

I feel his hand slide up my throat, his palm against my pulse, his thumb on my chin, easing the angle of my face up. Then his mouth is against mine, and my own mouth opens in response, almost automatic. Everything is in slow motion. There is a slow, long hiss of air in through both our noses, and yet there is no thinking. There is all this time but there is nothing in my mind except the dizzying, falling out of the sky, spiralling ocean of what-the-hell-is-going-on.

We are kissing. And it is horrible and terrible and beautiful and amazing. Like something I desperately need to stop, but could never stop. And it is messy and wet and hot and burns across my skin, and I am shaking with it, with the adrenaline rush and the heat. And when I finally pull away long enough to look at him, we are in the wreckage of us, like a bomb just exploded in everything we ever knew, and we are staring at each other and I try to speak, but can't. It's not happening. It's a dream I'm about to wake up from.

'Oh my God, Jam.' I push my hands against my eyes so hard I see stars.

'It's OK,' he says. 'We don't ... we shouldn't ... I'm sorry ...'

'Oh man, no.' I sit up, hands still pressed against my face. 'No no no no.'

'I know,' he says, sitting up too. 'I'm sorry, I'm so sorry.'

'I'm not one of your girls, Jam. You know that, right?'

'Of course I do.'

'We can't ... We can never ... Why did that just happen?'

'My fault,' he says. 'Totally my fault.'

I let my hands drop into my lap, open my eyes. As soon

as I look at him, he looks away, down at my legs and his, where they are still tangled together.

'You're too … important to me,' I say, fighting for breath. 'You're the most important person in my life. I've never loved anyone the way I love you. What … why would you do this?'

'Bea, please … ' He looks almost like he's going to cry. He reaches for my hand but I pull it away.

'No!' I shriek.

I dive for the door, pull at the zip so many times that in the end he has to help me with it, leaning over me in such a way that I yell at him again.

'Where are you going?' he says as soon as I am standing.

'I don't know,' I say, tight-throated, plunging off into the darkness between us and the beach. I know I'm going to throw up; I can feel it. I don't quite make it on to the open sand before it happens, spectacularly; so much liquid it's hard to believe it was all inside me, pulsing out of me again and again in waves. I'm on my hands and knees by the time I feel his hand on my back.

'I'm OK,' I say. 'Just leave me alone.'

'You're not OK.'

I fall into the sand next to the puddle on my side and cough out the remaining waves. They have the deep iron taste I have learned to dread.

'How long has it been happening, Bea?' I hear him say, and when I open my eyes he is wiping my mouth with his the hem of his T-shirt, studying dark streaks of blood in the moonlight. 'How long has it been happening?!' And he is shouting now.

'I don't know.' I shake my head, cough out some more. 'A few times since we left.'

He wipes my mouth again. 'Why didn't you tell me?'

Somehow it seems easier to let my eyes drop closed than to think of anything else to say. And then it gets dark; gets really, really quiet. Gets so that it's like I'm not even there at all.

Nadir

I wake up and blink at the ceiling for a few seconds before I remember. The first thing I do is try to get up and out of bed, but when I push the green sheet off I get tangled in a transparent tube and realise I'm hooked up to a drip stand. I notice Jam then, in the chair next to the bed, asleep with his chin on his hand, legs splayed, white T-shirt streaked in dark stains of dried blood.

I watch him for a moment. Despite everything, the fact that he kissed me is what I think about first. He kissed me and maybe I kind of kissed him back. It seems like a dream now.

Outside the window behind him there is early morning light. The world hasn't ended, though it feels like maybe it should have.

'Jam.' My voice breaks the silence so suddenly it scares me. His chin falls off his hand and he opens his eyes, only a little at first, sitting up in the chair, leaning forward over his legs.

'You're OK,' he says, voice rough, but I don't know if he's asking or telling.

'What happened?'

'They said an ulcer in your stomach ruptured. They were talking about maybe having to give you some blood.' He swallows. 'You lost quite a bit.'

There are streaks of blood on his arms. Green curtains are pulled across on three sides of us.

'Where are we?' I ask him.

He looks around at the green curtains. 'The hospital in Seville. You were transferred from the medical centre at the base in case you needed surgery.'

I feel the panic choke me. 'I don't want to have surgery again. If they cut any more out of me there'll be nothing left.'

'It's OK,' he says, shunting forward. 'The bleeding stopped. You were . . . bringing up so much and then you were just unconscious and I was . . . God, I was so scared.'

His breath shudders in, then out, as he looks at the floor.

'They want to keep you here for observation,' he adds.

He touches my arm then, so I twist over on to my side away from him, pulling the sheet over my head, wrapping my arms around the scars on my carved-up stomach, listening to the beeping and hissing of the hospital sounds that I have learned to fear so deeply.

'You idiot.' I flap the blanket down off my face and

glare at him. 'Why did you have to freak out and get me landed in hospital?'

His eyes widen. 'Bea, for all I knew, you were about to die on me – what did you expect me to do?'

I stare at the ceiling tiles and think about that.

I frown. 'How did you even get me to the medical centre?'

'I carried you mostly. That Russian guy, Kazimir, helped me. He ran all the way, soaking wet, in his pants. I think he and Fin were skinny-dipping when they saw us.'

'Oh man.' I feel a laugh almost sneak out of me. 'Fin's going to kill me,' I say.

'I know, right?' says Jam, smiling a little too, but then it fades.

'What time is it?' I ask him.

He checks his watch. 'Almost seven-thirty.'

I widen my eyes. 'We're going to be late!'

He's so surprised he just watches me for a moment before he says, 'We can't go, Bea.'

'What?' I laugh. 'Of course we're going.'

He shakes his head. 'You're too sick. You need to stay here and get better. And I'm staying with you.'

'No way. That's not happening. I've missed out on enough in my life because of this crap. I am not missing this. *You* are not missing this.'

'Bea, it doesn't matter. None of it matters until you're well enough.'

'You don't understand.' I sit up, straining my pummelled stomach muscles so badly that I yelp and my eyes water and he goes to help me before I wave him away. 'They told me that this – that being in space – would reset my immune system. It could cure me.'

'What?' he says, frowning deeply. 'How are you only just telling me this?'

'I don't know,' I bark at him, then soften, shaking my head at myself. 'I don't know if I even believed it was true really.'

He leans back in his seat. 'But now you do?'

'I don't even know, but taking the chance suddenly seems more important. I'm getting worse, Jam, and if it carries on like this ...'

He looks at me steadily. 'Yeah, I get that,' he says, pushing a blood-streaked hand through his hair. 'I definitely get that.' But now he is watching me pull the plastic tube out of my arm, his face this frozen mask of horror.

'Bea, no,' he groans.

'Jam, seriously, we're getting out of here. Where are my clothes?'

I can tell he thinks about trying to argue with me again for a split second before he realises it's impossible and gives up the fight. Instead, he looks around, picks up a bag off the floor and hands it to me. My T-shirt is crusted hard with blood, but it only looks as bad as it

265

does because it's white. That's what I tell myself anyway as I pull it on. I struggle with the tie on the hospital pyjama bottoms. It's double-knotted so tight that no amount of picking at it with my fingers seems to make any difference.

'I may have to just style these out,' I end up saying, laughing. 'Let's go.'

We slowly pull back the curtain. The ward is empty except for an old lady slumped and asleep in the bed opposite, so we head across the shining tiled floor to the big swing doors at the end and find the lifts. I stab my finger at the call button and we stand waiting while a phone rings somewhere out of sight.

Other people begin to gather to wait for the lift and a woman in a white coat glances at me then looks away, then looks back again, slowly tracking up my body, taking in the hospital pyjama bottoms and crusty Ventura T-shirt and bruised arms and unbrushed hair. God, if anyone tries to stop me right now I'll scream. I've never had a fight in my life, but I feel like it could happen now if anyone tries to keep me here; the adrenaline of it is running through my limbs so hard I'm trembling. Jam must sense it because his hand finds mine and squeezes it, and I feel myself calming again, as I always do, as I always have done at his touch, and as the lift doors open and we step inside, we exchange a look before fixating on the floor.

On what we think is the ground floor we side-step our way out of the lift and walk-run across the forecourt of the reception area to the automatic doors that kick us out into the belting Spanish sun.

'Freedom!' I say, letting my head drop back so that I can feel the heat on my throat. By the time I straighten up again and squint at Jam, he is watching me.

He runs around the car park showing people the logo on his T-shirt, in the hope that they might tell us which of the line of waiting buses we should get on. I stand in the heat peering up at the huge rectangular hospital with its green-mirrored windows. It seems like it can't possibly take long for them to send someone after me, or call security on the two blood-stained kids terrorising people in the car park.

'Bea!' Jam calls me, and when I look he is pointing at a bus that is about to pull out, waiting for me at the door.

I climb into its air-conditioned interior and try to ignore the way the four passengers near the front watch me in horror as I pass. I sit near the back and Jam sits next to me.

'Goes to Santo Domingo,' he says. 'Nearest village to the base. I'm pretty sure I heard someone say the base does supply runs to there, so we should be able to get a lift back.'

I watch out the window as we lurch out of the car park

and leave the hospital behind, leaning back against the seat, the sweat drying on my neck.

'Bea,' says Jam. 'About last night ... I wouldn't want you to think—'

I don't wait for him to finish before I say, 'I don't think anything,' and I fake a breezy smile that, judging from the way he looks back at me, I totally fail to pull off. Then I go back to looking out of the window, so I can be left alone to think the things I said I wasn't thinking, mostly that the entire geography of my life suddenly seems upside down and inside out and I can't imagine anything ever being the same again.

I don't even register that I've fallen asleep until the bus brakes are hissing and my head is sliding forward off Jam's shoulder. The driver is shouting something down the almost empty bus.

'We're here.' I pull on Jam's arm. He is rubbing his face, sweaty haired and still mostly asleep. I climb out of the bus on shaking legs, pulling him after me, and feel immediately buried under the weight of the heat.

'This is the main plaza,' says Jam. 'The base vehicles are bound to pass through here at some point. Let's eat something.'

I make a face. 'No time. We're already nearly two hours late.'

'You're eating something,' he says firmly, so I follow him. He's still holding the bag with my jean shorts in; I take it from him and fish out my dog tag. For some reason when I lift it on over my head I lose my balance for a moment and he takes my arm, steadies me.

We sit outside the only place that's not derelict, which looks like one of the little agri-workers' cafeterias we have at home and Jam studies the whiteboard menu on the wall.

'What can you eat? I can't remember what the doctors used to say to you when you were bad. Soft things, right? Nothing hard to digest?'

I look up at the domed roof of the church opposite. Right at the top there is this huge messy stork's nest.

'Just order anything,' I say, flapping my hand. 'I'm sure it'll be OK.'

He raises his eyebrows at that but then points to something on the whiteboard, which the waiter writes down before leaving. I look back up at the bird's nest just at the moment that the huge stork makes a crash landing into it.

'They get everywhere.' I smile and Jam looks up at it for a moment.

'How long have you been ill for, Bea?' he says, still watching the bird.

'I told you – not long.'

'So, did Bexley know?'

'I guess he . . . he saw me puking once or twice.'

He sighs, shakes his head.

'What?' I ask, just as two milky coffees in glasses arrive.

'I'm just finding it pretty difficult not to be mad at him right now. He used the fact that you're in love with him to get with you while Mali was away, because he knew he could get away with it.'

'Jam!' I feel my mouth drop open. 'That is not how it was. He didn't even know that I was in love with him so how could he have used that?'

His gaze goes middle-distance.

Something clicks. 'Or did he?' I say.

There's an infuriating delay before he says, 'I told him. Months ago. Because he was flirting with you all the time and he thought it was harmless. You were never going to be able to move on or even be … open to someone else while he was giving you just enough to keep you thinking about him all the time. I thought, stupidly, that he was actually going to back off. I didn't realise he'd use it to his advantage like this. I guess I misjudged the kind of person he is.'

The waiter arrives with pieces of toasted baguette on two plates, a little bowl of something that looks like pulverised flesh and a bottle of oil in a tall green bottle. Once he's gone, we both just stare at the food between us.

'He's not like that.' I shake my head. 'You've got it wrong.'

'Really?' He raises an eyebrow.

I pick at the corner of my toast, considering. 'To be honest, now that I think about it … I'm not sure I like either of us, him or me, as much as I did before.'

'What do you mean?' He frowns, leaning forward like I'm a puzzle he's trying to crack.

I shrug. 'Now that I know he'd cheat on Mali, I guess he's not who I thought he was. Now that I know I'd betray my best friend, I guess I'm not either.'

He sighs. 'Bea, seriously,' he says, shaking his head. 'Why did you do it?'

I carry on picking at the corner of my bread, searching my head for the true answer to that. 'I feel . . . I've always felt like he's one of the only people who really sees me.'

He squints off into the distance again and says, 'I see you.'

And I say, 'I know you do. But you don't count.'

'Why don't I count?'

I can't answer that. I just sit forward, slide my plate closer, and say, 'What are we meant to do with this food?'

I answer my own question by looking around and catching sight of the guy at the next table drizzling oil all down his bread and then spooning out the red contents of the little bowl on top.

'Where do you think this vehicle will be?' I say, pouring my oil.

Jam sighs and takes the oil I pass him. 'Let's face facts – we will have been cut by now.'

'You don't know that.' I press the fear of that possibility back into my chest, where it had threatened to leap out.

His face is inscrutable behind his hair, but I watch

him spoon out the red stuff on to his bread in silence. I suddenly realise how heavy my limbs have gotten.

He watches me stare into space for too long and slides my plate at me. 'Eat,' he says.

I pick up one of the pieces of bread and take a bite. It's mashed tomato, the red stuff; almost like a tomato jam but not sweet. It's actually pretty good. At that same moment I see two people in grey La Verdad uniforms, carrying a huge net bag of oranges each, walk into the plaza.

'Look!' I say to Jam, pointing. 'It's them!'

'Go!' he says. 'I'll pay.'

And I run for them.

We drive in past the campsite, and I notice how much emptier it is. There's rubbish in piles, blackened rings from campfires, even some abandoned tents. They drop us off along the main trunk road on the base and point the way to the training centre.

Which is when we hear footsteps, pattering on the tarmac behind us. We turn just before they get to us, before they start passing through and over us like water. The rest of the recruits – running.

Even though it seems like the hardest thing I've ever had to do, I make myself start to run with them, but I'm slow, my limbs leaden. Most of the rest of the pack pass me, but Jam stays running beside me.

We get close to the training centre and there are two

Ventura lieutenants with stopwatches and handhelds sitting on chairs under a shaded canopy, watching as the recruits run over the line. I slide my eyes to them as I pass and, sure enough, one of them presses the klaxon on their megaphone and points at me and Jam. We wait for a gap in the runners and cross to him as he looks us up and down.

'I've watched this group run nineteen laps,' he says, after a long silence. 'This is the first time I've seen you.'

'We just got here,' I say. 'We were . . . held up.'

He watches us, motionless as a statue, before he says, 'You got "held up"?'

Jam says, 'She was taken to hospital last night. They thought they might have to operate. She nearly had a blood transfusion.'

He watches Jam for a few seconds, then looks back at me.

'And yet here you are,' he says.

'I was discharged this morning,' I say. 'Well, I left. I knew I needed to get back here.'

'Which hospital were you in? Sevilla?'

We nod.

'And you left, and drove back here?'

'We got the bus,' says Jam. 'Then found the supply van in Santo Domingo.'

'And you think you can just join in?' he asks. 'On lap twenty? Does that seem fair?'

I look at the last of the runners, who are just appearing

out of the heat shimmers on the road, stumbling along, barely on their feet, wet with sweat. And I know that, of course, it's not fair.

'With respect,' says Jam, 'we spent the night at the hospital, wondering if Bea was even going to make it and, against all advice, took ridiculous risks to get back here. She's in no condition to be doing this anyway. Cut me if you like, but don't cut Bea. If it's bravery and strength you're looking for, you'd be crazy to cut her.'

Another silence while he stares at Jam, who bites his lip as he pulls his dog tag up and over his head. I can do nothing but stare in horror but, just as he's about to hand it over, the lieutenant waves his hand and says, 'Carry on, recruits. Let's see what you've got.'

And we are running before I can even digest what just happened.

It's not long before I'm soaked in sweat and panting. I am leaning sideways to spit out the gluey gunk in my mouth when Jam circles back for me.

'This is full-on nuts, Bea,' he says.

I can't speak but I force myself upright just as we are lapped by a few huge superhumans, one of whom slows and runs backwards for a few seconds before saying, 'How are you here?'

Even though my lips are starting to go numb and I can't particularly focus my eyes, I look up at Kazimir as he falls into step next to us.

'She refused to stay in the hospital,' says Jam.

'That doesn't seem sensible,' says Kazimir in an even voice, a slight flush along his cheekbones, but not even the faintest sheen of sweat.

How is he making this look so easy? God, it's infuriating. Is he even human?

'Nobody asked your opinion,' I manage to puff out, but I'm so out of breath he doesn't catch it.

'Keep it up. I'll see you round there,' is all he says, loping off like a gazelle.

I've been getting slower and slower and I notice now that Jam is taking these tiny steps to stay with me. I've got pins and needles in my hands and spreading down my arms; I can feel the sweat dripping down my legs. I notice a drop of sweat break free from the front of my hair and fall straight to the road beneath with an audible sound. Something in me is just about to crack when we get out past the concrete wall and suddenly we are next to the ocean, a wind that is slightly cooler than the broiling heat breathing over me. I look out at the horizon, focus on it, and somehow my feet keep following each other. I am still moving. Slowing all the time. But still moving.

And then I feel it. The knotting in my stomach, the inevitability. I grab Jam's hand to steady myself just before I bring up the hot contents of my stomach, coughing the last of it into a star-shaped red splash on the sandy ground.

'Oh man,' says Jam, and his face is pinched in fear when I look up at him. 'This is crazy. We need to get you back to hospital.'

I shake my head. 'I'm not giving up.'

'Bea, please . . . '

'Half the reason I'm still in this world at all is because I won't give up. I don't. I never will.' And I go to start running again, but he holds my shoulder and makes me turn back to him.

'I keep thinking about what your mum said,' he says, and his voice cracks. 'About me holding you in my arms. About me coming back without you.'

I look at him. 'That's crazy,' I say.

'I know,' he says. 'But sometimes your mum's been weirdly right about these things. Remember how she said something bad was going to happen the night they came for my dad?'

'What?' I bend and spit into the dirt. 'No, she didn't.'

'She did. We were just sitting there watching TV and she showed me her hands and she was shaking and I asked her why and she said she wasn't sure but she just felt like something bad was going to happen. And that was the night they kicked the doors in.'

We look at each other then, read years of history in each other's eyes. Even though we never talk about it, I know that the fear we felt that night is something we both carry around with us every day, just under the skin.

'It's like she . . . ' He swallows. 'Maybe she has a sixth sense.'

'She's the last person who would have a sixth sense,' I say, and I am staring down at the puddle of sick. And then I laugh. 'It's not blood. Not this time. It's the tomato.' I grab Jam's arm and pull him on.

We trudge along next to the sea, along the perimeter of the facility, past houses on square plots of lawn that look fake and out of place, which must be where the scientists live. We are pacing back along the length of the Array when there is this weird clunking sound, followed by a loud, low hum that fills the air and travels through the ground and into my body.

'What the hell is that?' Jam says and turns a circle as he runs. 'It's changing position,' he says, nodding towards the Array.

I can hardly lift my head but I look up at it, at the barely perceptible movement of the vast satellite dishes against the blinding blue sky. We see two recruits then, laid out on the sloped ground next to the fence, side by side.

'Hey!' they yell, waving something at us.

Jam jogs close to them and they put something into his outstretched hand with a clink – two dog tags. I keep running because I know if I stop I'll never start again.

'Don't do that,' says Jam to the two guys. 'You can do it. You can keep going.'

'No way,' says one of them in this feeble voice. 'Seriously, can you ask them to send that buggy thing for us? I don't want to die out here.'

We're on the last stretch up to the training centre again, running along next to the vast, circular facility reservoirs when we hear the rending, roaring sound of a supply shuttle coming in to land out on the vast strip beyond the spaceport. The thunderous sound somehow spurs me on; a strange kind of fuel for my utterly spent spirit.

By the time we are back at the lap line, I am breathing so hard it is rattling my voice box. Jam hands the dog tags to the lieutenant and says, 'They asked if you could send the buggy.'

The lieutenant just nods and says, 'Give me your numbers.'

We exchange a look before we show him our tags.

'Well, B-37-16 and B-37-37, you certainly are lucky if nothing else. We just made our last two cuts for today,' he says, letting the dog tag chains unspool between his fingers. 'We'll see you tomorrow at oh-nine-hundred hours. Go celebrate.'

Radiant

This might be the greatest shower of my life. I hang my head in the warmish flow, feeling it turn colder. It feels so good to wash it all away – sweat, dirt, blood, vomit; the half rotten stench of the hospital.

Walking back to camp I realise that, weirdly, all I want to do is be with Jam. Despite the whole mess of last night, it feels like he is the only person in the world who could possibly understand the insane mixture of feelings I have right now. I get a flash of his face last night then, the smile on it just before he kissed me, like he was suddenly a beautiful stranger, and yet also the person who knows me most in the world, all at the same time. I start planning the excuses we'll make to get away from the others as I'm walking back over the squashed dune grass and eddying sand of the campsite.

As I get closer to our camp, I hear unfamiliar voices. Or not quite unfamiliar. And then I'm rounding the corner of the tent and I'm standing there looking at someone sitting on my camp chair, shoved up right next to Jam's.

'Carmen,' I say.

She looks at me. 'Hi, Bea,' she says. 'Surprise!'

'What are you doing here?' I ask, shifting my eyes to Jam for a moment, clocking the way he watches the side of her face with a smile as she talks.

'I came to pick up my sister,' she says. 'She got cut yesterday. So I thought I'd come and say hi before I leave in the morning.' She looks back at Jam, picks up his hand and moves it into her lap, while they smile at each other.

'That's great . . . ' I say, blinking in surprise at the anger I am barely repressing, pulling my strapless top up where it is slipping down. I look at Jam again, trying to catch his eye, but he doesn't look my way. Then I look across at Mali, who is sitting in her camp chair with her legs in Micah's lap.

'Who do I have to kill to get a drink around here?' I ask.

Mali raises her eyebrows and jumps out of her seat. 'Nobody, recruit!' she says, saluting. 'You're through to the final day! We're celebrating.' And she starts rummaging in the storage boxes.

'I wouldn't celebrate yet,' I say, sighing as I wring out the two still completely blood-stained Ventura T-shirts (mine and Jam's) that I have just washed out in the shower and hang them over the apex of the tent roof. 'You should see the people we're up against now. Basically superhuman androids – the kids who grew up here or on haulers.'

'Are the Russians still in?' asks Micah.

'Of course they are,' I say, as Mali hands me my drink. 'Kazimir ran twenty-nine laps today, in the same time that everyone else ran twenty.'

'And we ran one,' says Jam.

'Well, I'm amazed you even managed that,' says Mali. 'I can't walk to the beach without collapsing. And I didn't spend the night at the hospital.'

'What happens tomorrow?' asks Micah.

'We get cut?' I shrug, and take a sip of some ridiculously sweet wine. 'I think us normal human beings have had our chance.'

'I wouldn't describe you as a normal human being,' says Micah.

'Oh great,' I laugh, staring into my drink. 'Thanks, Bexley.'

There's this beat then, way too awkward, that's only broken when Jam checks his watch and says, 'I was going to take Carmen up to the dune, to see the launch, if you wanted to come?'

'You guys go,' says Mali, shooting me a wink. 'You've seen one rocket launch, you've seen them all.'

'Um, OK,' says Jam, standing up and stretching, arms over his head so that his too-small T-shirt rides up and I end up looking at his tanned stomach.

Carmen holds out her hand for him to help her up and when he does she says, 'Thank you, Joram.'

'Joram?' I snort. 'Nobody ever calls him that.'

'I do,' says Carmen, stepping close to him. 'I think it's beautiful.'

And I watch them walk off into the pinkish light.

'I'm going to take a shower,' Micah says, kissing Mali and glancing at me briefly as he passes.

Mali slings her arm around my neck and pulls me close, making something inside me twinge, probably whichever organ it is that processes guilt packing up from overuse. 'Now we've got rid of the boys, let's get a good spot for sunset,' she says, grinning. 'I haven't had a date with my best girl in way too long.'

We sit on the top of the nearest dune. From there we can see the broad stretch of flat ocean, the endless sand from one end of the world to the other. Down on the beach about a hundred metres up, the Russians are sitting at the water's edge. We watch Kazimir stand up and yell something at the sky before dancing around and swigging from a bottle of wine while the others laugh at him.

'Twenty nine laps in forty-two degrees?' muses Mali, watching him. 'With that kind of stamina . . . '

'God, Mals, gross.'

'Really?' She raises an eyebrow at me. 'You don't think he's hot?'

'Maybe if you're into vampires.'

'Well, OK, I just thought you might be making the most of it a little, like Jam is. Considering your choices are probably about to become a lot more limited.'

I shrug.

'That idea doesn't bother me. Falling in love's too … complicated for me. Too unpredictable. Too inconvenient.'

I know she's looking at me, but I can't bring myself to look back.

'Oh my God,' she says, eventually, like she has just worked something out. I swallow fear. 'Spill! You met someone, didn't you?'

'No,' I say, glad that it's the one thing I can be honest about.

'Then what? I can see it in your eyes. Something's happened.'

'I've just been thinking about it all a lot lately. Of course I have, what with the way things would be on the Ventura, if I made it. And the more I think about it, the more I think I would be glad the decision wouldn't be mine. That I'd be partnered with someone and that would be it,' I sigh. 'I can't be trusted with that decision. I'm not sure that anybody can. It's one of the most important decisions of our lives and we make it based on what? Instinct?' I shake my head. 'It's stupid. There're too many opportunities to fall in love with the wrong person, or have the wrong person fall in love with you. And then you just end up in a mess. Like my mum.'

'Oh,' she says, leaning back and nodding like this explains it. 'Oh OK, I get it. Your mum. Look, Bea—'

But I'm saved from hearing whatever she was about to

say by the loud rumble of the thrusters starting up out at the launchpad.

When it quietens again, Mali changes tack and says, 'Tell me what it's been like – life on the road with our boys. Have you managed to keep them in line?'

I laugh. 'Yeah, it's been . . . it's been good.' And suddenly it seems like there are all these things, huge things, that have happened – with Micah, with Jam – and I can't share any of them with her, even though she's my best friend. Then for a moment I can hear it in my head. I can actually hear myself saying: *Mali, I'm so sorry, I have done the most stupid, stupid thing and ruined everything we had, everything that was so, so important to me.* But I don't, because I can't, because it's all my fault, and it would hurt her, and how can I do that to her? So I just hang my head and watch my hands pushing into the sand.

And she says, 'I can't get over Jam. Suddenly he's this, like, ladykiller.'

'You have no idea,' I say, and out of nowhere I find I'm thinking about the sweet, soft strength of his kiss. I shake it off.

'I mean, it's not that much of a surprise to me,' Mali continues. 'I've always thought he was hot. Even when he was just Ryan Rees's weird kid and everybody was kind of scared of him.' She laughs. 'And then suddenly he was living in your house and you were horrified. Doesn't that seem strange now?'

284

I smile. I can't even remember that life.

'Anyway, I could always see his potential. Remember how much I fancied him when we were thirteen?'

I laugh.

'Then Micah came along and changed everything.'

I look out at the reddening sun, while we both take a drink.

'Can I . . .' she starts, 'can I ask you something?'

I sense the shift and turn to her. She is frowning, her lightly freckled brow creased.

'Sure,' I say.

'Did Micah . . . ' She shakes her head.

'Did Micah what?' I swallow.

'Did he . . . ' She laughs. 'I mean, this is stupid, but did he . . . cheat on me with another girl?'

'What?' I basically shriek. 'Of course not!' I laugh, terrified it sounds as super-fake as it feels.

She nods, looks out to sea, then back at me. 'Would you tell me, though?' she says. 'Even if there was no way I would ever find out, and you thought it was better that way . . . '

'Of course I would,' I say and, I know this is dark, but I justify it to myself by thinking about the fact that if he had done that, with anyone but me, I would have told her. No doubt.

'I know you would,' she says, making me feel a million times worse. 'It's just . . . he's been a little weird with me since I got here.'

'No, he hasn't,' I say, as the rumble from the thrusters intensifies.

She nods. 'He has. I missed him *so much* when I was in Canada. And when I told him that, I thought he would say the same, but he didn't. He just looked ... I don't know, I can't explain.'

She looks so sad right then and all I want to do is hug her, but I know I can't, not without the guilt that's sitting under my skin passing into her like an illness, not without the anger I feel at myself and Micah smouldering through my skin like embers. So instead I watch the glow from the shuttle light up her face and the beginnings of tears in her eyes before turning round to watch it arc into the atmosphere, leaving a trail of fire and smoke.

The Russians are howling at the shuttle like a pack of wolves.

I bite my lip. I should tell her. She deserves to know. But I might be gone soon and she'll still be here. With Micah. And she'll have lost him, all for nothing. So I take a deep breath, force a smile and turn back to her. 'There's nothing to tell, Mali, really. He's been fine. It's probably just ... the heat.' I shrug.

'The heat?' She couldn't look more unconvinced.

I cringe, hearing too late how ridiculous that sounds, but luckily just then there are squeaking footsteps in the sand behind us.

'Water's nice,' says Micah. 'I recommend it, Mals.'

She turns as he arrives and snakes her arm behind his leg. 'Are you telling me I stink?'

'Of course not,' he says. 'Just . . . '

She's already on her feet. 'I'm kidding. I'm going over there now.' And she pulls him into a kiss before plunging off down the dune towards camp.

Micah watches her go. I push my cup into the sand, screwing it in deeper. He sits next to me, gazing out to sea.

'How are you?' he says.

I genuinely have no idea how to answer that so instead I say, 'Mali's suspicious. She asked me if you'd cheated on her.'

'Jesus,' he says, scooping a handful of sand and letting it fall between his fingers.

'You have to get over it,' I say. 'I know the guilt is . . . bad, but you don't have the option of falling apart.'

He shakes his head. 'It's not just the guilt.' He lies back in the sand, staring at the sky. 'It's you,' he says.

'Me?' Panic shoots through me like a cold spear.

'After I picked her up and we were driving back, I realised that while she was talking, I wasn't even listening.' He puts his hands in his damp hair and pushes it off his face. 'I wasn't listening because I was thinking about you.' He levers himself up on his elbows, flips on to his front and looks at me. 'I can't stop thinking about you, Karlo.'

I narrow my eyes at him. 'Don't do that.'

He brushes at the sand just in front of him with his fingers. 'I keep telling myself to stop thinking about you, but it doesn't work,' he says. 'That night, and just ... everything. I wish I could forget about it, but every time I'm near you ... It's impossible.'

'No, it's not.' I almost shout it, standing up, walking down the dune towards the sea, feeling him following me, pressing my forehead because of the thoughts that are overcrowding my brain. He gets level with me and I turn to him. 'It's not impossible at all,' I say. 'I've loved you in secret for the last three years. I've lived with it so long, it's a part of who I am. I've grown crooked because of it. For you, it's new, it's only just happened, and already you can't bear it? I've got so much happening right now that this is the first time in for ever that you aren't all I'm thinking about. Can't you just let me be free of it for a little while? I'm so close to getting away without ever hurting her – you're not taking that away from me. I won't let you. So deal with it, Bexley. Just make it work.'

So weird but when I look at him in that moment it's like it's already the future and I'm looking back on this – him and Mali and me and the mess it nearly was already a part of my past.

I go to the water's edge and there are about a million little white shells there, right under my bare toes. Maybe I'm the only person who finds shells morbid; I can't help seeing them as bones. Looking at them now almost makes me cry.

'Why did say you were reading that book?' I turn back to look at him, at the parts of his hair at the front that have gone blond in the sun. 'You weren't. It's Jam who's been reading it.'

He smiles, starts to laugh. 'What does it matter?'

'Sometimes I just wonder if you say whatever will get you the most out of any given situation.'

He shifts his eyes to the side. 'Doesn't everyone do that?'

I look out over the water. 'Like, with me ... you knew how I felt about you, and maybe you were just curious about being with someone else ... and Mali wasn't here ...' I shrug.

'Karlo, it wasn't like that,' he says, and he takes hold of my arm, his fingers circling my wrist.

I look up at him. 'Mali adores every little thing about you. She talks about you almost non-stop. It drives me nuts sometimes how completely into you she is.' I'm still shaking my head. 'How could you do this to her?'

His mouth falls open in what looks like genuine shock.

'I know I did it too,' I tell him then, a wave washing in over my feet, 'but at least I did it because I was in love with you. Or at least ... I thought I was.'

And I guess it's only because I can't bear it any more that I run out into the water – ankle deep, knee deep, thigh deep, fully clothed into the sizzling waves. Then I dive out, hitting the surface and going under, skimming along just over the sandy bed and moving through currents that are warm and cold until I get to the surface again, five metres further out, rubbing the water off my face. I only realise then that Micah is front crawling out to me and just when he gets close I duck under again, start to swim away. I feel his hand graze my leg twice before he catches hold of me and pulls me back. I get to my feet and push his hand off where he has hold of my arm.

'We can hate ourselves for ever,' he says over the hiss of the surging water. 'Or we can just accept that it happened. Accept that you and I were ... an inevitable fact. There's probably one of your physics equations somewhere that explains the whole thing away. But you need to know that you're not easy to forget, Karlo. And also that now I know how it feels to lie to Mali, to risk losing her ... I'm never doing it again.' He rubs seawater off his face, before adding, 'I mean it.'

'Do you promise?' The current nearly unbalances me, but he takes my arm to steady me.

'I promise,' he says.

A wave gets me then, and by the time he pulls me back to my feet, I notice that there are three people standing on the beach watching us, one raising a tentative hand. My stomach sinks. Kazimir, Fin and Tara watch us struggle back to shore, both fully clothed and soaked.

'Hey,' I say into the awkward silence, wringing out my hair.

Kazimir just laughs.

Fin whistles through her teeth before saying, 'That looked intense. Should we ask what you were doing or ... not?'

'Swimming,' I say, fake breezy and like she just asked the world's dumbest question.

'Where's Jam?' asks Tara. 'Fin got cut today and we're leaving tomorrow so I wanted to say goodbye.'

'He went to watch the shuttle launch,' says Micah, and I turn to give him a look, watching it dawn on his face what he's said as seawater still drips off his nose and chin. 'I mean he ...'

But it's too late. She turns to go. 'I'll head up there and meet him on the way down.'

'No, don't,' I say. 'Come and have a drink with us. Jam'll be back at some point.'

She looks back round at us. 'I don't know ...'

'We have a lot of wine,' says Micah.

She smiles. 'Well, why didn't you say so?'

We're just pouring the wine out into plastic cups when someone steps carefully through the edge of the camp and then does this comedy double take at Micah.

'Micah?' he says, and we realise it's Ernesto, the guitar-playing Spanish guy. I had no idea he'd made it this far.

'Hey, man!' yells Micah, jumping up and shaking his hand. 'It's good to see you! Join us.'

Micah is almost mesmerising in his ability to switch modes back to acting as if everything is normal. It should be annoying, but something about it soothes me, like maybe we really can leave all this behind, putting it all in the rear-view mirror like a ghost town we never need to visit again.

Ernesto is already tuning the guitar when Mali gets back, clean and wet-haired. She spends a few minutes talking to the others before she goes over to Micah and kisses him.

'Your shorts are soaking wet.'

'Yeah,' he says, with a nervous laugh. 'I fancied a swim.'

She frowns. 'After you'd just had a shower?'

It seems like the volume turns down on everyone else and I can only hear them. Micah only answers her with a shrug and pours her a drink. This is probably the whole reason that she side-steps over to me straight after she hangs her towel up, still frowning. She looks at me once, then double takes.

'You're wet too,' she says, almost laughing. 'What happened?'

Kazimir overhears.

'They were out in the sea swimming in their clothes,' he says. 'Very strange.'

'I went out in the waves and kept wiping out,' I say, lying so quickly and easily it scares me, but then feeling the untruth burning under my skin as everybody watches me. 'Micah had to come out to help me.' Then I pick up my cup and tip it empty against my lips.

Jam gets back just then, appearing at the edge of the circle of awkwardness to create a whole new awkward of his own. I clock how coated in sand they both are, how sweetly flushed and happy Carmen's face is, how fiercely Tara is scowling at Jam, how Mali is just frowning down at her cup.

'Where's Oksana?' I ask Kazimir, more for something safe to say than anything.

'She's tired,' he says. 'After the running.'

'You're not?'

He slaps his chest. 'No problem for me.'

I laugh. 'You're not normal. We are so gone tomorrow.'

'You're wrong,' says Kazimir, shaking his head. 'I hear them talking about you. They expected us to be good. That's why they asked Concordia to send us. But you, you've surprised them.'

Against the background of Ernesto playing along to Simon and Garfunkel, I look across at Jam just as Carmen says something to him and he looks at her and kisses her. I watch it happening; watch it for way too long. I try to remember the way he tasted; realise he didn't taste of anything, almost like he was a taste I already knew, have always known.

'I saw them checking your file, heard them talking about you.' I realise Kazimir is still talking.

'That's great,' I say, but I'm not really listening, and I get to my feet so suddenly that it feels like everyone looks up at me. 'I'm sorry,' I say. 'I'm going to have to go to bed. I'm really tired.'

'Are you OK?' says Jam, half-standing too, concern in his eyes.

'I'm fine,' I tell him, holding his gaze. 'I didn't sleep last night so ...'

I dive into my tent and pull the zip closed, before anyone can question me any more. I lie there for a few minutes, deep breathing in an effort to stop my heart pounding. It's only after a while that I struggle out of my wet clothes, the salt already crystallising on the seams, and struggle into my sleeping bag in my underwear. I hear everyone talking so loudly that it seems like there is no possible way I could actually sleep, but it happens without me realising it, eventually.

I've no idea how much later it is, when I feel Jam crawl in next to me and shift around. I feel him lean up on his elbow and lean across a little to peer at my face.

'Bea?' he says, quietly, but I don't answer. 'I know you're awake,' he adds.

'Because you woke me up,' I say. 'Shouldn't you be with Carmen?'

He ignores me and says, 'You and Bexley need to do better at burying it.' Then rolls over on his side, his back to me.

'I know,' I whisper into the dark. 'I will. We both will. It's in the past now, believe me.'

I hear Jam sigh. 'God, I hope that's true. You've wasted so much time on something that never even ...' He sits up, looks down at me. 'I mean, you can't actually think it's a coincidence that you fell in love with the one person you know who is completely unavailable?'

I blink in surprise and sit up too.

We are so close that when he speaks I feel his breath on the skin of my shoulder. 'You must realise you only ever loved him because he was the one person who couldn't love you back. You don't want anyone to love you. You can't bear it. Strangers are OK. Strangers you can forget about. Strangers don't get anywhere near your heart, which is just how you like it. But when it comes to letting yourself love someone, you'll only do it if you're sure that they will never be able to love you back. They'll never be able to make it real.'

I look at him in the dark and my throat seizes. He might as well have grabbed a knife and carved a hole through every barrier I ever put in place to protect my heart. I know immediately he's right.

'Can you blame me?' is what I manage to say eventually. 'Both my parents have spouses or boyfriends or other children they prefer to me and spend all their time on. That's the first relationship you have. That's how you learn about love. I've learned I'm number five or six, at best, on anybody's list.'

Then he looks straight at me. 'You're number one on mine.'

That stops anything else I might have said; stops it all. All I see is the heat in his eyes; the rest of the world is dust.

'I . . .' I try to make words but nothing comes.

'Let me guess . . .' he says. 'I don't count.'

'I . . .' Still nothing, and all the time Jam is watching me, waiting, his expression hardening into something like anger.

And then he nods, like I just confirmed all the worst things he ever suspected of me.

He punches his pillow a few times before lying down, turning his back to me, his forearm over his head, like he's protecting himself from falling debris.

I lie there, trembling, pretending to be asleep and listening to him pretending too, for I don't even know how long.

Variable Star

'Group Two – welcome to the final selection day!' booms the redheaded Lieutenant. 'Psychological evaluation this morning followed by teamwork assessment in the afternoon.'

'That sounds like a hoot,' Caleb side-whispers to Jam.

We are sitting on padded benches in an airless auditorium. It seems we are going to be shown a series of documentaries and information presentations about Ventura, about La Verdad, about the Epsilon Eridani signal, while we are called into one of five adjoining interview rooms, where I'm guessing we'll be grilled by a shrink. It's only the final selection day adrenaline that's keeping me going after another mostly sleepless night.

On some kind of romantic offensive, Micah has taken Mali to Santo Domingo for the day, after they spent what seemed like most of the night keeping everybody in the vicinity awake with their giggling.

The first documentary they play is about the discovery of the signal. I can't help thinking about how completely amazing it must have been, the moment they first heard it. All those millennia on our own and then suddenly somebody out there is trying to talk to us. It sounds like pulsing static, until you fiddle with the levels and hear the high-pitched ones underneath, and then suddenly it sounds like music. To me, anyway. Somewhere in the crazy huge deal of this road trip I almost forgot that right at the heart of everything is this: I have always wanted to be here, in this amazing place, to know the answer to these questions: who sent the signal? What does it mean? What happens next? These are the most exciting, most important questions humanity has ever known, and the thought that I could be a part of finding the answer is almost too huge to comprehend.

Every ten minutes or so someone is called into one of the rooms, as someone else walks back out, usually in tears.

Just then the screen beeps again and I see it: B-37-37. My number. I look at Jam, and he is already looking back.

'Good luck,' he says, and even though he's been pretty much ignoring me all morning, he pats my leg. 'You'll be fine.'

The room I find myself in is a grey, windowless cupboard. There is a woman sitting in a chair, tapping wildly at her computer keyboard. She has her hair clipped back but parts of it are escaping.

'I'm Emma,' she says, without looking up. American accent. 'And you are?'

'Beacon Karlo,' I tell her. 'B-37-37, if you prefer.'

She looks up. 'That doesn't bother you?' she asks. 'Being known as a number?'

I just smile.

'Sit down,' she says, looking back at her computer, still typing away.

I sit in the seat opposite her.

'Tell me what brought you here, Beacon.'

I lean back in the chair and stare at the ceiling. 'Sometimes I'm not even sure any more,' I say.

'Oh?' She looks at me again. Her eyes are disconcertingly dark. 'Why's that?'

'Because things have changed so much since I first decided to come here.' I think about this some more. 'I've changed.'

'You have?' She glances up. 'In what way?'

I laugh. There's so much to say, I don't know where to start. 'I'd never really left the town I grew up in until this trip. I'd only gone to school and gone to work and that was it. And then suddenly, on the way down here, I realise there are all these other places and other people in the world, but there are still the same problems, it's still the same messed up world where the poor are poor and

the rich are rich and everyone's just trapped, and yet ... '
I shake my head. 'I've seen so much on the way here that, for the first time, just as I'm about to leave it all behind, I'm starting to see why it is that some people love this planet so much, despite its faults.'

I realise now that I'm rambling, which probably isn't helping convince her I'm psychologically sound. 'Am I allowed to ask questions?' I ask.

'Of course.'

'Is it true that my immune disorder is going to be cured by being in space?'

She blinks, but barely misses a beat. 'Most likely.' She nods, flicking her eyes down to her screen. 'Space travel alters the entire chemistry of the body to such an extent that it's to all intents and purposes a system reboot. In the case of an autoimmune condition like yours, this would probably mean it would disappear. The changes that would take place in your body would stay with you then, for the rest of your life, since you would never be returning. The factors we consider more pertinent are psychological. A person's likely reactions to stress, confinement and adjusting to a new way of life. Aside from fertility, what we're mostly seeking are people who have the psychological strength for this challenge.'

'And bravery,' I add.

'Bravery?'

'That's what Jam says you're looking for.'

'Jam?'

'Joram Rees. B-37-16.'

She types something. 'Do you know each other from before the process?'

'Oh yes,' I laugh.

She looks at me, waiting for me to elaborate.

'He's probably the person I know better than anyone, if I think about it.'

'Sounds like you're good friends.'

I nod, look at my hands in my lap, feeling my brow crease as I think about the kiss again.

'Do you believe in God?' she asks.

'Wow,' I laugh. 'That's a weird thing to ask.'

'Is it?'

'For me it is.'

'Why?'

'Because I never think about it.'

She nods, types, giving me a chance to think before I speak again.

'I don't think it's a question of believing or not. There are so many things I don't understand in the universe. Like, for example, I love physics at school. It's my favourite subject. It's the philosophy of the science world; so many of its questions are the biggest, deepest questions we have. Why are we here? Am I real? It's no accident that so many of its technical terms sound like poetry. Or they do to me anyway. But there is so much about it I don't understand, so I just have to take it on faith. Infinity, time, black holes, other dimensions, string theory, the many worlds interpretation – I can't even start to get my head around it. But that doesn't stop me trying. It doesn't stop me wanting to understand, even if I have to spend my whole life trying. Because I know how great it would be to even get close to an understanding of what it all means. And it's the same with life. There are just so many parts of it I don't get.'

'Like?' She smiles. She isn't typing any more; she's just watching me.

'Like ... love. What makes you want to put another person before yourself? What makes you care about someone so much it makes you feel ill? And why is it that even when you do love someone, you'll still do things that hurt them?' I swallow. 'Anyway, I guess for me, God, whatever he or she is, is just another massive thing I may never be able to get my head round, even if I wanted to. It's not a question of whether I believe or not. The possibility's just something too huge for me to comprehend.'

She doesn't type, doesn't even move, just goes on looking at me while I go on looking back.

Eventually she says, 'What makes you want to spend the rest of your life on Ventura?'

I think for a moment, unsure how to answer. 'I guess at first it just seemed like something I was always going to do.

I saw it on the TV and it just made sense. I thought: that's what I'm doing. It's the thing that has always been in my future, just out of sight, calling to me. And another part of me was just thinking, I'm going to get out of here and get a million miles away from all the crap I've called a life for the last seventeen years. And then of course there's the fact that it might cure me of the condition that otherwise, in the next however many years, will probably kill me. But then I got here and it got real for the first time and I realised I wanted it in a deeper way. Not just to escape, not just to cure me, but because this is something I should do, something I want to do, something I'm right for. And now I've seen a little more of this planet, and have finally fallen in love with it just at the very moment I realise how doomed it is, I have even more reason to leave it behind. Because I know that this mission, making contact, finding whoever or whatever we find out there, might be this world's best chance of surviving. Does that make sense?'

She looks at me, her face unreadable. 'Thank you, Bea. You can go now.'

I somehow manage to stand, with what I've just admitted to her, and to myself, still surging in my veins.

Jam's gone when I get back out to the low-lit auditorium, and I find I'm staring at his hat, where he's left it on his empty seat, holding the shape of his head, darkened at the front where he grips it to put it on.

A door opens down at the front and I watch Jam come out of it, head down, his hand on the back of his neck. I stand as he comes back up the stairs, taking them two at a time but slowly, heavy footed.

'How did it go?' I say, my anxiety so bright and hard I can taste it.

He stands just in front of me, puts his hands on his hips for a moment, lets out a long breath.

'Not sure,' he says in the end.

At lunch we sit with Caleb and Ernesto and the Russians while they make fun of the psychologists and their questions. I don't recognise most of the questions they say they were asked, except the one about God, and why we want to be part of the mission.

'What did you get asked?' I say to Jam, tuning everyone else out.

'Can't remember really,' he says, but I notice that he hasn't even taken a bite of his sandwich.

After lunch we are bussed out to the facility reservoirs. Jam sits next to the window and leans his head there, knees up against the seat in front, hat tipped low over his eyes. I can't ask him if he's OK again without being annoying so instead I listen to Caleb telling the people across the aisle about how his mum was part of the original research team working on decryption of the signal, just after they discovered it.

'She was a grad student on placement from MIT.' He shakes his head. 'Talk about right time, right place.'

I look out of the window as we skirt the spaceport, where one of the shuttles is just being towed in from the landing strip, trailing clouds of steam from its rear, cooling system almost overloaded from the heat of re-entry.

The buses pull up at the first reservoir, where there are ten uniformed facility operatives. Without explaining anything they call out numbers that divide us into groups of twenty. This takes long enough for me to look around and notice a floating platform sitting in the middle of the lake. Identical piles of items – rope and large empty water containers – are spread at regular intervals around the shoreline.

I've already guessed what they'll ask us to do when the booming megaphone announces that we have twenty minutes to design a way to get our entire team onto the pontoon in the middle, using all the items in each pile.

The klaxon sounds to mark the official start of our twenty minutes and we race to the shoreline. Ernesto is the only person in my team I know, and he's full of bright ideas, but somehow I've ended up being the only person on my team who isn't fluent Spanish-speaking, even though I swear they're in a serious minority here, which is how come I end up squatting next to the items, staring at them, a calm coming over me as I establish the fact that there is no way enough material here to make a boat that will hold twenty people. I look up and see other teams lashing the containers together into a raft. Some of my team members start counting up the containers to work out how many wide and long our raft should be. I stand slowly, feeling my ankles click as I do.

'He never said it had to a boat,' I say to myself, then again louder, to them, 'He never said it had to a boat.'

Ernesto gets still for a moment and touches the arm of the girl nearest him so that she stops talking and looks at me too. 'What are you thinking?'

I tell them my plan and I'm amazed when everyone pretty much immediately agrees we should try it. It takes us almost the whole time to figure it out, to tie the knots, to argue over whether the rope is going to be long enough and whether this will work, but by the time the klaxon sounds we're about ready and streaming sweat.

'OK, everyone knows what we're doing, right?' I say, squinting around at them in the harsh sunlight. 'José is the strongest swimmer so he'll go up front and once he anchors the rope we all know what to do.' I see some cynical faces and take a deep breath, 'We can do this if we work together. Everything is energy. All we need to do is match the frequency of the reality we want and we can't help but get that reality.'

Ernesto is watching me, nodding as he says, '*La filosofia de Bea.*'

And I say, 'No – it's physics. And it was Einstein who said it.'

He laughs. 'But the right words in the right moment.'

Next to him this girl called Maripaz is nodding too and it spreads around the circle in a way that makes me flush.

The first five groups have been given the signal to start, and are mostly sinking on lumpy, badly thought-out rafts. No one has made it to the pontoon by the time the klaxon goes again to mark the end of their turn.

Jam's group is one of the next five and when I look at the messy pile of containers in front of them fear starts scuttling in my chest. But they don't climb on their raft like the others do; instead they hang on around the perimeter of it and start kicking in the water, driving the raft out towards the pontoon.

'Yes,' I hear myself saying, louder than I meant to, my fists clenching so hard that my nails are driving into my palms, but then the raft is falling apart before my eyes.

Jam keeps swimming, keeps dragging, even though it looks so hard I swear I can feel the burn of it in my own muscles.

'No,' I say, stamping my foot so that the rocks shift beneath it while I'm watching the way Jam is still swimming, still pulling, and calling to the others to keep going. And then the klaxon tears through the air and he lays back in the water, looks up at the sky, before starting to swim back to shore, stopping once to push his hair out of his face and glance over at me, squinting across the distance between us.

We're next and we're the only ones who haven't made a raft, who have instead made a long line of floats spaced out at intervals. I'm third in line, running in with my float in my arms and swimming while I hold onto it. It feels like I'm swimming for ever, burning with adrenaline. It takes José longer than I thought it would to get to the pontoon but then he stands and hauls at the rope, reeling people in like fish, speeding us through the water. Once I get there I get out too to help him pull our teammates out of the water, but then the klaxon goes and there's only six of us out, with fourteen more still strung out along the rope. I stop, stand, sniffing and dripping and looking around, then I realise that there's another entire team already on the other side of the pontoon, air-punching and celebrating, Kazimir standing amongst them. Ernesto slams his hand on my shoulder so hard it makes me jolt in shock.

'*Que bien*,' he says, whistling through his teeth, adding, 'We did good.'

But I'm pretty sure it's not good enough.

I almost don't have the energy to swim back, but when I finally reach the shore I lie on the rocks and stare up at the sky to where a tiny wisp of cloud is sketched across the blue. It feels like it's the first cloud I've seen in Spain.

Afterwards, we are shepherded back to the buses and, even though I fight against the tide of people to try to wait for Jam, I don't find him.

Back at the canteen I move among the buzzing nervous crowd, listening to people laughing about what a mess most people's rafts were. I think a lot of the laughing is to cover up the fact that it's just sinking in, just dawning on us, that the course of our whole lives is about to be decided on what basically amounts to three days of quizzes and games.

By the time I feel Jam take hold of my arm I'm so overwhelmed I just fold myself into him, both of us still damp despite the heat. He rests his chin on my head and I feel his voice in his chest rather than hearing it.

'You did so well,' he says.

But I can't speak to say anything in reply.

Just then the tannoy rings out a sliding scale of beeps and the Ventura Com computerised voice says, 'Will all recruits please proceed to the main gate for the posting of the final selection. Thank you for being a part of the volunteer program for the ESA's First Contact Mission Ventura. Good luck.'

And then it repeats the whole thing in Spanish.

'Oh God, this is it,' I hear myself say, as everyone starts to file out of the door. 'This is really it.' And fear begins to pound in my throat as I lock eyes with Jam.

We arrive at the gate, where the rest of the recruits and what looks like a million members of the press and drones and cameras and who knows what else are gathered around the information screen, waiting. A hot gust of wind, sea-scented, plays across my skin, and suddenly it comes to me.

'This is the end of the adventure,' I tell Jam, and his steps slow with mine. 'People like us don't go into space. It was fun while it lasted, to think of us doing something as crazy as that but . . . ' I reach up to pull him into a hug, pressing my face against the skin under his ear. He smells so much like home I could stay there for ever.

'You never know, Bea,' he says against my shoulder, and I blink hard against the heat of threatening tears.

I step away, force a smile, take his arm, thread mine under his, as we walk out of the open gate where we see Mali and Micah waiting for us in the mad scrum behind the press barriers.

'Good luck!' Mali shouts, but then covers her mouth with both hands like she's about to cry.

Just then there's that series of beeps again: the start of a giant dot matrix countdown from ten, that same robotic voice booming out of the speakers.

'*Ventura Com would like to thank everyone who participated in volunteer selection for First Contact Mission Ventura. The standard was extremely high. We are now delighted to present to you the three hundred lucky young*

310

women and men who will make up our first generation. Please join us in welcoming them to their new future.'

Three.

Two.

One.

And then the numbers appear.

I can't focus my eyes enough to read them; the thought of reading through to the end of that list without finding myself is too much. Instead I look around and spot Ernesto air-punching, Kazimir and Oksana high fiving each other, as if they didn't know it all along. But I swear it all happens in slow motion as Jam turns to me and says, 'Bea, you made it.'

I look at his face, at the trembling smile I have never seen before, and then I look up at the screen. There's my number: B-37-37. I made it. I stand in a state of shock. Then I look back at Jam.

'And you?' I ask, almost no voice.

He shakes his head.

'You made it though, Bea,' he says, breathless. 'You made it.'

'But you didn't,' I croak.

He shakes his head. 'Don't worry about that.'

'Don't worry about that?' I can hardly breathe. The world is spinning around me.

I'm vaguely aware of Kazimir, Caleb, Mali and Micah waiting to congratulate me. But all I can see is Jam.

'We can talk to them,' I say, throat tight. 'We can make them change their minds.'

He shakes his head. 'They've made the right decision,' he says. 'They probably saw right through me. I only tried out at all to be with you.'

I feel the heat of the tears in my eyes and when I blink they spill down my cheeks.

He shakes his head. 'Don't,' he says. 'It doesn't matter, Bea. Of course they want you – they were always going to. And this is it, this is your chance. And I am going to be so so so happy for you. Even though I have no idea how I'm going to get through even one day without seeing you, let alone the rest of my life.'

I shake my head, throat tight, eyes spilling. 'But what does any of it matter without you?'

How is it that it only now becomes clear in this moment? How is it that it took this to show me the truth that has been in my heart the whole time?

We stare at each other for what feels like for ever, reading every emotion that passes across each other's face. I reach for the front of his shirt and pull him closer, pull him down until he is stooped all the way over, my hand on the side of his face, pushing his hair back, my thumb on his lip, a sob hitching in my throat even as I feel his hand on the small of my back and press my mouth to his because it is the only way to say all the things I can't find the words for.

And then we are kissing and kissing and kissing right there while everybody watches and I don't care and neither does he because nobody, absolutely nobody, exists in this whole universe in that moment, in the moment that we are simultaneously finding each other and losing each other for ever.

Entanglement

I don't even know how long we go on kissing, but every passing second only makes it clearer that even eternity wouldn't be long enough. At some point I realise how far I am pulling him down to me and I jump into his arms, wrap my legs around his hips so that our faces are level while he links his hands under my legs, and even though I must be heavy he makes it seem so easy, so perfect, that I feel like I belong there, that I always have. I push my fingers into his hair, knocking his hat off. The feel of his lips, super soft on mine, goes straight to my heart and makes it ache.

But something eventually makes me aware of the cameras that are closing in around us, of Mali telling them to leave us alone, and suddenly there is this scary woman in a red jacket and clown make-up standing next to us while a low drone swirls the air into a whirlwind with us at the centre of it.

'Nicola Rodriguez from Worldwide Television Network,' she says. 'Can I ask you for your story?'

'No,' I say, barely looking at her as Jam lowers my feet to the ground and I take his hand, pull him away. 'No you cannot,' I yell back at her when she makes as if she's going to follow us.

'Where are we going?' asks Jam.

'Anywhere,' I say. 'Anywhere where it can just be you and me.'

He looks back to where the others are following us at a distance, to where the drones still swoop in low circles and the press are rounding the recruits into groups to be filmed.

'Might be difficult just now,' he says, smiling but sad-eyed.

'Guys –' Caleb catches up to us – 'I'm throwing my last party on Earth at my place. I have passes for base. The press aren't allowed through so they won't bother you there.'

Jam and I share a long look. All I want to do is be alone with him. But it's all we've got.

On the walk to Caleb's I say nothing. I feel like a tornado came and sucked my life up into it and dumped it a thousand miles away. All I can do is thread my fingers through Jam's and press my face against the top of his arm, half listening to the conversations going on around me.

In Caleb's garden there are lights up in the trees and

I'm relieved when I hear Nick Drake playing rather than party music. I end up lying on my back on the brown grass while most people are inside gathered around the TV. Jam only managed to leave me at all because he said he was getting me a drink, otherwise I wouldn't have let him.

'Hey,' breathes Mali, sitting next to me on the grass, cross-legged. 'It's amazing,' she says, touching my arm gently. 'That you made it. I mean, Bea, come on, out of tens of thousands of people? *You* made it.'

I don't answer; I just look at her.

'You don't have to go,' she says. 'If you don't want to.'

'I don't know what I want any more,' I say.

'I didn't know about you and Jam,' she says, letting a smile creep on to her face.

'Nobody knew,' I tell her. 'Not even us.'

'Has it been going on this whole trip? I knew there was something different with you – why didn't you tell me?'

I shake my head. 'It only just happened.'

She pulls her bare legs up in front of her and hugs them to her chest. 'Even though the timing completely sucks, I'm still glad it finally happened. For his sake, if nothing else. All the years he's spent loving you.' She shakes her head.

I frown at her as she carries on. 'I've always wished anyone would love me the way he loves you.'

I'm so speechless I can't look at her. I feel hot tears forming.

'Oh Bea, I'm so sorry. I always thought you knew. I didn't—'

'Guys, you have to see this!' Caleb calls us from the big sliding glass door into the house. I let Mali pull me up and walk me over there, holding me upright with the arm she tightens around my shoulders.

Inside, the huge TV is showing footage of Jam and I kissing, while the sand swirls around us and his hat drops off and it looks for all the world exactly like it felt: like nobody else in the world exists. A caption reads: 'The Doomed Lovers of Mission Ventura.'

'Guys, that is so hot,' says Caleb, shaking his head. 'You are literally my heroes right now.'

I find myself looking across the room to where Jam is standing, flushed in the face and looking at the carpet, returning my gaze when he feels it on him.

'You realise you need to call your mum, right?' says Micah, his voice a little tight as he looks across at me, then looks away again. 'If that's on the TV here, it's probably on the TV there.'

'I'll call her soon,' I say. 'It's not like I'm flying out tomorrow.'

'I fly out in two days,' says Kazimir, matter of fact. 'Transfers are every two days for the next three weeks. You have to sign up to available seats.'

'What?' I let out a panicked laugh. 'When did we get told this?'

'Today.' He shrugs again.

I feel the room spin as I sit on the nearest chair, my head falling into my hands. But then someone is prising my fingers away and it's Jam, holding a drink out to me. I look up at him and he looks down at me and everything else is out of focus. I take his hand and pull him outside. We walk all the way down the garden and out through the gate in the back fence.

We find ourselves staring out across a field of wind turbines that stand crazily tall, chopping at the air.

'Oh, what the hell is going on?' I yell at the sky, kicking at the gravel underfoot so that the stones shift against each other.

'I know, right?' is all Jam says.

'A day ago everything made sense and now . . .' I shake my head. 'Now nothing does. And now I have to leave you behind. And, you know what? A few days ago I would have been able to live with that. Well, I think I would have. But that was when I didn't know . . .'

'Didn't know what?' he says, super quiet.

'Why didn't you tell me how you felt?' I ask him, going to him and taking both his hands so that he turns to me in the twilight. I pull him to me. The proximity disorientates us both, throws us off-topic, renders it so that we can only look at each other, studying eyes but mostly mouths, lips.

I notice how he brings his lower one up to meet his top one, almost pouting.

'Maybe it's for the best that you're going and I'm not,' he says, sighing hard so that I feel the rush of air on my lips. 'I mean, I guess I can't really spend my whole life seeing you with him, or whoever else ... wishing it was me.'

I look up at him, at the pain on his face, and suddenly it is dizzying how beautiful he is, as he turns and walks away from me, leaving me watching his back and feeling like leaving him is impossible.

'Look at this,' he says, pushing his fingers through the fence of the next-door house, bruising the jasmine. I come up next to him, smelling the perfume in the air, and breathing him in, and it takes me a while to realise what I'm looking at. Light on water.

'A swimming pool,' I say.

'Yeah,' he says. 'Who the hell has a cultivated lawn and a swimming pool in a world strangled by water shortage?'

'Space research scientists, clearly,' I say, sidestepping to the gate and sliding the unsecured bolt across, before looking at the windows of the house, all shuttered, nobody home. I walk towards the dark pool, hear Jam follow me. The sound of frogs and crickets surround us. I pull my T-shirt up and over my head, drop my shorts and turn back to him. 'When was the last time you swam in an outdoor swimming pool?'

He pretends to think. 'Um, never?'

'Exactly.' And we are both smiling, but then I notice his gaze shift to my chest and he loses his smile, frowns a little, deadly serious.

I love having his eyes on me, even though it's almost impossible to bear. I watch him drop his hat on a sun lounger, then reach back to pull his T-shirt off over his head, messing his hair, only looking at me sideways, shyly, before he pulls at the buttons of his shorts and drops them. When did he get so beautiful? And how did I not notice before? His immaculate, shining skin, so tight over the secret machinery of his muscles as he stands there, completely unaware that he is making every imaginable beautiful angle, hips, shoulders and jaw illuminated by the twilight. We take each other in, and one of his chest muscles twitches under my gaze.

He steps towards me, gets close enough so I can feel his body heat, and for a second I wonder if I'll die, but then he takes another step, past me, doing the most beautiful dolphin dive into the water. All I can do is follow him.

When I break the surface, he is treading water in front of me, pushing his hair out of his face, pulling towards the far end in three long strokes, but then turning back to me, smiling. 'Water feels so good,' he says.

And it does, but I swear I can't think about that. Not as I get close to him and we are face to face. Instead all I can do is look at him, at how different he looks, almost like he has changed so much during this trip that I can hardly recognise him now. It could be the tan I never saw him with before, the way his dark hair looks when it's wet, or maybe how much his mouth distracts me now that I know how good it feels to kiss him.

'You said you'd never lied to me,' I say. 'But you never told me how you felt.'

He frowns, shakes his head. 'Do you want me to tell you that I love you? That I've loved you as long as I've been capable of that kind of love? That nobody else in the world has ever seemed real to me the way you do? That for years I lay just on the other side of that partition wall with my fingers pressed against it because I needed to be as close to you as I could get? Why would I say that now? What would be the point?' And he turns to swim away so that I have to take his arm to pull him back to me, my heart thudding. And then I am close to him, which is the only place I feel I can be. 'Please don't go,' I whisper.

'If I stay here, all I'm going to want to do is kiss you.' He says it against the water's surface, then looks up at me, squinting a little.

'Good,' I say. 'Because I don't think I can bear it if you don't.'

He blinks slowly, gently slides his hand along my jaw, a tremble in it I can feel, and we are looking at each other for so long, watching the shine of each other's eyes. All of this, so that in the end I am spinning out completely even before the moment he leans in slowly, waiting for me to lean in too and then it is happening. He is happening to me and I am happening to him.

I've no idea how long we've been kissing by the time he lifts me on to the side of the pool, with a strength that takes me by surprise, then plants his palms on either side of my legs and lifts himself, still kissing me as I lean all the way back until I am lying flat on the grass on the edge of the pool.

I've never been kissed like this before. It is so full, so open, so hungry. And I'm vaguely aware that both of us are making these noises like this kiss is the most delicious thing the world has ever known and no amount of it will ever be enough.

I twist into him, against him, until he is under me, and I sit on his hips, look down at him, smooth his wet hair back from his face, while he watches me. I've never let anyone look at me like this, look this long. I've never wanted to look back. His beautiful broken lip shape, the dip in his chin, the carved out lines of his collarbones and shoulders – like an angel I could never have imagined.

I take his hand and lay it over my heart. He bites his lip, but doesn't break eye contact.

'Suddenly it feels like I've never done this before,' he says, but with no real voice.

'Feels like that for me too,' I say, and we smile at each other, letting it grow slowly. 'Maybe it's because it's never been like this.'

'You're not – what was it? – taking my soul?' He raises an eyebrow and suddenly I want him so much it hurts.

I swallow, watching his lips. 'Feels more like I'm giving you mine.'

He moves his hand back on to the side of my face, his thumb on my mouth, pulling me in and around until he is above me, then pausing, almost sending me crazy with it as he studies my face, super serious.

'Don't you want to?' he says, slight frown.

'So much.'

'You look scared,' he whispers.

'I am. Aren't you?'

'No and yes,' he says, right against my lips. 'No because it's you, and yes ... because it's you.'

And I fall back into kissing him and right now I swear we are like two beings trying to occupy the same space so that we aren't two any more. I think suddenly I know where my soul is located because I can feel it.

It would have been so easy to leave my life behind a day ago. And now suddenly, in the space of a moment, it's impossible.

Perihelion

I only realise I've dropped into a shallow sleep when Jam shifts position and it stirs me into opening my eyes under a multi-coloured dawn sky. My face is right against the skin of his throat and it feels like the perfect place. He moves his hand down my shoulder and I pull back a little so that I can look at him. I move my fingers down his bare chest, but then feel the chain of his dog tag. Its significance washes over me, leaving me cold. There's no way I can leave him. Not now. Not after last night.

Like he's reading my thoughts he lifts it off just then, takes my hand and opens it gently, finger by finger, like a flower, before dropping the tag into my palm.

'You can take it back for me,' he says.

I stare at my hand, without closing it.

His hand goes to my hip, then to my stomach, where he delicately traces the shining pink K-shape of my surgery scars with his finger.

'I love these so much,' he says, before I can say anything.

'They're your story. The story of you. The story of how brave you are. The story of how you never gave up. I'm so glad you'll always have them with you, to remind you. That way, if things get tough out there ...'

'I'm not going,' I say, realising right then that it's true. 'How can I now?'

He is utterly stilled, looking at me so long and so serious before he says, 'You have to go.'

I shake my head.

He watches me, his expression so sad, almost like he could cry. I touch his mouth, the sides of his face, take a glossy lock of his hair between my fingers, try to deny to myself that my eyes are filling with tears even though they are, unstoppably. I hear a bird singing and look up to see it sitting on a corner of the roof, above it the clouds and the sky. I force myself to look back at Jam and he's watching me like I am something he has already lost.

It's only once we are standing in Caleb's kitchen, and Mali and Caleb and Micah and Kazimir are leaning against his island drinking coffee, laughing as they look us up and down, that we realise we are covered in crusts of orange mud.

'Ah, mud wrestling? That's where you've been?' says Kazimir, raising an eyebrow.

'Skinny dipping in the Rigsons' pool would be my guess,' says Caleb, with a ridiculous wink.

Micah leans against the counter and stares at the patterned floor.

Mali brings me coffee and then beams at me. Her hair is wet and she smells like fruit.

'This place has the most amazing shower,' she says.

'Is that a hint?' I sip at the inky coffee, grateful that she knows me well enough to have filled it with sugar, but when my focus shifts to the kitchen wall behind her, where a big square clock reads 8.22 in blue numbers, it turns so sour I can hardly swallow it.

The shower is amazing. So hot, so strong. I watch the mud make an orange puddle around my feet before draining away.

I get out, get dressed too quick, while I am still wet. I sprint down the stairs and find Jam sitting on the sofa alone, as though he's been waiting for me. I climb into his lap, press my face against his ear, tighten my arms around his neck, feel his hand move up and down my back. There are no words.

Mali and Micah have gone back to their tent, but Jam walks with us to the gate and then we stand there, hands linked, me wondering how I will ever manage to walk away from him even for a few hours.

'I'm just going to go in and tell them that I'm withdrawing,' I say.

'No, Bea,' he says. 'Don't do that.'

'Come on,' says Caleb. 'You'll see him later.'

'There's no point,' I say. 'I'm not going.'

'Bea.' Jam squeezes my hand again, while Caleb shifts his weight, unsure where to look.

'Listen,' Caleb says eventually, super quiet, like he's aware how peripheral he is in any of this. 'You may as well come in and hear what they have to say today. It might make your decision easier.'

'I've made my decision,' I say.

Jam is smiling and sad-eyed when I turn to him, but he pulls me a few steps away and leans close.

'I know it feels like everything's changed, Bea,' is all he says. 'It does for me too, but the reasons for you to go are still the same. They haven't changed. You have to do this. I know you know that, just as well as I do – right?'

Maybe I do. Maybe that's why when he leans in to kiss me I almost don't want him to, because suddenly I can't stop imagining that I am collecting them, every one of them, like a series of jewels. All the many beautiful kisses like this that were scheduled into the future that may no longer be mine.

As I walk away I look back at him again and again, standing completely motionless and watching me leave. I'm just about to run back to him when the gate guard hits the klaxon on his megaphone and tells us to line up.

I end up standing next to Kazimir and I feel him giving me a side-glance, smiling slyly.

'What?' I ask him.

'Your life is complicated,' he says. 'I think it's a good thing you're leaving it behind.'

We get herded out to the Training Centre and sorted into groups of fifty. Caleb and I get put in the same group, along with Kazimir. It doesn't look like there's that much method to it except that I notice that it's equal numbers male and female. Our group ends up in the auditorium again, where Lieutenant Dean presents another slideshow about the Ventura. The artificial gravity (which I don't understand entirely, but it has something to do with the momentum from the propulsion), the floor plan, which shows living quarters, the canteen, Medical, Production, Factory, Engineering and Docks. Right at the top of the ship is Command. Suddenly it seems immense enough to get lost in, and tiny enough to feel trapped in, all at the same time.

The slideshow finishes and Lieutenant Dean invites questions.

'What exactly do we know about the signal?' asks a guy at the front.

'We know three things for sure,' says the lieutenant, marking them off on her fingers. 'It is purposeful, it isn't natural and it is coming to us from the vicinity of the Epsilon Eridani star system. We don't know what type of alien is sending the signal, but the exciting part is going to be finding out. First contact, once we make it, will be the most significant moment the world has ever known. The knowledge we stand to gain, and the discoveries that we make along the way, are going to be the keys to ensuring the future of our planet, and the human race itself.'

'How long will it take to get to the source of the signal?' asks a girl at the back.

'We predict that it will take around three hundred and fifty years.'

Epic silence. Although we already knew this, hearing it now that it's real is different.

Lieutenant Dean scans the room, smiles and says, 'Although it won't be us who get there, one day our descendants will return to Earth with the glorious news.'

'Seven hundred years later,' says a guy, without putting his hand up. 'What will Earth even look like by then?' He turns a little to the audience. 'Will it even still exist?'

'This is the reality of long-distance space travel,' says Lieutenant Dean, like it's the most ordinary thing in the world. 'Our mortality is our barrier. This multi-generational model is what makes it possible. Ventura will be the first of its kind. A space civilisation, you might say.'

There's so much to take in. Here's how it breaks down: volunteers will be assigned Service roles on board which they will have to work in for three years. Service roles are the real dogsbody jobs that nobody else would want to do – cleaning, hauling rubbish, laundry, cooking in the canteens. Volunteers will also be assigned a life partner. The person they will raise children with. Two. Both the same sex. Made in a lab and implanted.

Suddenly I get an image from this morning – Jam smiling as he watched me kiss each of his fingertips. The contrast to all this is so stark that vomiting starts to seem inevitable, and I begin to plan an exit route. An American girl at the back puts her hand up.

'Why is this all so crazily authoritarian? I mean, lab babies and slavery?'

Lieutenant Dean laughs. 'There's no slavery, recruit. The Ventura is a paramilitary vessel. Your work detail and your role within the breeding program would make up part of what is considered your duty.'

'Our duty?' the girl comes back with. 'What if we really don't get along with the person we're assigned to? What if we like someone else more? These are partnerships of convenience, right? So we'd be allowed to see other people?'

The lieutenant's smile only slips slightly. 'We believe that well organised and planned ties of community, on both smaller and larger scales, will be essential to the success of the mission. Your partnerships will be decided on genetic and personal compatibility. We'll pick personality types we believe will make effective teams, and genetic combinations that will create optimum offspring. You can see why this would be important – your children will be our future crew, and they'll need to be strong.'

'That didn't really answer my question,' says the girl, after thinking about it for a few seconds.

The Lieutenant looks like she's trying extremely hard not to roll her eyes. 'Eight hundred and eighty eight people are setting out on this mission, occupying the same couple of square kilometres for the rest of their lives, in harmony, as well as procreating just the right amount to replace themselves effectively and create a future crew. It's just too important to leave to random chance. Everything will be strictly controlled for the welfare and wellbeing of all. It will be a different kind of life to the one you've been used to, and there may be some drawbacks. There will also be some benefits. Perhaps it might be helpful if we broke into smaller discussion groups? That way we can air our doubts or worries and then put them to rest.'

I end up in a group with Kazimir, and we're all sitting in an awkward circle. I'm staring into space, completely distracted by memories of last night when the guy next to me asks Kazimir, 'So I'm guessing you've been on a lot of haulers?'

'I grew up on a hauler,' Kazimir says, not even the slightest hint of a smile. 'Only returned to Earth for brief shore leave. Visit grandparents,' he says.

'What a weird childhood,' I say it without thinking.

He turns to me and watches me for a few seconds before he says, 'Maybe, but the truth is that we never have anything to compare it to, do we? Our own is all we get to experience.'

I shrug.

He smiles slowly. 'Mine was very similar to the childhood you will be giving your own children. But yours won't have the shore leave. Or any life choices.'

I watch the amusement on his face and match it with a frown. 'I'm not going to worry about my purely theoretical children just yet, but you've made your point.'

'What's your father's job, Kazimir?' asks another girl.

'Security Operative on Concordia Industries' hauler vessel Soyuz 32 up until now. Chief of Security Ventura from two weeks ago.'

'Security?' My mouth is dry so when I swallow it clicks. 'As in, protection? From what?'

He rests his pale gaze on me. 'From each other. From ourselves. Fighting, endangering others, endangering the mission, rule-breaking.'

'What happens to people who break the rules?' the first guy asks, half-laughing but the sound is mostly like fear.

'They are put out the airlock.' Kazimir nods, looks around the circle at the horrified expressions on everyone's faces before he says, 'I'm joking, by the way.'

We all laugh then, but it's definitely uneasy.

'What about video calls?' asks another girl. 'Is the connection really bad?'

'There are no real time coms with Earth after two days' travel.' He leans forward, with his forearms resting on his spread-apart knees. 'After two days we can only send data drops. I believe once we exit the system we won't even be able to do that. We will have networked devices on board so we will be able to communicate easily with each other, but Earth . . . ' He shakes his head. 'You'll just have to say your goodbyes.' I wouldn't have found that idea particularly hard, until recently, and now it seems impossible.

'Excuse me.' And I get up, head for the door, don't look back, don't stop until I am in the *servicios*, staring down the toilet bowl, willing it not to happen right up until the moment that it does and I am staring at the blood.

After lunch, we are issued with our uniform. We'll be given pyjamas, underwear, recreation uniforms, formal, everything, but will spend most of the time in this ridiculous all-in-one jumpsuit type thing and matching cap, grey, branded with the Ventura logo just about anywhere they can fit one in. They will have our names stitched on to them too and I try hard not to think about why that is, as well as why the cloth they're made of is flame retardant, reinforced and thermally insulated.

'These are going to be a nightmare to use the bathroom

333

in,' says Maripaz, the girl from yesterday. 'Whose idea was it to make them a one-piece?'

'Health and safety,' says Lieutenant Dean. 'You'll get used to it.'

I look at myself then in the mirror. My uniform feels so heavy on me, it's like I'm wearing chainmail.

They want us to stay in them for the rest of the day. It turns out they haven't thought this through, because we're in southern Spain, and it's August, and it's the middle of the day, so within minutes we are all literally pouring sweat.

'There's AC in the gymnasium,' says Lieutenant Dean. 'You'll be fine once we get there.'

Walking across the yard with the sun beating on us, I swear I almost puke. When we get to the gymnasium, it is pretty much no cooler at all.

I don't realise Kazimir's staring at me until I notice him smiling in my peripheral vision, and re-focus on him.

'What?'

'You are a little warm?' He smirks.

'Well, I don't get why they made them this thick,' I say, pulling open more popper buttons.

'You don't?' Same amused smile. 'Really?'

I roll my eyes at him. 'Well, obviously I know space is cold, but doesn't the ship have heating?'

'When outside temperature is less than minus two-sixty degrees, even with heating it gets a little cold.'

I narrow my eyes. 'I know about space. Don't patronise me.'

He holds his hands up. 'Just talking.'

'Just talking? Really?' I suddenly feel so angry it feels like something slipping through my fingers. 'Well, perhaps it's best if you don't talk at all,' I tell him.

'I didn't mean to upset you,' he says, emotionless, more than a hint of superiority.

Something inside me snaps.

'Whatever, man!' I'm suddenly yelling. 'Who the hell *are* you anyway? We're not all second-generation space androids with a daddy letting us in the back door. Some of us are real people who came here thinking we had a fair shot. Perhaps we should have realised all along that people like us don't get a fair chance. Ever.'

'And yet here you are.'

'Oh aren't I lucky?' I spit back at him. 'To be standing here with you.'

All the time I've been speaking, he's just been watching me, almost expressionless, pale eyes on mine like he is trying to read something in them. It almost happens in slow motion when he reaches his hand out and touches my arm.

'I know it isn't easy for you,' he says.

I throw his hand back at him and glare, before storming away. He comes after me, takes my arm again, and I turn and plant my hands on his chest, shoving as hard as I can.

335

He's like a solid wall, but I surprise him enough that he overbalances a little and takes a step back.

'Recruit B-37-37!' Lieutenant Dean's voice booms across the gymnasium. 'Step out into the hallway and wait for me.'

I'm sitting on the floor with my head rolled back against the wall when Lieutenant Dean comes out, closing the door behind her and staring down at me. She looks all set to launch into a lecture, before something changes her mind and she lowers herself on to the floor to sit next to me.

'Why are you so determined to put your future here with us at risk?'

I sigh. 'Because I'm not sure I want a future here.' God, it feels good to tell the truth.

She studies my face. 'I've seen your file, recruit. You came through as a level 1.'

'What does that mean?'

'That, from your personality profile, you were identified as someone highly suited to the mission.'

'I don't even get why anyone would think that.'

'Resilience. Strength. Courage. Determination. Intelligence. Drive. These were the things that we were looking for, and we found them in you. It's not going to be easy – any of this. But we believe you're up to it. You're exactly the kind of person we want.'

I look down into my lap then, watch my hands twisting there.

'Why didn't you think Jam was up to it?' I ask eventually, voice quiet.

'Who's Jam?'

'Joram Rees. B-37-16.'

She shrugs. 'It's likely his profile wasn't right, which could have been for numerous reasons. But in any case, we aren't keen on recruits being friends, relatives, boyfriends, girlfriends. We theorise everything will be more effective if this is a clean start for most of you.'

'Caleb's mum is up there,' I laugh. 'Kazimir's dad.'

'That's different,' she says. 'They're not breeding program. Milly Lomax and Karim Sherbakov are Mission Specialists. Two of our best. It's hardly a surprise that their children have a genetic predisposition to be suited to this too. But we also needed to find the people we could never have predicted – the ones whose particular set of characteristics and experiences have combined to make them the kind of person who will lead our community, our new civilisation, into its future. People like you.'

She doesn't say anything else; she just looks at me, gets up.

'Come back in when you're ready to join us,' she says.

By the time I walk back into the gymnasium, everyone is playing some kind of dodgeball touch-football game, and it involves one team holding hands and running across the court while the other team attempt to take them out with tennis balls. Ironically it's Kazimir who is on the end of the line closest to me as they pass, and when he offers me his hand I have this surge of anger. But I take it anyway.

At the far end, an American girl who's on our team tells me that we're winning.

'I don't even know the rules,' I tell her, turning away.

She pulls me back around. 'It doesn't matter,' she says. 'Just listen to me and do what I say.'

'Why?' I shrug. 'What's the point?'

'For the team,' the guy next to her says, with a Spanish accent.

'We just need to get to the other side one more time without any of us getting hit,' says the girl, super intense and sweaty. 'We need to watch out for ourselves and each other.'

'Unless the test is whether we can actually survive in these uniforms, I don't want to play.' I know I sound childish, but I can't help myself.

'Just look out for your team,' says Kazimir, and I'm glad to see he actually has to wipe sweat off of his top lip. Maybe he is human after all.

I make a face, but I take his hand again and we run back across the court with all we have. Time shifts and everything happens in slow motion. My arm is nearly ripped out of its socket when the guy two along from me hauls a girl tight to his side to avoid a bullet-like flying ball. We're almost halfway when I see one that is about to connect with the American girl's shoulder, so I yank on her arm hard, pulling it down so it misses her.

By the time we get to the other end, everyone is hugging and I'm joining in.

'Thank you,' yells Lieutenant Dean through her megaphone. 'Please proceed to the facility office if you haven't yet signed your contract and booked your transfer. Once you've done that, please turn in your uniform so that it can be personalised and report back here in good time for your window. Welcome to Ventura, recruits! Any questions?'

I raise my hand. 'What was the point in playing that stupid game?' I ask her, still panting.

'Well, since you ask –' she raises an eyebrow – 'we're observing interaction and alliances from the team-building exercises, which will partly inform compatibility. So, you may be standing in the same room as your future partner right now.'

People whoop and make stupid noises. Caleb nudges me.

'How about it, Beacon? I can see you and me making beautiful music, can't you?'

I make a face at him and then catch Kazimir's eye across the room just as he looks away.

I can't even contemplate thoughts like these. It's all irrelevant now I suddenly and irrevocably know the real thing.

And that nothing else will ever come close.

*

I'm standing in the Facility Office, with the world turning to dust around me.

'Say that again,' I tell the guy sitting behind the desk.

'We recruited three hundred and twenty-five, for three hundred slots. We had to account for possible fall-away. This is our final slot and, as you can see –' indicating the line of people behind me – 'we have other people who would take it. You need to sign up now if you want it to be yours.'

A frenzied murmur breaks out among the people standing behind me. My legs threaten to give out. I slump forward over the desk and try to breathe.

'What's happening?' Hands pulling me back to my feet and it's Kazimir. 'What's wrong?' But I can hardly hear him over the buzzing in my ears.

I basically yell, 'They're telling me there's only one remaining volunteer place. So I need to sign up for it now or lose it.'

And he says, 'So sign up.'

I shake my head. 'I can't.'

'Just stand out of the way then,' says the girl behind me in the queue, rolling her eyes, then saying to the guy behind the desk, 'You can't seriously want someone who's this reluctant to go.'

Kazimir tightens his grip on my shoulders. 'Jam asked you not to go?' he asks.

I shake my head. 'He wants me to go.'

'And does he know you well?'

'Better than anyone,' I say, but the words break open and turn into a painful sob.

'Well then,' says Kazimir softly.

'They're telling me I have to go tomorrow though,' I say around hitching breaths. 'Tomorrow!'

'Step out of the way!' says the girl again, louder, another eye roll.

'Have some respect,' Kazimir tells her over his shoulder, adding, 'I doubt very much that you are the kind of person Ventura want anyway if you don't have basic manners.'

'I'm not going,' I tell him.

'You're going,' he says, turning back to me, super sure of it.

Even though I'm shocked I manage to say, 'You don't . . . you don't know me.'

'OK,' he concedes. 'But I do know that, until last night, this was what you wanted. Can so much change in one night?'

'You don't understand,' I say.

'Beacon, this is your life. You feel it. I know you do. You were made for this.'

I stand there wiping each tear as it falls, but they keep coming.

'Even if I did go,' I manage to say, 'it would have to be in a few weeks, once I've got everything . . . sorted. Once I've had a chance to say goodbye.'

He's shaking his head. 'You're only making it harder. For you and for him.'

I think about that. It sits on me like a rock.

'You want to do something painful, you do it quick, right?' He mimes pulling a plaster off his forearm, complete with sound effect.

I watch him, then look away, out to where dust whirls past on the wind.

'What's the alternative?' he says. 'Stay here and spend the rest of your life wondering about it?'

Precession

We're standing on the beach, looking at the water when I turn to Jam and say, 'I ... I'm shipping out tomorrow morning.'

I watch his face, the way it fades from shock to sadness and still he manages to say, 'That's great, Bea.' He swallows, then takes this one long breath that shudders in then out.

He takes my hand, just my fingers, looks down at them, and suddenly I can't imagine what it was that made me stand there in that office and agree to sign that contract; agree to get on the shuttle tomorrow morning.

'I don't know what made me do it,' I say, my voice dropping octaves into the pain that thrums in my chest. 'I didn't know what to do and I just ...'

He's shushing me, pulling me closer, stilling my hands, smoothing them out where they have formed into claws.

'It was the last spot and I didn't know what to do. I didn't know what to do. I wanted more time ...' There's

343

so much more to say, but suddenly it feels like if I start explaining, I'll never stop.

'You did the right thing,' he says, his hand on my head, smoothing my hair back from my face. 'You did exactly the right thing.'

'No.' I shake my head.

'Yes,' he says against my lips, then kisses me, making me close my eyes so that more tears spill out. I feel like I could cry a million tears and still they'd come.

'You need to speak to Joella,' he says.

'Yes,' I say, sniffing, swallowing, squeezing his hand. 'Let's do that, let's go now. I'll ask Micah if we can borrow the car and we'll drive to Santo Domingo.'

'Can't you call from the base?'

'Probably, but I want to go. Somewhere it can just be you and me.'

'OK,' he says, and he frowns a little, smiling at the same time, his emotional weather just as thrown into chaos as mine.

I change my clothes in the tent, and when I get out, blinking, Micah is standing there.

'Jam and Mali went to the *servicios*,' he says, looking at his feet and then at me. 'I probably won't get another chance to speak to you before you go, so I want you to know that I'll miss you, Karlo.'

'I'll miss you too,' I say.

'And I'm sorry.'

'What for?'

'For all of it.' He looks out over the roofs of the abandoned tents. 'But if what happened with us is even a small part of what finally pushed Rees into telling you how he felt then I don't regret a thing,' he says, smiling but sad-eyed. 'All his mooning about like there was no other girl alive.'

I bite my lip.

'Looking at you together, it's ... ' He looks across to where Mali and Jam are now walking together through the detritus of everyone who's already left, and they are deep in conversation, then slowing and stopping, her pulling him into a sad-looking hug.

'It's what?' I manage to say.

'It's just a shame it happened too late, I guess.' And then he steps close to me, pulls me into a hug I'm not expecting, but one it turns out I need, from the friend I only just realised I have. Close to my ear he says, 'Any amount of a good thing is a good thing, right? Promise me you'll remember that?'

I nod, sniff. 'Remember your promise then,' I say. 'To never lie to her again. To try to be even half as great as she thinks you are. You won't coast through on looks for ever.' I hear him laugh against my ear, but feel him nod.

We let each other go, just as Jam and Mali arrive back.

'I'm just going to change my shirt,' says Jam, and he ducks into our tent as Mali folds me into her arms.

'Oh, Bea, if doing this is what makes you well,' she says, 'then I'm so happy for you.' She pulls an arm's length away and studies me, pushes hair off my face. 'Even if right now I have no idea how we . . .' She doesn't go on, and when I look at her and find she has tears in her eyes, it makes me ache with bottomless sadness. She takes my hand and kisses my knuckles, pulling me back close to her to where she says, super quiet, 'Be good to Jam tonight. It's going to be so hard for him.'

And I want to tell her how hard it's going to be for me too, but then I realise it's me that's making it all happen.

Driving along the road to Santo Domingo at ninety with the windows down, I turn to Jam and say:

'I'll miss driving so much.'

And he says, 'Yeah?' And then, 'You're good at it.'

And I say, 'It's pretty much the only thing I've ever been good at it.'

And he says, 'That's not true.'

And I feel myself blushing, which never happens.

'I didn't mean that,' he almost laughs. 'Well, not just that. I mean a lot of things. I mean science and maths and, well, most things at school. Also just . . . standing up for yourself, standing up for what you believe in. Doing everything you can to protect the people you care about, even when it's impossible.'

I cut a glance at him. The shirt he's wearing is my favourite of his; it's a checked pattern but mostly sea green, tight on his narrow waist. He has his hat tipped forward on his head and is moody in side profile.

He shifts his eyes to me. 'What?' he says.

'Looking's free, ain't it, cowboy?'

'Sure is, mam,' he says, touching the front brim of his hat.

I want so much more of this, of us just being us. And suddenly it feels so incredibly, desperately unfair that this one night is all there will ever be. I notice the dirt side road, heading off down between two fields of solar panels and pull into it so hard the wheels squeal and spit gravel in our wake.

'Where are we going?' he says, eyes widening.

'Anywhere,' is all I say, while the borders of bending yellow flowers and crazy sisal plants close in on us tighter and tighter until I stop and haul on the handbrake, pulling myself up from behind the wheel and moving on to his lap, pushing his hat off backwards so I can kiss him, no hesitation. He yanks the car door open, spilling us both out on to the gravel. I pull him against me and I couldn't care less about the dirt and rocks that dig into us. It's just me and him and the earth beneath us, and that's how it was always meant to be.

*

'Joella, it's me.'

She doesn't reply right away, and I share a look with Jam.

'I'm calling from Spain, so I don't really have time for the silent treatment.'

'You lied, babes,' she says. 'Why would you lie about a thing like that?'

'I guess I –' I squeeze the phone receiver in my hand – 'I didn't see the point in telling you when I might never have been chosen.'

'And now what?' she says. 'You're actually going to outer space?'

I take a deep, steadying breath. 'I am.'

'When are you coming back?'

Another breath. 'I'm not.'

'OK.' She sounds flat, completely robotic. 'When do you leave?'

I cringe, brace myself, realise I'm never really going to be ready for it. 'In the morning.' I try to sound upbeat.

Silence. Then, eventually: 'Tomorrow morning?'

I nod, before realising that of course she can't see me, and so I find enough voice to say, 'Yes, tomorrow morning.'

Jam rubs me across my shoulders, then his hand comes to rest on the back of my neck. There's nothing from her end but silence, then some breathing which might actually be crying. I don't remember her ever doing that.

'Is Joram going too?'

'No.'

Another silence, but I think I hear relief in it.

'We saw you on the TV,' she says then. 'Both of you. You were quite famous for a few minutes.'

'Oh yeah?' I try to sound upbeat.

'Everyone was a bit ... well ... confused, I suppose,' she says. 'None of us even knew you'd gone to Spain to do that and then ... there you were. The Doomed Lovers of Mission Ventura. That's what they were calling you.' There's another question waiting in the silence that she finally gives voice to. 'How long have you loved each other like that?'

'Not long.' I shake my head. 'Or ... ' I hesitate. 'Or maybe always. Always, probably, but we didn't know about it until ... ' I turn a little and realise Jam is watching me, sad mouthed. 'We didn't even know it ourselves until it was already too late.'

'I could have told you,' she says. 'But I didn't think you wanted to know. Seems like I was wrong about that. Seems like ... ' She trails off but I wait for her to continue. 'Seems like maybe I never really knew much about you or what you wanted at all,' she finishes, and I blink tears on to my cheeks just before I say, 'The thing is I don't ... ' I turn to Jam and he gets it without me having to say it. He nods and slides out of the cubicle.

I take a deep breath in, then blow it out in a rush.

'Joella, the thing is . . .' Suddenly I can't say any more. It just hurts too much.

'The thing is – what?'

I swallow a few times, finally manage to make my voice work. 'I don't think I can go. Now . . . with Jam and everything . . . I suddenly feel like I have something so amazing in my life and I . . .'

'So don't go,' she says, her voice louder, as if she is holding the phone closer.

I smile, but there are tears on my face as I listen to her voice.

'I know how much you always wanted to do something important . . . to get out of here . . . do something better with your life. But if you think that this . . . that *he* is what will really make you happy – then stay!' She almost laughs. 'What even made you tell them you would go?'

'I don't know. Nothing. I don't even know any more, except they said I would be well. That living in space would reset my immune system and I could live a normal life. A long life.'

Silence. So much silence I hear the line clicking, hear a long, low whistle I didn't notice before, and in my mind I travel a thousand kilometres to where she is before I say, 'I'm definitely not going.' And I feel relieved.

More silence, and then:

'Bea, you have to.'

350

I screw my eyes shut as hard as I can while she keeps talking.

'I understand that you've fallen in love with him and that yes, you could have a wonderful few years together. But then what? He'll watch you die, Bea. Because that's what will happen. We both know that. We've always known it. My God, if you have a chance to live, you have to. For his sake as well as yours.'

I don't answer. I just let out this long miserable hum while the tears pour down my face and make it itch and burn.

'Jam's had to lose so many people, babes. You know that because you know how sad he was when he came to us.'

'And now I'm making him lose someone all over again.'

'He's losing you either way. Sooner or later, he's losing you. He'd rather lose you this way, believe me.' She gets quieter again. 'We'd all rather lose you this way, if those are the only choices. And they are.'

'But I'll never see you again,' I choke out. 'I'll never see Jam. I'll never get to . . . ' But I can't even get it out. Our eyes meet through the glass door of the cubicle then and he lays his hand on the glass between us. I lay my hand where his is; blink a flood of tears down my cheeks. 'How can I lose the most wonderful thing I've ever known when I've only just found it?'

'Because it's what's right for you, babes, you know it is. Loving someone . . . being loved . . . it can feel like there's nothing you can't do, nothing you can't beat together, but it's not the real world.'

We listen to each other's silence, or near silence, for a moment before she says, 'It's funny,' and I hear a sound that might almost be a laugh. 'Your name.'

I frown. 'What about it?'

'Do you know why we called you Beacon?'

'Because you could see the Brecon Beacons from your window, you said.'

'I made that up.' That almost-laugh again. 'I never knew why I liked it when Dylan suggested it, not really. It just felt right. But now I know.'

I blink in confusion. 'Mum, I . . . '

'That's what they called it back then, you see. This signal. They called it the beacon. When they first discovered it. Which was just around the time you were born. I guess this is what you were always going to do. I've always known you were going to do something amazing. I've always known you weren't mine to keep. I guess, in a way, that's why I could never bear to get too close. I was always so afraid of losing you.'

Just then my credit runs low and I hear the beeps. 'I have to go,' I tell her.

'OK,' she says, letting out a long shuddery breath. 'I love you, babes, OK? Be safe, OK? Be happy. I'll always be thinking about you. I know how strong you are, I know you can do this.'

I blink more tears. 'I love you too. And Joella – Mum – I . . .' Suddenly I'm not sure quite how to put it. 'You're right that love can't change the way things are, but it *can* help, so … please get rid of Ianto? Wait for Ryan. Despite everything that happened with him –' I can hear her crying – 'he and Jam are still the best thing that ever happened to us – you know that, right?'

'I know, babes.'

'Promise me?'

Which is when the phone cuts off. Jam watches me pull the receiver hard into my chest while I add more tears to the ones already drying on my cheeks. He pushes the door open and steps in close to me, rubbing my shoulders and swaying with me.

We follow signs to Cabo Santo Domingo, and stop in an empty, sandy car park where there is a broken sign lying on the ground that says 'Playa Paloma Luxury Beach Bungalows'. The bungalows themselves stand around like ruins, their old thatched roofs collapsing into haystacks.

'I wonder what happened,' I ask Jam, taking his hand as we wander through the ruins.

'That's what happened,' he says, nodding out at the horizon where there are a thousand orange lights studding the sea, as if there was a city out there, sitting on the surface. 'Some kind of nasty-looking facility.'

'Seabed mining probably,' I say. 'There are basically

353

mountain ranges under the sea, and some of them are full of cadmium which they need for the solar panels so . . . ' I shrug. 'You can guess how that goes. Only problem is the amount of sediment it stirs up kills just about everything, and turns the sea brown.'

I realise then that I can hear it. The humming, clanking, grinding out at sea.

The resort's four-poster sunbeds are still there. There's no padding on them any more, just wooden slats, but they still have their white curtains on each corner and they stir in the wind as we get close to them, ghostly and beautiful. We sit on the edge of one, and Jam touches the grazes on my shoulders from the gravelly ground.

'I'm sorry,' he says into my broken skin.

'Don't be,' I say, pulling his hand so that his arm is tight around my waist. 'Don't even be a little bit sorry.'

I only notice the lighthouse then, right on the end of the cape. It is so old-fashioned, like something from a book.

'Look at that,' I say.

We watch it beam its light out into the sky, across the sea, then back round on to us, making the curtains iridescent.

'A beacon,' says Jam. 'Like you.'

He kisses me, goes to kiss me more, but I pull away a little, stop him.

'Tell me something,' I say.

He looks at me, waits for me to go on.

'If it was reversed,' I say, 'if you had been picked and I hadn't – would you still go?'

I watch the light travel across his face once.

'If you had suddenly realised that you had this beautiful, perfect thing,' I go on, 'that had been right in front of you all this time, would you give it all up and walk away?'

'Yes,' he says. But I know he's lying.

'You wouldn't,' I say.

'I would,' he says. 'Because this is something too huge, and too important to give up being a part of. I can't ask you to stay and then realise I'm the reason that you gaze up at the stars and get this sad look on your face for the rest of your life. And I know that's what would happen. And –' he squeezes my hand – 'it's different for you, Bea. You can be well.' He looks away from me. 'Otherwise, one of these days you won't make it, and I can't . . . ' He shakes his head down at where our hands are joined. 'There is just no way I could watch that. Don't make me do that. Please. I can't even bear the thought of losing you that way. I wouldn't survive it.'

I shake my head; bite down on my lip in determination not to cry again. I get up and walk a few steps away from him, disconnecting from the heat of his body and feeling immediately lonely without it. I'm so glad I feel his hands on my shoulders just then, and I turn and look at him, at the sad twisted look on his beautiful face, the shine in his eyes.

'I know it's wrong,' I say, 'but part of me just wants to spend whatever time I have with you, even if it's not long. No amount of time would ever have been enough anyway, because I love you.'

I've never really said those words to anyone before, and maybe I never will again. I seriously doubt I'll ever mean them this much anyway, even if I live to be a hundred years old. We watch each other in the rhythmic passing light from the lighthouse. I step closer and pull at the front of his shirt, pulling it apart so that his first snap opens, then continue to pull so that each one pops, never taking my eyes off his.

I lay my ear against the skin over his heart, ready to die there. I guess not all of the massive mysteries of this world take hundreds of years to answer; it turns out that one of them at least can become clear in a heartbeat.

It's slow and steady and beautiful this time. This time there are these still moments that make me ache with regret that we didn't start doing this sooner. But yet I know that it would never have been enough. Afterwards he closes his arms around my waist and kisses the back of my neck and our bodies dovetail like we were made for each other.

I watch the curtain blow across the fading stars.

'Somewhere,' I hear myself say, 'somewhere there's an alternative universe where it's you and me, and we have this amazing life together, where we love each other every day, for the rest of our lives.'

I feel him tighten his grip and breathe deeply.

'But just not in this one,' I say through my tightening throat. 'Not in this one.'

Theory of Everything

The sun comes up and, even though it feels like some terrible ticking clock, I devour every millisecond of its journey. Every tiny shift in colour, every tinge in the clouds, every glint on a distant wave.

'It's like music,' I hear myself say.

I'm sitting in Jam's lap, my head leant back against his shoulder, eyes half closed.

'It is,' he says, kissing my neck. 'Sad music.'

'I'm sorry I'm going to miss your birthday,' I say, and suddenly it seems unbearable that he will turn seventeen without me. 'Promise me you won't go back to Wales – there's nothing for you there.'

He half laughs. 'So where should I go?'

'I don't know.' I shrug. 'Go to Russia and try to get on the haulage program. Just don't go home.'

'OK,' he breathes against my hair.

'Or you could find Carmen,' I say, surprising myself, and despite the fact that the thought of him with her slides under my ribs like a red-hot knife. 'I think she really likes you. And she's cool. You could have a good li—'

'Bea, stop,' he says, gently.

'You got dealt such a crappy hand in life, Jam, but I don't want you to accept it. Make the world deal you a new one.' I move away a little to look at him and lay my hand against the side of his face, beautiful in the sunrise light. I smile at him and he smiles back, melting me. 'You are so beautiful when you smile, Jam; I just wish I'd seen you do it more.'

And he says, 'You've seen me do it more than anyone else has.'

And I say, 'Aren't I lucky?'

And just before he kisses me he says, 'Luck's got nothing to do with it.'

It was pretty much impossible to leave. Jam almost had to drive me, even though he doesn't have his licence, because suddenly I just couldn't do it. And now here I am, in the tent, trying to decide which two things will be my essential items – packing my medication and toothbrush and clothes and everything else into a bag I'll leave here and never see again and wonder what'll happen to it – while the others sit outside in silence, as if they're at a funeral.

'Thanks for this,' I hear Ernesto's voice say.

'Sure man, no problem,' I hear Jam say. 'I'm happy to do it.'

When I stand up out of the tent, Jam is holding his dad's guitar by the neck, right in the middle of handing it over to Ernesto.

'What are you doing?' I frown.

'He's taking it as one of his personal items,' shrugs Jam, as Ernesto takes hold of it gingerly, now unsure.

'It's your dad's. Won't he ...?' My throat goes tight. 'Won't he mind? Don't you want it?'

He shakes his head, half-smiles. 'I like the idea of it going with you.' He sighs heavily, squints in the bright morning sunlight.

There is such a hard ache in my chest that it's agony to breathe.

We walk to the main gate and I nearly run straight in without even saying anything, without even looking back, just because it's so impossibly hard that all I want is for it to be over.

Micah lays his hand on my shoulder.

'I heard you were a couple short so I got these printed in Santo Domingo.' And he holds something in the space between us. Photographs – the one of him and me at the monastery, me in front of the mountains, one I didn't know he'd taken of me and Mali laughing on the beach. The last one is of Jam and I standing talking on the ferry over here, looking at each other in such

360

a way that I can't believe I never realised I was in love with him.

'And every classic 1970s album is on your data key,' Micah adds. 'So you'll never be able to forget this trip even if you wanted to.'

'I never want to forget it,' I say, managing a slight smile. 'Thanks, Bexley.'

And he kisses my cheek and backs away.

Mali pulls me close and I breathe in the smell of her, the scent of her hair, like medicine.

'Bye, beautiful girl,' she says, and then, 'I'll be missing you for the rest of my life, you idiot.'

'I . . . ' I start, and then just for a moment I am thinking that I have to tell her what I did. Suddenly the weight of it buries me like a rockfall. All the truth and love she gave me seems ruined by the lie. Will I leave and spend my life regretting not taking this one last chance to be honest with her? And then I realise – it doesn't matter. If it sits on me for ever and blackens me like rot on fruit, that's my problem. I'd only be telling her for selfish reasons. I'm used to secrets – I am one, after all – and this is just one more I am going to take with me to the stars.

'You're the best friend I ever had,' is what I tell her, just as she pulls away.

'Are you sure?' she says, raising an eyebrow and glancing in Jam's direction. 'But, look, I am honoured to have been second best,' she says, backing away, pointing at my face. 'You'd better remember me,' she says. 'Or else.'

I smile. 'Like I could forget,' I say, swallowing something hard.

I take Jam by the hand and pull him away, just as Kazimir and Oksana pass us. Kazimir offers Jam his hand and shakes it.

'Good luck, man,' says Jam.

'And to you,' says Kazimir, and he is gone, striding off towards the bus to the spaceport like all of this was nothing.

When Jam looks back at me he smiles, which is not what I was expecting.

'I don't even know what to say,' he says. 'There's way too much to even ...' He shakes his head, all beautiful bashful cowboy.

'You've said it all,' I tell him. 'You've said every wonderful thing a person could say and more.'

He shakes his head, glances up, looks down again.

'You realise that, in a way, this is perfect,' I say then.

He frowns.

'You know how life is,' I say. 'Things would have got in the way. Everything would have got more difficult. It all just would have become too ... real. And let's face it, we both know I probably would have done something stupid to mess this up,' I say, almost laughing. 'Come on, we both know it. But now I get to leave in our perfect moment, and keep it that way, in my heart and yours. For ever.'

He makes a face I've never seen before and I realise he is crying, lovely mouth creased, tears leaking into the corners of his eyes. It's only now I realise I am crying too, as I push his tears away with my thumbs.

I pull him down to me and I am kissing him, kissing him and kissing him, and then I'm not, I'm just leaning my forehead against his.

'We're entangled, Jam, if people can be. My molecules and your molecules. Even when we're a universe apart, I know I'm always going to feel you,' I manage to gasp out. 'I'll know when you're sad, I'll know when you're happy, I'll know when something huge happens to you in life and I'll always know you're OK because if you weren't, I'd feel it. If something happened to you, I'd feel the light of you blink out. And one day maybe that will happen, or maybe you'll be the one to feel my light go out. I'm always going to feel you and you'll be able to feel me.'

And then God knows how but I manage to drag myself away and suddenly I am walking, one foot following another, walking away and not looking back, swallowing a million gallons of pain that nearly stopper me up completely, slowing and telling myself not to, picking up pace, slowing again, the spaceport bus swimming out of focus before I can get there, before I can grab hold of the edge of the door, haul myself up, throw myself into a seat and lean my head against the window. I force myself to look at him, watch him standing there, as Mali takes hold of his hand in both of hers and Micah comes to his other side and puts his hand on his shoulder and we just watch each other as the bus door hisses closed and we lurch away and I turn my neck until it hurts to get every last sight of him before he fades into the churned up sand and dust. I close my eyes and slump against the glass.

At the entrance to the spaceport, we submit our data keys, our personal items and our printed photographs. I glance at Kazimir's and notice they are all nearly identical shots of him, alone on the beach. He sees me looking and says, 'I didn't have any; had to take them all yesterday.'

He laughs a little, but I don't think it's funny.

In the women's changing room with Oksana, I pull my uniform out of its vacuum pack and change into it. I can't stop shaking.

'You are feeling OK?' she says. 'Very hard to leave someone important behind. We all have to do it some time.'

I study her wide snaking plait and say, 'You get to bring Kazimir with you though, which is helpful.'

She shakes her head. 'We were flown out together by Concordia, but before that we never met. I left parents, sister and boyfriend on hauler Soyuz 29.'

'Why did you do that?' I blink in surprise.

'Because the direction of our life goes here, and theirs goes there.' She shrugs. 'That's just how it is.' And she takes her clothes to a bin marked LEAVE DISCARDED CLOTHING ITEMS HERE and drops them in.

I walk through the giant hangar of the spaceport on the way to the transport out to the shuttle and I'm still shaking hard, even though we're in our heavy uniforms, and now also in a metallic mesh spacesuit that I have been ratcheted into and that makes it nearly impossible to move. I'm carrying my helmet under my arm. This transport is like a golf buggy that we are loaded on to. It is open to the air and I watch the swallows dart across the sky as we pass under them.

At the shuttle we get out, walk to the tower. All I do is stare at the shuttle, at the charred parts on its fuselage from its previous re-entries. It is larger than I expected, towering into the blue morning, waiting to take me away.

A tight, airless lift takes us up the tower, and it hits me suddenly, with no warning.

'I can't do this,' I shout, my own voice tearing out of me, unbidden. 'Why did I . . . ? I can't . . . I can't leave Jam . . .'

I am falling against the wall, into the corner, when Kazimir drops his helmet and takes my arms in his hands, super awkward as it is in these ridiculous suits, and pulls me back onto my feet.

'You can do it,' he says. 'You got this far, so I know you can make it the rest of the way.'

'No,' I nearly spit at him, shaking my head. 'I have to go back.' I feel the tears come then. 'You have to let me go back.'

I watch him shake his head. 'No, Beacon,' he says. 'This is just the step. A difficult step, but one that takes you into the rest of your life. Into a good life.'

I close my eyes and shake my head. 'No, I ...' But suddenly all I feel is weak. All I feel is that I am already a million miles away and rising fast.

The lift doors slide open and at the same time I open my eyes. Don't ask me why, but for a moment I am lighter.

The ground crew strap us in. There are ten of us on either wall of the tight cabin, lined up along its side on a row of seats perpendicular to the ground, so that our legs pull painfully to the left and I already feel at odds with gravity. Kazimir sits opposite me and watches me steadily. Then suddenly we are alone and the doors are closing.

The thrusters start and I shriek, squeeze my eyes closed in fear at the way it rattles inside me, vibrating my teeth and bones. When I manage to open my eyes, I see Kazimir, raising his hand to tap the side of his helmet. All I do is shake my head but he widens his eyes and taps it again so I push at the side of my helmet, looking for something, until I hear a beep, and suddenly his voice is there.

'It's all normal, recruits,' he says, looking at me but

clearly addressing the others who are new to this too. 'Just the thrusters. We'll be on our way in just a few minutes.'

That makes me breathe, several long deep, shaky breaths that bring the world back into slightly more focus, despite the fact that the vibrations are getting stronger.

Then there's another surge, a grinding, a clanging, a sickening lurch.

'That's lift-off,' says Kazimir, his voice now the only thing I'm clinging on to. 'You may experience some motion sickness. That's all normal.'

It surges in me then.

'Oh God, I'm going to puke,' I hear myself shriek down the com.

'All normal,' says Kazimir, still super calm. 'If you have to vomit, just remember to purge your helmet using the button at the top left.' He points to it.

My head begins to pound. I manage not to puke, but the whole thing is agonising. It seems like for ever before the vibrations ease and suddenly there is peace, quiet, a penetrating cold.

'This is orbit,' says Kazimir.

I close my eyes, trying to picture Jam, Mali, Micah, even Joella, all the way down there on the planet I'll never see again. But they are already so far away and my throat tightens. All that's left now is living with the consequences of a choice I may never know was right.

Then suddenly someone is unclipping my helmet. I

scream, expecting to implode in the vacuum of space, to feel my blood begin to boil away, or at least to drown in a lack of oxygen. But then I realise there is air and it is only Kazimir. He pushes me against my seat and says, 'Just breathe normally, you're fine.'

Then he points to the porthole and says, 'Look.'

And when I turn, there it is: Earth. There is the planet that I have spent my whole life on. And my God, it is beautiful from here. It is more precious and delicate and iridescent and magnificent than I could ever have imagined. And tears burn in my dry eyes.

'What did you bring?' asks Kazimir, but I have no idea what he's talking about so I just stare back.

He pulls open the Velcro on a flap behind my head and says, 'It's OK to see your personal items?'

I nod.

He pulls out a book.

'*Tender is the Night*,' he reads. 'Cool. I've never read it. Maybe I can borrow it. I brought a book too. Russian poetry.' He grins. 'Want to borrow mine?'

'I don't speak Russian,' I say.

'I can teach you,' he says. 'We'll have time.'

He reaches for the flap again and frowns. 'You only brought one item?'

I shake my head, feel the panic surge in me, try to twist back to rummage in the flap myself, keep struggling until he helps me reach. But once I shove my hand in there, I find it, right in the corner; I feel the sharp edge of it even through my glove. I cup it in my hand like a captured moonbeam, and then show him. B-37-16. Jam's dog tag.

Just then it comes alive, takes flight. I hadn't even realised we were in zero gravity but we are, and it is dancing away from me, and I am so amazed all I can do is watch it. It is Kazimir who reaches for it in the end, who clasps it back into his hand and delivers it into mine.

'You'll want to keep that,' he says, closing my fingers over it like he is closing a flower, before swimming down the capsule to the guy at the far end who is struggling with his helmet.

I turn to the porthole and look out of it, at the planet tracking silently by underneath us, sun glinting on oceans far below.

Acknowledgements

Many, many thanks ...

To NASA's website and *Encyclopedia Britannica* for the astrophysical inspiration, and to the *New Scientist, Scientific American,* and podcasts like Radiolab and Invisibilia for getting me excited all over again about science in general.

To Sam Swinnerton for being just the editor I need, for seeing this book exactly the way I do, and for being prepared to log some serious Skype hours getting it right. Also to Kate Agar for encouraging me to give Bea the story she deserved, and to all the other talents at Hachette, in the UK and elsewhere, that make my books beautiful and get them into people's hands.

To everyone at Madeline Milburn Literary Agency for all the energy and positivity and hard work they continue to put into championing my books, and especially Alice Sutherland-Hawes, for answering all my (crazy) emails so quickly and so honestly. It's massively appreciated, and I'm so glad to have you in my corner.

To all my fantastic translators and editors in other territories. You do a job that is so challenging, and you do it so beautifully that my story is able to resonate in languages I know not a word of. I feel so privileged that that is the case.

To all the booksellers, book bloggers, bookish people of Twitter, and bookstagrammers – whether you're hand-selling, reviewing or photographing my books looking their best, I am so grateful for your support and the little moments of joy you bring to my days.

To the school where I work and everyone in it, for talking books with me, for reading, for writing, for the candid opinions and the cheerleading.

To my friends and family near and far for all the many and varied shades of support, and for repeatedly telling me you're proud of me, even when I'm not. It helps!

To my husband for giving me so many amazing stories to tell about best friends and lovers and people who belong together. It's no accident that I always end up writing about love.

To my star and my sky, for being a sight for sore eyes at the end of every long day, and for being braver and cleverer and funnier and more filled with joy than I could have hoped. I look forward to the future now I know there are people like you in it.

And to you, my readers, wherever you are in the world, for completing my stories by making them into movies in your mind. They're nothing without you.

Kate Ling was born and brought up in London
but over the last ten years she has worked in school
libraries on three continents. Like her characters,
she knows how it feels to leave everything behind
and journey into the unknown.

Kate currently lives in Spain with her husband and two
daughters. She loves eating seafood on the beach and
running while listening to podcasts about space.

kateling.co.uk
@katelingauthor

'It is that quick, that strong, that beautiful.
And it is also totally impossible.'

Years after Ventura has begun its mission, the founding
crew are hailed as heroes. But for Bea's great-granddaughter,
Seren, having never experienced Earth haunts her. She longs
to have the sunshine on her skin – it's something she feels
she needs to stay sane. But when you're hurtling through
space at thousands of kilometres an hour, sometimes you
have to accept there are things you cannot change.

Except that the arrival of Dom in her life changes
everything in ways she can barely comprehend. He becomes
the sun for her, and she can't help but stay in his orbit.
To lose him would be like losing herself . . .

'I longed so hard for all the things that make life life,
*and I never thought they'd be mine. But now ... now
they are. Now I have something to lose.'*

Seren and Dom have fled their old lives on board
spaceship Ventura in order to be together. They crash-land
on a beautiful, uninhabited planet, which at first
seems like paradise.

There is no one to answer to ... no one to ask for help.
And with each new day comes the realisation
of how vulnerable they truly are.

This planet has secrets – lots of them. Uncovering them
could be the key to survival, but at what cost?

Find your place

Want to be the first to hear about the best new YA reads?

Want exclusive content, offers and competitions?

Want to chat about books with people who love them as much as you do?

Look no further . . .

bkmrk.co.uk

 @TeamBkmrk /TeamBkmrk

 @TeamBkmrk   TeamBkmrk

See you there!